Anne Isabel Staffor̲... ...n in
March 1901 and e̲... ...Ladies College
and Newnham, Cambridge, reading for the French and
Russian Triposes. After a short spell as an assistant mistress
at Selhurst Girls' Grammar School in Croydon, she studied
Russian Social History for her Ph.D. at King's College
London. She spent the vacations studying art in Paris, and
has illustrated some of her own books. In 1926 she married
Tom Simpson Pedler, a barrister, and had one son, John,
who was in the Diplomatic Service.

She became well known for her social and welfare work,
which she also brought into her novels, in particular *Silver
Street* and *The Great Mrs. Pennington.* She drove an
ambulance during the war and was in charge of an East End
Citizens' Advice Bureau. Here she became so interested in
the problems of dockers and their families that she made a
study of Bow and Poplar, writing *Light Me a Candle* and
Bess, novels set in the East End in the 19th century, and *A
Match to Fire the Thames,* a study of the Match Girls' strike
of 1888 at Bryant and May's factory in Bow.

In 1957 she went on a lecture tour of Burma and Pakistan,
and studied women in social work in Vietnam.

She wrote a total of 24 books; novels, social history and
even two pony books for children. She died in 1966.

SILVER STREET

ANN STAFFORD

Greyladies

Published by
Greyladies

ISBN   978-1-907503-55-9

Set in Sylfaen / Perpetua
Printed and bound by Charlesworth Press, Wakefield.

SILVER STREET

KALEIDOSCOPE
TEN-THIRTY A. M., NOVEMBER 11th, 1918

Vera.
A small girl with flying pigtails skidded along the oil-cloth corridors, clashing open class-room doors. "It's over. It's over. It's over," she shouted and ran on, while the shrill, uncontrollable, uncomprehending excitement of schoolgirls blazed up behind her.

Howard and John.
Two subalterns linked arms, swung dizzily into Trafalgar Square, charged through the roaring crowd, leant against the cold, bland lions, vowed eternal friendship, and were swept apart for ten years.

Beatrix.
A V.A.D. probationer stood on the fringe of the crowd at Roehampton, crumpling her apron and choking back tears. Over ... after one week ...

Isabel Snow.
A greyish-haired W.A.A.C. was kissed by an elderly Major in the lounge of the Ritz. She gulped down her brandy and soda and joined in the cheering, muzzily aware that for her more than the war had ended.

Robert.
A thin boy in shabby flannels stood in a cold attic bedroom, miserably turning over a pile of snapshots. They were men,

these schoolboys in khaki. He was eighteen to-morrow—
and the War was over to-day.

Susan.
A long-legged girl pedalled an ancient bicycle furiously
down the steep hill leading to the Market Square of a
Wiltshire village. She wore no hat over the red hair that
was cut square across the nape of her neck. A coat collar of
shabby grey tweed was turned up round her ears. In a few
minutes the church clock would strike and she would be
too late to see the end of that chapter because she had been
dawdling and dreaming of the next.

Alice.
In room C.33 of the Ministry of Pensions, work was still
going on. The girls were stacking buff papers in lop-sided
piles, cramming blue forms into wire baskets, opening and
slamming filing cabinets. At her desk, Alice Gedge stood
and watched them, one hand ready to pounce on the buzzer
whenever the mutterings became audible. She was waiting
for the desk telephone to ring, but when it sounded she
could hardly lift the receiver. Every one looked up in a
medusa stillness, hands suspended over baskets, pens over
inkpots, fingers over typewriters.

"Yes, sir ... Speaking, sir ... In ten minutes. Certainly, sir
..." The receiver slipped back into its rest with a ping. "You
may go in ten minutes. It's over," said Alice, turning to face
the room again.

Then she sat down quickly: the room was suddenly dark:
the narrow oblong window at which she had so often stared
for reassurance split up into odd triangles of light. She shut
her eyes, and, as she opened them again, the scene jerked
back into focus and she saw, with sudden exasperation, that

one pert junior clerk was fox-trotting down the narrow ink-stained table, scattering baskets, blotters, pin trays, pens and ink-pots. Alice brought her forefinger imperiously down on the buzzer.

"Stop that row this minute," she said. "Joan Drew, you must be clean crazy. Get off the table. Clear up that mess at once. You can make all the noise you want in ten minutes."

"That's right, Mrs. Gedge, there's a good time coming…" shouted someone.

"What'll you do, girls?"

"Oo cares? Ain't it enough the blinking war's over?"

"Marry your boy, dearie."

"Have a good time …"

"What'll you do, Mrs. Gedge?"

"What'll happen to us girls?"

"Us?" said Alice. "We'll go home, I suppose."

"Go home, dear, wot to?"

"What for? When we can earn good money?"

Alice said: "Do you suppose any one in their senses will want to give you ninnies a job when the men come back?"

"That's right, Mrs. G. Keep the Home Fires Burn—ning … Leave the work for the Heroes … "

"Work!" said Alice. "There's not one of you wants a job except for the fun of it. The War's been your good time all right, it has. And no mistake … It's back to your homes for those that's got them. And back to the wash-tub and the pram for me."

"Catch me …"

"We'll have our bit of fun first …"

"Beginning now!" "Pack up Yer Troubles in Yer Ole Kitbag … " "Keep the Home Fires … " "It's a long, long way to Tipperary … " "There's a long, long trail a windin' … " Everybody was singing a different tune, and somebody had begun to cry ... The girls drifted out into the passages.

Alice went round the long room, tidying methodically till all the papers and baskets were back in their places and the room looked as though the Armistice had come and left it unamazed.

"I don't know," said Alice, half aloud, as she, too, went down the passage to the cloakroom. "Peace at any price, I say ... But I daresay we shan't be that thankful when we've had it a bit. Bound to be upsetting." She reached her own peg where her hat and coat hung; she pulled on her blue felt, twisted a fur round her neck, decided against taking her umbrella, and went out by a side entrance.

CHAPTER 1

I
ALICE'S WAR

ALICE GEDGE was twenty-seven in 1918, and her skin was pink and white in spite of overwork. But her grey eyes had fine lines at the corners. Her hair was naturally fair, with a wave of its own, and she had been one of the first people to go in for bobbing. Alice always wore sober, well-cut coats and skirts and she had kept the trick of wearing her hat at the appropriate angle and the habit of good shoes and gloves which she had acquired as a lady's maid. She had gone to Lady Boyd as a girl of nineteen, in the height of pre-war prosperity. But before very long she had impulsively married Thomas Gedge, a chauffeur who was often at Everton Court when his master was there as a guest. Her marriage had been one of the sensations of the servants' hall. Most of the men envied Thomas aloud and some of the women were jealous of Alice; but the housekeeper, who was a good judge of a man, told Alice she was marrying beneath her. And Alice did not listen because she was captivated by Thomas's sallow good looks and by the idea of being independent. She was married that autumn and Lady Boyd told all her friends that she had lost a treasure. She gave Alice an oak dining-room suite and her wedding dress, and she was kind when Leonard was born early in 1912 and Dulcie eighteen months later.

Alice and Thomas had hardly begun to differ when the War broke out and Thomas, always an adventurous man, joined the Navy. He looked grand in uniform and was very amiable when he came home on leave. But he was not often on shore. Alice went to live with her mother-in-law in London and Lady Boyd helped her to find war work in the Ministry of Pensions and continued to give her, though less and less frequently, the coats and skirts, hats and shoes she discarded. By 1917, when Thomas was demobilised with a stiff leg and a very small pension, Alice had been put in charge of one of the filing rooms at the Ministry, where she managed the work and controlled twenty odd girls of all dispositions and classes with admirable efficiency.

But Thomas came back to the flat which Alice had found, to two children he hardly knew and to an Alice who had grown, under the pressure of responsibility, into what he called derisively a strong-minded woman. He complained that he had no comforts except what he found in the nearest public. Alice, in all the newly-found strength of an unaccustomed wage earner, complained that Thomas was unpatriotic; and Thomas said that he had done with patriotism now that his leg was shot to pieces. He stayed in bed most of the day, while a neighbour obliged by minding the children, and every evening he went round to the 'Three Feathers' to discuss strategy and explain how he got his wound. There were nearly always plenty of people to stand him drinks, but fortunately he had a very good head.

At first Alice used to look forward to evenings at home with Thomas: she wanted to hear his terrible tales of submarines and torpedoes and horrors at sea: she wanted also to tell him exactly what had happened in the Ministry that day. But the evenings that Thomas did spend at home were so unsuccessful and his comments on her activities so scathing that she gave up any attempt at this kind of friendship. She began to nag and Thomas, in return, made a point of scoffing at her in public. But in secret he was immensely proud of her—holding down a grand job like that and looking so smart. Plenty of fellows would be glad of her company: in fact he wondered whether Alice had any followers and if there had been any goings-on while he was away.

Sometimes he tried to find out; but his obscure gibes never found a mark. Alice could keep her own secrets. Thomas could never make her swear that she had always been faithful, as he sometimes tried to do when his friends at the 'Feathers' had been extra generous. But he could never make her admit that she had not. So Thomas was unable to decide whether she really were speaking the truth when she said that all the War had meant to her was a lot of hard work, cruel anxiety about Thomas and a shortage of food.

But there had been one evening, in the blackest days of 1916, of which Alice never spoke and seldom thought. She had collided with a small grey officer in Oxford Circus. They had both been struggling unsuccessfully for the same 'bus and, as Alice stepped despondently on to the curb again, he had said: "Let's take a taxi." They had. But the taxi had not taken Alice home: instead, it took them first to a restaurant and then to a small hotel. He had gone back to the Front the next morning and Alice, who had known passion but never tenderness before, saw him off at Victoria and went early to work and wept in the cloak-room. He had given her a card and asked her to write sometimes. But before the first letter was posted, his name was in the casualty lists.

As Alice came out into Whitehall on Armistice day, she remembered him and stood still. Then she walked on again. "The things us respectable women do—when there's a war on," she sighed, and paused again to look down Whitehall— a river of khaki and black, into which every side street and every building was still sending fresh streams. 'Buses were islanded in it, balloons and flags and streamers bobbed up and down above it. Then she shrugged her shoulders. All these celebrations! Time enough to go celebrating when she had got dinner for Thomas and the kids. If she didn't, ten to one nobody else would. That Mrs. Watkins from upstairs had a head like a sawdust doll, and Thomas, as like as not, would be off to the 'Feathers' directly they opened.

An almost empty 'bus, driven by a Pacifist and conducted by a Communist, went grinding slowly past her. She boarded it and it took her away from the crowds, through emptying thoroughfares, towards Paddington, and it did not stop when the maroons went off at eleven. But in the Edgware Road, it was commandeered by a swarm of officers and girls. While they badgered the driver to turn round, Alice climbed off and plodded away towards a tram which was going up Silver Street because the driver lived out that way and wanted to get home.

Silver Street ran with Roman directness through quiet squares whose tall houses had turned into genteel flats and cheap hotels; it left these behind and ran on, over the railway bridge, past narrow side streets edged with barrows of fruit and winkles, past fried fish shops and pawn shops and furniture shops, up the hill, where the infirmary and the cemetery were, and on to a desolate fringe of untilled fields where new suburbs would soon begin to sprout.

The tram rattled through the empty streets, lurched over the railway bridge and stopped: the north end of Silver Street was always crowded, but that morning a solid mass of people blocked the road. Alice got off and began to elbow her way towards her own street, Tuffnel Road. It was deserted. No children were playing in the gutters, no hawkers were hammering on doors, no neighbourly quarrels were going on in front gardens. Only a few dejected flags flapped from front windows to celebrate the Peace.

Alice hurried on, past the Household Stores, now shut for the day. Her flat, three rooms and half a wash-house, was at number ten—a small square two-storied, six-roomed house, exactly like all the others, except that its paint was brighter and the garden tidier. Mrs. Watkins from upstairs, who obliged with the children, had already gone out and Thomas himself was hanging over the gate and scowling, while the children squabbled round his legs.

He wanted to go straight off and said so. But Alice paid no attention to him. She gripped a child in each hand and went through to the kitchen, where she rescued a pan of stew and a pudding from the stove.

"A lot of use you are!" she said to Thomas. "Can't even give the kids their dinner. Besides, I'm not going to lug kids in and out of the crowds. Not likely."

" 'Oo's askin' yer to?" said Thomas defiantly. "Mother'll take 'em," he added. "I arst her." Alice thought this over, and agreed. She knew that old Mrs. Gedge's rheumatism was so bad that she could not escape from Leonard and Dulcie. But she insisted on dinner first.

After he had helped Alice to clear the table, Thomas put on the remnants of his naval uniform and took the children over the way to their grandmother. Then he tucked Alice's hand under his arm and swaggered off to the 'Three Feathers,' where he began his celebrations with beer and Alice's with port and splash.

Alice always said afterwards that the rest of that first Armistice day was a blank. But she stuck to Thomas somehow. At midnight, she brought him home, got his boots off, left him snoring on the bed and went round to old Mrs. Gedge's to collect the children. They were packed up ready for her, wound in shawls and sleeping on the sofa with their mouths open. Old Mrs. Gedge hoped Alice had had a good time and said that the noise was nothing to Mafeking night. "Believe me, dearie . . ." she began. But Alice was far too tired to listen.

II

AFTER THE WAR WAS OVER

WHEN Thomas woke up the next morning, he found Alice standing grimly, hands on hips, at the foot of the bed.

"Well, Thomas," she said, "so it's over."

"Wot's over?" grunted Thomas.

"The War," said Alice.

Thomas said: "Wot's the blurry war got to do with me? Bin over for me a long time now. I done my bit, 'aven't I? Ought to be proud of me, you ought."

Alice sniffed. "I've been proud of you all right," she said. "I've kept you for a year on the best I could get."

"You ought to be thankful to 'ave me to keep," said Thomas, indignantly. "Me with a medal an' all."

"I'm proud and thankful all right," said Alice. "Covered in glory, you are. But we can't live on it."

" 'Ow do y'mean, live?" said Thomas, sitting up and holding his head.

"Well, somebody'll have to keep us, won't they?" said Alice.

"Keep us?" said Thomas. "But the Ministry'll carry on for a bit yet, surely?"

"Oh no," said Alice, "I'm through with that. That was War Work, that was."

"Well, you can git another job easy enough," said Thomas. He lay down again and closed his eyes.

"Job," said Alice. "You wait till all the other heroes like you come back home looking for jobs. There won't be

16

enough jobs to go round soon, without us women with a man to keep us hanging on to them."

" 'Old 'ard, Alice, 'old 'ard," said Thomas, pushing back the bed-clothes. " 'Oo's got a man to keep 'em?"

"I have," said Alice. "Meaning you."

"Don't talk so silly," said Thomas loudly. But before he could begin to say what he thought of Alice the children screamed and she went through to them. Thomas lay on his back gaping at the gas-blackened ceiling. Then he sat up and cursed.

He was a man who had done his bit and more than his bit. What he wanted was a good rest. He had a snug home, a real snug home—if Alice would only leave well alone and get on with it. And now here she was talking silly.

Thomas looked proudly round the small bay-windowed room with its flowery wall-paper and lace curtains. It was a very well furnished room indeed. The bed had large brass knobs to it and there was a fine oak wardrobe in one corner and a piano—which refused to fit into the living-room—in the other. A green plush armchair stood in the window beside a wicker table with a nice fern on it. The plant rocked dangerously as Thomas turned over and settled to sleep. A real cosy home, it was. Why worry ... Alice would get over it.

But Alice did not. Thomas tried arguing with her. He told her over and over again that he had done his bit and was entitled to a quiet life. She could earn more than he could, so why shouldn't she carry on? There she was, enjoying bossing folks round, so why not do it in an office and be paid for it instead of upsetting a man's home? At first Alice argued back. She said she had taken a job as war work, to do her bit, and a nice profitable bit it had been. But now that the war was over, she had no right to a man's job. Thomas had—and his leg wasn't bad enough to prevent him taking one. He could go and get it and she would mind the babies. But Thomas could never hear her out without swearing. So Alice gave up arguing. She also gave up working.

Thomas got hold of his mother, his sister-in-law and an aunt of Alice's and sent them round to talk sense into her. They came, separately and collectively, and sat round Alice's fire and told her she didn't know when she was well off and poor Thomas was in a bad way. Alice went on with her washing and ironing and gave them cups of strong black tea. She listened to them quietly and said: "Daresay you're right," when they had finished. One by one they went away and slipped in to see Thomas to tell him that they'd made Alice see reason and she'd soon come round.

But old Mrs. Gedge knew from the first that Alice would go her own gait and nobody else's. She hobbled across to number ten on two sticks, was helped into the rocking-chair and promptly went to sleep by the fire. When she woke up, she said: "Mind now, Alice, I don't blame you. Wot I say is as it's a man's place to keep 'is family, that's wot I say. Besides, it don't do a man no good to 'ang about the way Thomas does. I wouldn't 'ave it, neither. But all the same, seeing you like office work . . ."

"Matter o' conscience," said Alice, turning red and picking fat Dulcie out of the coal scuttle. Mrs. Gedge nodded and mumbled. Dulcie screamed with rage until the old lady took her on her knee and let her nibble the smooth, worn handle of one of her sticks. That was the last Alice heard of the matter, for Mrs. Gedge told Thomas straight that he was wasting his breath. "There's no turning 'er," she said.

Thomas stayed at home till his gratuity was exhausted. Then he made one more effort to persuade Alice to find a job. When that failed, he went out resignedly to find one himself. But there was a glut of chauffeurs, able-bodied men without the limp Thomas had acquired and with the polish he had lost.

1919 turned into 1920 and Thomas went drearily from one indifferent job to another. The War had used up all his ambition and drained away most of his energy. He went out an alert, adventurous creature; he came back a heavy, apathetic man, who no longer minded what sort of work he did. He was incapable of looking ahead. All his interests were primitive: he only wanted enough to eat, a few drinks, a warm bed with a woman in it. He accepted Alice phlegmatically and took the children for granted.

But at last, in 1921, he settled down into regular work at a small garage out Hampstead way. Thomas often took night shifts and stayed in bed during the day. Sometimes he did theatre work and came back at two or three in the morning. Sometimes he got up at dawn to finish repairs that had to be done to time. The pay was poor, but the erratic hours suited him. He still wore the blue-bordered flannel vest of naval days, and swaggered round to the 'Three Feathers' whenever he could.

Alice continued to stay at home, minding the children and the flat in the same efficient way that she had cared for Lady Boyd and managed her staff at the Ministry. But the efficiency gradually took on a tinge of bitterness. The War which had so stunted Thomas had stretched and strained Alice's ability and fed her ambition. She could not take life at Thomas's pace and, as he could not be prodded on and she had no work of her own left, she slaved fanatically for the children. She ceased to love them in the warm and casual way she had loved them when they were babies: instead, she cared for them as a trainer might care for champions. Good food, good clothes, good manners, she could and would give them, whether they liked it or not.

Good health they obviously had, and if they only had brains—Alice cherished and dreamed over every childish hint of intelligence—then they should have their chance. Sometimes in the evenings, when Thomas was either out or dozing by the fire, Alice sewed or darned and thought of scholarships and colleges. She had a secret account in the post-office in the children's name and, as soon as Thomas's back was turned, she would pick up his evening paper and turn to the racing news. For there was no harm in having a gamble—just once in a while. On the Derby now. That was none of your shady tipsters' frolics. The Derby was a National Institution, said Alice, cheering up.

CHAPTER 2

1921   DINNER TIME IN TUFFNEL ROAD

NOVEMBER rain sluiced down Tuffnel Road, stopping up the drains with banana skins and cigarette stubs and cabbage stalks and silver paper and all the other odds and ends that were continually escaping from the small rickety dustbins. It battered the privet bushes in front gardens, flattened out the brave chrysanthemums in the flower-beds of number ten, filtered between faulty slates into nearly all the attics, and collected in dismal puddles by every back door in the street.

It was half-past twelve, and the smell of mixed cooking hung over the road. There were three or four dinners going, on stoves or gas-rings or oil-cookers, for the three or four families who shared most of the houses, and they varied from sheep's head and onions to bacon or fried fish. It was an encouraging kind of smell, and Thomas sniffed it appreciatively, hoping for sheep's head, as he turned the corner from Silver Street. The rain had soaked through his coat already and his trouser-ends dripped into shoes that squelched at every step. But Thomas was pretty well used to being wet, and he intended to go to bed after his dinner, anyway, for he had been on night duty all that week.

He unhitched the loop of string that fastened the gate of number ten and banged the gate behind him. Alice opened the front door as he stretched out his hand for the knocker.

"My goodness," she said, "you're a bit wet, aren't you? Here, give me your coat. What do you think you are, a dog, shaking yourself all over my clean floor?"

Thomas let her take his coat and cap and elbowed past her without speaking. He sat down in the rocking-chair in front of the kitchen fire, shook off his shoes into the grate, found a cigarette in his waistcoat pocket, lit it and asked what there was for dinner.

"Tripe," said Alice, moving a shirt from the clothes-horse and hanging Thomas's coat over it instead.

"Well, let's 'ave it, there's a good girl."

"There's Len and Dulcie not back yet," said Alice. "I don't want to dish up till they get in. They'll be drenched, poor mites."

"Well, you can give me my 'elping now, can't you?" said Thomas. "I don't want to wait for a couple of kids, do I? I pay for the food, don't I?"

"I should've thought you'd've had patience for five minutes, Thomas. How can I bring the children up proper, with nice manners and all if they come in and find their own father guzzling in an armchair by the fire? Why can't you help by setting a decent example?"

"Blast them kids," said Thomas. "You don't give me no peace about them. I can't 'ardly get me smokes and a drink because of them … you take every penny I 'ave off me … Why should they 'ave new boots and be dolled up to go to school when I go wet and 'ungry to me work? I tell you wot, Alice, if you don't look sharp and give me me dinner, you'll 'ear such langwidge and the kids'll 'ear such langwidge that you'll be sorry you crossed me."

Thomas leant back and shut his eyes. He had said his final word and knew it was a winner. He boasted in masculine society that he never laid a finger on his wife. But he did not explain that he had found out, within three weeks of marriage, that his vocabulary was the best weapon he possessed. There was a streak of gentility in Alice and a really full-blooded oath made her sick.

Alice dished up drearily, scooping Thomas's portion out of the pan, and slamming potatoes into the gravy so that it splashed over the edge of the plate. Two of the best dishes were warming in the plate-rack, but Alice ignored them. She had arranged to give her family dinner on a nicely-set table, with a fresh white cloth and the spoons and forks laid cross-wise and the last few chrysanthemums in a pink and gold vase in the middle. The vase had been a present from some of the girls in the Pensions, and it matched the pink walls and the curtains. For Alice's kitchen was a parlour as well. The mahogany sideboard given to her by Lady Boyd stood next to the door, with a photograph of Thomas in uniform on it beside a large electroplate biscuit barrel. The rocking-chair had a pink silk cushion in it, and there was a bright red Indian rug by the window. But what was the use of having things nice when Thomas spoilt it all, gobbling up his dinner by the fire instead of sitting up to the table properly? Better not bother with the extra dishes, she thought, and save the washing-up.

Alice planned this kind of really nice dinner several times a week—whenever she knew that Thomas would be in, in fact. But it very rarely materialised.

As Thomas's last mouthful disappeared with a plop, the gate slammed again and Alice put down her saucepan and let in the children. Both of them had on sensible boots with strong soles, mackintoshes and sou'westers. They began a long, incoherent story about teacher directly they were inside the door, and it rippled on while Alice took off their wet things, smoothed Len's hair, blew his nose, combed Dulcie's fair hair that she took such pains to curl, tweaked her dress straight and drove them through the kitchen to the sink (hidden behind a japanned screen) to wash their hands.

Thomas planked his plate down on the floor and glowered at them.

"All this spit and polish," he said. "Brushing your 'air and washin' your 'ands. 'Oo do you think you are? Lord and Lady Fauntleroy?"

"Now, Dad," said Alice, "you know very well …"

"Garn," said Thomas, closing his eyes again. The children, recognising danger-signals, stopped chattering and ate their dinner warily, with one eye on Alice, who was apt to be particular about manners. Neither of them said anything till the food was safe, but then Len began rummaging in his trouser pockets. He disentangled two dirty blue cards from a mixture of string and toffee and pushed them over the table to Alice.

She said: "Mercy, what's this?" and before she could find out, Thomas took them from her.

He peered at them for some time, turning them this way and that. Then he growled: "What's this? 'Medical Inspection … You are requested to attend … examine your child … Leonard … 2.30.' And another for Dulcie. Must be daft. There ain't nothing wrong with Len. Nor Dulcie neither. Look 'ow they eat. Seein' doctors is all my eye. Don't you go, Ma, nor you kids neither. They can't make you."

Dulcie giggled. "Teacher can," she said. But Len said, "Aw, it don't cost nothin', Pa," going to the core of the matter at once.

"If any child of mine … " began Thomas violently, and Alice hustled the children out of the room into the dark little passage that always smelt of damp clothes. She flung on their mackintoshes, helped them to lace their boots and drove them out into the rain. The school would still be shut for the lunch hour, but better the wet streets or the puddles of the dripping playground than the warm kitchen with Thomas's language in it. But when she got back to him, he was asleep.

II
HUBERT STREET

MISS ISABEL SNOW pattered down Hubert Street towards the gaunt school. She wore pepper-and-salt tweeds, because she thought them business-like, and a smart hat and high-heeled shoes as a tribute to London. The realisation of middle age had overtaken her unexpectedly two years before. At forty-five, she had been jaunting round Italy in gay clothes that accentuated her spreading figure. At forty-six, she had suddenly come home, taken a small flat in Alfred House at the good end of Silver Street—so cheap and central and a nice address—and given herself up to social work.

As a Care Committee Worker (voluntary) attached to three elementary schools and Secretary to one, it was her business to see that parents carried out doctor's orders, that sick children had holidays, that underfed children had free dinners. She managed Hubert Street school entirely, and kept an eye on two others. But Hubert Street was, as she said, her best school: the children were a good type, their parents decent folk. She wore her second-best coat and skirt when she attended its functions and did not bother to change when she came back from Medical Inspections; nor did she wear her special "good works" clothes when she visited in the neighbourhood.

She was a little late on this particular afternoon and the big hall on the Infants' Floor was empty, for the children had already gone to their classrooms. The high-pitched drone of lessons had begun and, as she went down the passage, she could see rows of bent heads through the half glass doors.

By the time she had climbed three flights of stairs, from INFANTS to GIRLS and on to BOYS, she was a little out of breath. She hurried into the small staff-room set aside for the occasion, acknowledging an absent-minded nod from the doctor and a supercilious smile from the nurse.

Miss Snow pulled up a chair to the table, snapped open her attaché case, picked out a bundle of blue case sheets and yellow report sheets and a large shiny black notebook. She took off her good coat and hung it over the back of her chair, smoothed out the collar of her heavy silk tailored blouse, folded her gloves, tried the nib of her pen and turned to the nurse.

"Has the doctor seen any yet?"

"They're coming up this minute," said the nurse, shuffling and re-shuffling a pack of white cards. She was a small sallow woman in a white but crumpled overall and an uncompromising blue felt uniform hat. In her opinion, Care Committees were unnecessary and their representatives had no business at medical inspections. She took Miss Snow's presence as a personal affront. On the other hand, the doctor, a large mellow woman, saw no objection to it and would even stay for a cup of tea and a semi-medical gossip afterwards. Then Miss Snow stood, temporarily, on Olympus; she, too, shared in the ordering of lives. All the slights and snubs and jeers, the slammed doors and broken promises she met when she went visiting ceased to matter.

As she turned over her papers, she wondered if this would be a lucky afternoon, with a cup of tea and a talk at the end of it. But nurse said that there were more cases than usual.

Nurse got up.

"Ready, Doctor? ... Rosie Adams and Johnnie Brown, please. Come along, now hurry up. Just take her dress off, will you, Mother?"

Rosie's blowsy mother peeled a scarlet velvet frock off Rosie's fat arms and shoulders and edged her suspiciously towards the doctor.

Doctor Ethel Hawkes laid down her pen and looked over the stout grubby child.

"Sorry, Mother, but you'll have to take off far more than that," she said.

Rosie's mother began a grumble: "Nurse said, to take off 'er dress ... she's that subjec' to colds ... "

"And how do you expect me to see her chest through all that flannel? Come along, quick. Let's have it all off.... What's your name? Rosie? Well, Rosie, you're too big to cry. That's it. Four petticoats and stays and a vest ... No wonder she takes cold." Her stethoscope went quickly over Rosie's chest, and as she took it away, the child let out a bellow. Dr. Hawkes immediately popped a wooden spatula into her mouth. The roar was cut short and changed to angry sobs as the weapon was withdrawn and tossed into the waste-paper basket. The doctor waved the pair away.

"Nothing whatever the matter," she said, "except too many wraps. One vest in future, Mother, and one petticoat, if you like. But keep them CLEAN ... Next, please."

The affronted Rosie and the still more affronted parent backed away. Propelled by his angular, bad-tempered mother, Johnnie Brown took his place by the doctor and stood and shivered while his narrow little chest was thumped, his unhealthy throat examined, his eyelids drawn back from his pallid eyes.

" 'E ain't never ailed nothink," said his mother loudly. " 'E only coughs from 'abit. I don't know what you want to drag a 'onest woman up 'ere for, for nothink, as if you was the Prevention of Cruelty. I ain't never touched 'im. 'E's all right."

"That'll do." Dr. Hawkes pulled Johnnie's thin shirt round him and buttoned it up. "He needs care," she said. "To begin with, his throat's in a bad condition, but before we touch it, I'd like his chest thoroughly examined. Now go along to that lady over there, and she'll arrange it for you."

She tossed a slip of paper across to Miss Snow, ignored the protests of the mother and told nurse to send for the next case. Miss Snow spent five minutes trying to persuade Johnnie's mother to do as she was told and take the child to the Tuberculosis Clinic, and when she finally went, she made a dreary note in her book ... 'Follow up. Child T.B. unlikely to get treatment.'

At this rate, she thought irritably, they'll never get through the case list in time for tea. She looked up to see how the next patient was getting on and saw with relief that the mother was an energetic, capable young woman of a very different type and the children nice sturdy youngsters. Not likely to take up the doctor's time.

'Now there's a really nice woman,' thought Miss Snow. 'No nonsense about her. She looks almost a lady ... Fancy, white gloves ... and those shoes ... they weren't bought in Silver Street either ... respectable, though ... none of those nasty sham pearls. Of course the voice gives her away ... But the children, they might be *anyone's* ... that's a good sensible frock ... and knickers to match ... and a Liberty bodice ... and proper combinations. So *clean* ... it's not often you see clothes a *real white* here ... '

"Well, Mrs. Gedge," said Dr. Hawkes (and Miss Snow in her corner nodded to herself: you could hardly call that young woman 'Mother,' like the rest) "so this is Dulcie? She looks in splendid health ... still, we'll just see ... Ah, there are one or two teeth, I think, that need attention, but that's all. The boy next ... that's good sensible dressing ... Come along, sonnie, and let's look at your chest. Well, I think we'd better get the dentist to look at your mouth too. They're both fine, Mrs. Gedge. You get them off to bed early?"

"Seven sharp," said Alice beaming. "They have a real good dinner when they come home from morning school and as much tea as they can eat at five, and then just milk and biscuits after they're bathed."

Dr. Hawkes smiled back a companionable smile; Alice was so enthusiastic. "That's grand," she said. "I congratulate you, Mrs. Gedge. If you'll go to that lady over there, she'll arrange about the dentist for you. Will you explain to Mrs. Gedge, Miss Snow?"

Miss Snow smiled at Alice too. There was some pleasure in helping someone who was glad of advice, so eager to be helped, so grateful for appointments with the dentist, so proud of her children. Miss Snow noted names and addresses enthusiastically: Alice went off with Len and Dulcie at her heel: the dreary procession of children and mothers continued. There were boys who were 'that 'ighly strung' and girls who were miserable with tonsils or incoherent with adenoids and a string of small children with streaming colds (so that Miss Snow hurriedly pulled out her eucalyptus and sprayed her handkerchief). And others were fed on 'wot we 'ave ourselves, a bit of kipper or pork and a drop of stout,' and even more were perpetually under-nourished and some were perversely fat and blooming in spite of wrong feeding. There were no dirty heads or verminous clothes, because the Hubert Street children were 'good class.' But the room gradually filled with a warm, sour human smell.

"Thank goodness that's over," said Dr. Hawkes, as she sent away the last case. "Open the windows, will you, Nurse? Ah, tea ... splendid. Come along, Miss Snow. Can't you stop, Nurse? What a pity. Still, we won't keep you."

When the nurse had gathered up her papers and her coat and clumped away down the stone stairs, Dr. Hawkes pulled her chair closer to the small fire, hitched up her skirt, crossed her knees and lit a cigarette. She handed her case mechanically to Miss Snow, who, as usual, shook her head.

Dr. Hawkes said: "That was a remarkable young woman."

"Mrs. Gedge?" Miss Snow lowered her voice. "Do you think, Doctor," she said, "that they can be her own children? I mean, when I saw her first, I really thought ... but, of course, directly she spoke ... very superior though. And, of course, as I saw from the Case Sheet, her husband's a mechanic, quite a poor position ...two pounds ten shillings a week, I think. But the children, they look so different."

"Oh, they're her own, right enough," said Dr. Hawkes. "No need to invent a romance, Miss Snow. The real thing's far more interesting ... a woman, in a district like this, but with our sort of standards, bringing up her children on next to nothing ... with healthy bodies and good manners and fine ideas ..."

"I wonder," said Miss Snow, "whether they'll rise ... beyond Tuffnel Road, I mean? I wonder what she was before she married ... if the girl takes after her, she might do anything. I wonder ..."

"I wonder," said Dr. Hawkes, out of an infinite experience of brave beginnings, "whether she'll keep it up."

CHAPTER 3

I

1923   SPRING

MISS SNOW had been in Italy again since the Christmas of 1922, chaperoning a niece about Rome, Florence and Siena. Now she was back, looking much the same, for she had reached the age when the years only deepen their tracks. The English March felt cold and hopeless: Alfred House needed re-painting: the view of the tramlines and the railway was grimmer than ever.

Miss Snow had meant to have a couple of days of inquisitive idleness before she settled down to her routine of voluntary work, committees, bazaars and bridge. She usually enjoyed coming home, finding a pile of letters containing appointments and invitations, agendas and telephone messages, hearing the detailed and intimate news of every flat in the block from the maid she shared with half a dozen other households. Mrs. Black was generally so good: there would be hot toast and a good cup of tea waiting and bacon and eggs for breakfast. But when Miss Snow rang, no one answered and she had to let herself in with her own latch-key—so providential that she had carried it with her all that way. She found a cascade of letters and bills on the hall linoleum, thick dust in every room and a blotchy note on the sitting-room mantelpiece: "Mrs. Black as trouble with her stomak she is goin into ospital and cannot oblige Regrets."

So Miss Snow had to dust her own flat, make up her bed and go out to get a meal at the Willow Restaurant round the corner, where one dined (three courses, coffee extra) for one-and-sixpence. On her way back to the flat, she met

31

young Mr. Dean from next door, who told her that Mrs. Black was very bad, that her sister, who had been obliging him, was a slattern, so that he kept on finding bacon and eggs on his supper plate, that the people downstairs were going and that the top flat was let at last. And what did Miss Snow think of it? But Miss Snow said she was too tired to think at all and went straight to bed in a state of exasperated depression that lasted over night and enveloped her again in the morning.

Over a boiled egg, she decided to go straight to the office and work till lunch-time. After that, she would try to find a good daily woman. For there was no point in taking a few days to look round in when there were no home comforts in the background. It would quite spoil a nice play to know that there was no supper waiting for her at home.

So she put on her old pepper-and-salt tweeds and went round to the local Care Committee Offices. The paid officials, curt, decided young women, whose chilly competence was utterly inimical to voluntary workers, had all the upper part of the house. But on the ground floor, there was a long, inconveniently narrow room, with cream walls and blue curtains, set apart for the voluntary workers, and outside it there was a garden into which they were also allowed and where one of them persistently tried to grow bulbs.

This room had no desks, but there were files along the walls and there was a large table round which everybody worked. On a busy afternoon, it was very difficult to avoid mixing up case papers, upsetting ink or jogging a neighbour's elbow. But Miss Snow, who had not been brought up to be business-like, did not find it at all inconvenient, and besides, as a senior worker, she had acquired the head of the table for her own use. As she came into the room, she was pleased to see that an extra large and bulging folder (marked HUBERT STREET ... MISS SNOW ...) was laid at her usual place.

She lit the fire, for she did not believe in being chilly: she gave her services for nothing and considered that the L.C.C. owed her as much gas as she liked to burn. Then she hung up her coat, put on her spectacles, adjusted her pen and started to go through the case sheets. And she began to feel happier, for at last she was back in her own niche and the pile of papers was ample proof that no one filled it quite as well as she did.

As she sorted them out, scrutinising the new ones severely, shaking her head over well-known offenders, she kept up a continual murmur of comment: "Dear, dear, Johnnie Brown again ... to go to a Special School ... Well, we all knew it would come to that ... Violet Pope, appointments not kept ... well now, there shouldn't have been any trouble there ... I can't understand that ... these professional workers will rush things so. I shall just have to go round myself ... Gedge, spectacles, two shillings owing. Mother says cannot pay ... Gedge, now let me see ..." For a moment Miss Snow's memory wavered. Then she picked up the papers again ... surely it was that very cold afternoon in the autumn ... no, not last autumn, the year before, of course. Well now, was it really nearly two years since she had been surprised by Alice Gedge ... a green hat, a grey coat and skirt, white gloves and shoes not bought in Silver Street. And the children might have been anybody's. She turned back to the beginning. There it was, Gedge, Leonard and Gedge, Dulcie, of 10 Tuffnel Road, followed by the Doctor's splendid report and her own: "Mother extremely pleasant, superior and refined. Home excellent and well kept ..." There were no other entries until the beginning of 1923, when Leonard, now eleven, had been sent up as a special case, because his eyes were clearly defective. The doctor had ordered glasses and noted that his condition was poor. The professional Care Committee worker, visiting in Miss Snow's absence, had added an unfavourable comment on the child's clothes and another about his mother: "Inclined to be tiresome. Says cannot afford three-and-sixpence for specs. Might pay sixpence a fortnight. Home poor." When Miss Snow turned up Dulcie's record, she found the child described as under-nourished. She was getting extra milk at school. Miss Snow gave an impatient little sigh and tossed the papers into the pile she had marked for visits. After all, Dr. Hawkes had been right ... Mrs. Gedge had not kept it up. It was just another back-street tragedy. But she might as well go and investigate it ... You never knew with professional social workers ... it was surprising how often they were wrong.

II

THREE O'CLOCK IN TUFFNEL ROAD

THE FIRE in the kitchen of number 10 was nearly out, but the coat and skirt hanging in front of it were still heavy with damp from the early morning shower. There was just a handful of small coal in the bucket, enough for a tiny fire, but it would have to be hoarded for next morning. Alice wondered if there were enough gas left to heat an iron without putting another penny in the meter. Then she decided that it was a pity to waste gas on a skirt that no ironing would dry, when she herself would be so much better for a cup of tea before she went out again.

She dragged the clothes-horse nearer to the stove, pulled a faded pink wrapper round her shoulders and put her feet on the hob. As she settled herself more comfortably, she remembered the dishes that ought to be washed up, the darning that should be done for the children, the unswept kitchen. If she made an effort, she could do out the kitchen quite easily before the children got back from school. There were three hours before she need start; she only had to be in Oxford Street at six-twenty. But at half-past six, she would be scrubbing the marble paving in the vestibule behind the wrought-iron grill that kept the public out of Everyman's Stores, while the people whose day's work was finished passed to and fro, peering in. It was a pity to waste that last flicker of warmth from the embers ... the cleaning might just as well wait another day. Alice's head sagged forward and she dozed.

The front door bell rang three times before she heard it. Then she dragged herself up reluctantly and half started towards the hall. But she sat down again. It might have been her bell, but again, it mightn't. 'I've got no money for them, anyway, whoever it is,' she thought. The caller had taken to the knocker, and the thumps shook the house. "It'll be for Mrs. Watkins, I shouldn't wonder," Alice said as the stairs creaked. There was a scuffle of carpet slippers in the passage, blurred voices, then a pause. The front door did not slam and the carpet slippers came down the hall again. Mrs. Watkins from upstairs pushed open Alice's door and put a grey, frizzed head round it.

"Lidy to see yer," she said.

"What from?"

"I dunno. Why can't yer answer yer own bells?"

She shuffled off again. Alice sighed. There was no escape. Friendly callers were rare in the afternoons, and the others were not easily persuaded to go away once they knew their victim was in. So she rolled up the pink wrapper and flung it behind the mangle, pulled on her damp skirt, flinching as the wet coat fitted clammily over her shoulders, pushed one shilling, one sixpence and three coppers behind the alarm clock and went out. (You never knew. Once let the Rates or the Rent or the Care Committee or any other collector see money and they took it off you, whatever you said.)

Miss Snow was impatient: she had been waiting for five minutes on that particular doorstep and she had already waited just as long on three others in the same road. None of the people she had visited had been at all glad to see her or been willing to take her advice. So she had not been able to prove her own efficiency as a visitor, and in consequence her sympathetic interest had curdled: it was only curiosity that made her ring Alice Gedge's bell. But she felt that Alice Gedge ought to redeem an afternoon of unprofitable calls.

And then Alice opened the door, an Alice who looked just like any other Tuffnel Road housewife. Her face was as dirty, her fair hair as unkempt and threaded, surprisingly, with grey. She held the door in just the same way, poking her head round it with the same sullen expression on her face.

"Why can't you answer the door?" Miss Snow said, disappointed and therefore resentful.

"It's my door," said Alice. "I suppose I can do as I please."

"You've no business to keep people waiting on a cold day like this," said Miss Snow. "I suppose you know that there's still two-and-six owing on Leonard's glasses?"

"Oh, from the Care Committee, are you?" Alice said. "Well, I can't let you have it to-day. I'll send it to school by Len on Monday."

"You might just as well give it to me now," said Miss Snow. "It's got to be paid, you know."

"It's only Thursday to-day," said Alice desperately.

There was a frightened note in her voice that made Miss Snow look more closely at her. She had let the door swing open and Miss Snow could see that her coat was wet; it was the same coat that she had worn two years ago. But now the stuff was frayed and there was a patch under one arm.

"D'you think," said Alice suddenly, "that I like being in your debt? Come Monday I'll pay you. I don't touch my money till Saturday."

"You needn't pay it all at once," said Miss Snow, more kindly, her interest kindling. "We don't want to press you. But if money is owing, we must find out why ... the circumstances ..."

"It'll be all right Monday," said Alice again, and then the shower that had been threatening all the afternoon broke in a scurry of rain. Miss Snow, who had turned to go, hesitated on the bottom step.

"And I've forgotten my umbrella," she said.

Alice pulled open the door unwillingly.

"You'd better step inside," she said, "if you'll excuse my kitchen, that is. I'm not straight."

Rather to her own surprise, Miss Snow did go in and followed Alice down the narrow brown passage.

It was so dark that by contrast Alice's untidy kitchen was almost cheerful, though the paint was dirty, the curtains needed washing, the floor was unswept and the fire out. Alice pulled up the rocking-chair for the visitor, gave the ashes a despairing poke and cleared the clutter from the end of the table.

The rain spattered on the windows, and Miss Snow was so thankful to be spared a wetting that all her interest in the Gedge family welled up again.

"You know, I remember you so well, Mrs. Gedge," she said, "although it's nearly two years since I called. It was just after Leonard had that double tooth out. Dulcie had a little trouble with her front ones, too, didn't she? I do hope they're all right now?"

"Fancy you remembering! Len's ever such a big boy now. You'd hardly know him. And Dulcie, too, she's growing. Too fast, I sometimes think."

"That's just what Dr. Hawkes said. I see she's having extra milk. But I hope she's quite well?"

Alice did not answer at once. She went on mechanically tidying away the odds and ends that had been left to lie about for weeks. Then she turned round.

"Neither of them are as well as they were," she said in a tight, hard voice, "if that's what you mean. Mr. Gedge was out of work all winter. We're through our savings. I ought to've cut down and done with less for all of us sooner. But I didn't. I haven't paid up the back rent yet. But there, we mustn't grumble Mr. Gedge's got taken on at Lord Douglas's workshop for ex-service men ... it's not much of a job ... only two pounds a week. But it'll be steady. And I've been in work myself most of the time this last month or two ... cleaning at Everyman's. I'll let you have that two-and-six for Len on Monday."

"Never mind the two-and-six now," said Miss Snow. "Do you mean you've been scrubbing floors?"

"And polishing them afterwards," said Alice. "Six-thirty to ten, it is. After they're shut."

"But that work's much too rough for you. Why didn't you try service? Oh, not a resident place, of course, but there's always such a shortage of reliable dailies," said Miss Snow, remembering as she spoke that she wanted one herself.

"Charring's such chancy work," said Alice. "They told me at the Labour that regular cleaning was what I ought to try for. Besides, I've never done much housework, not on a big scale."

Miss Snow said cautiously: "But supposing I could get you some daily work ... cleaning and a little cooking ... ?"

Alice said with equal caution: "I'm not up to fancy ways."

Miss Snow's enthusiasm blossomed under opposition.

"Just plain cooking, sweeping and dusting, a little silver to clean, perhaps," she said persuasively.

"Oh, silver," said Alice, "I'm used to handling that. I can clean all right. And if it were plain cooking ... But would it be regular?"

"Well, we should have to try it," said Miss Snow. "Twelve-and-six a week I pay. For a little morning work and two evenings a week. But in the block of flats where I live two or three of us usually share a maid. I daresay you could fit in another family or two. In that case you could count on a steady thirty shillings ... Of course, some have less done than others."

"If you're looking for somebody ... ?" said Alice.

"My woman left me yesterday," said Miss Snow. "I'm doing for myself now. So if you'd like to try it ..."

"Have you no-one to clean up for you to-day?" said Alice.

"Miss Snow said: "Oh, I can manage."

Alice reached out her hand, extracted a penny from behind the clock and thrust it recklessly into the jaws of the meter.

"You'd like a cup of tea before you start home," she said. "I know what it is when you've been on your feet all afternoon. The kettle'll boil in a minute. I'll give in my notice at Everyman's to-night. But I mightn't be able to help you much in the evenings just till I've finished down in Oxford Street. What time would you like me to come in the mornings?"

"That'll be all right," said Miss Snow. "But if you could be round by eight …" She watched Alice make tea … thank goodness she heated the pot, had the kettle on the boil and measured the tea. She took one of Alice's best pink cups and sipped gratefully.

"You don't know the address yet," said Miss Snow. "But it's not far. Alfred House …"

"I know it," said Alice, "I pass it on my way to Oxford Street. That great block looking over the railway at the good end of Silver Street."

Miss Snow nodded and put down her cup; she fumbled in her bag. "Here's my spare key," she said. "You'd better have it and then you can get in without waking me. The rain's stopped. I'll have to get on."

"I don't seem able to say much," said Alice, "but I'm *grateful*…"

But Miss Snow picked up her attaché case and scuttled off, wondering whether she had been an utter fool—engaging a strange woman, without references, and giving her the key of the flat. Well, thank goodness her best silver tea set, worth fifty pounds at the very least, was locked away in the bank. And she would not get it out until she had got to know Alice Gedge a good deal better.

When Miss Snow had gone, Alice shut the door with a clap and hurried down the passage, rolling up her sleeves as she went. She dragged out the mangle to get her apron from behind it and turned the furniture out of the kitchen. She filled a bucket at the sink and scrubbed the floor, humming abstractedly. She washed down the table and climbed on a chair to take down the dingy curtains, and she had started to polish up the sideboard when the children came in.

"Now, Dulcie and Len," she called, "take off your shoes in the passage and don't bring your dirty feet over my clean floor." She stepped cautiously over the damp patches to the door and handed first one child and then the other over the shining oilcloth to the kitchen table.

"What's up, Ma?" said Dulcie. "We haven't had a turn-out for ever so long."

"Marge and bloater paste, Ma," said Len. "What's come over you. 'Ave you won a fortune?"

"Miracles do happen," said Alice, "so may be one day I'll win a sweep. Not that I've done it now, that's to say. But you eat up your tea and don't gabble."

"You must've 'ad a bit of good luck. Come on," said Len, "where did you get it?"

"Lady of the name of Snow, young curiosity," said Alice, "if you must know. I'm stopping at Everyman's and going to do for her and her friends. There."

"Well, if you 'ave come into some cash," said Len, "I wish you'd give me a tanner. Teacher's been chasin' me again for sixpence on account of my glasses."

"I'll give you the lot on Monday—that'll be two-and-six. But no tricks, mind. 'Cause I shall look in when I'm passing and ask teacher if she's had it."

"Coo," said Len, his dreams of the picture palace and unlimited toffee fading hurriedly. "But wot's the use of givin' teacher two-and-six when the ole girl'd take a tanner?"

"Because I choose," said Alice. "I don't like owing for things."

"Coo," said Len again, and tipped his mug over his nose. He was a small dark child with sallow cheeks and thin legs. He took after his father in looks and character and after his mother in intelligence. At school, his teachers thought highly of him; he would be up to scholarship standard. But he was

41

not popular with his form, because he drove a hard bargain in knives and pencils and cigarette-ends and cigarette cards and coupons.

He pushed the last bite of bread into his mouth and pulled a very dirty page of *Comic Cuts* from his pocket. He had acquired it in the gutter, been scolded twice for reading it in class and hoped to trade it off to-morrow for some stamps.

But Dulcie ate her tea more slowly, swinging her legs in their torn stockings. Her fair hair, that Alice no longer bothered to crimp, hung in limp, unbrushed plaits. Her small round face was so hollowed and shadowed that her likeness to Alice was absurd. She was a quiet child and no one was sure whether she would turn out to be extra clever or extra stupid. Alice was fonder of her than she was of Len, but all her hopes were set on the boy. Girls, come to that, didn't get much of a chance in this life.

Alice cleared away the tea things. "Dulcie," she said, "I've got to go out. Tell your father to put back the furniture when he comes in. And keep your feet off my floor. And mind you're in bed by the time I'm back. Both of you."

Dulcie said: "Oh, Ma, must you go yet? It don't take you all that time to get to Oxford Street." .

"I'm looking in at my new place on the way," said Alice. "Tell Dad there's a bit of ham left for him in the meat safe."

II
MISS SNOW'S TREASURE

ON her way down the Street, Alice called in at the General and Household Stores, which stocked everything from tin baths to cocoa, and smelled of bacon and tea and paraffin and paint.

"I'm starting in on a new job Monday, Mrs. Sims," she said to the proprietress, a heavy, flabby woman who spent her time behind the cash desk working out accounts, "so I'll be paying up what I owe you in a day or two."

Mrs. Sims flapped over the pages of a dirty little cash book. "That's aw' ri', Mrs. Gedge, dear," she said. "There's only a few shillin's standing against yer. I don't want ter press yer, yer know, dearie. An' if there's any little thing yer wantin' in the meantime ... I'm always one to oblige, yer know. Especially if yer' in work. I mean ter sye, we all got ter live, 'aven't we?"

Alice ordered a tin of cocoa, a pound of bacon, some soap flakes and, as an ultimate extravagance, a pound of butter.

Mrs. Sims made a note of it. "Well, dearie, it must be a good job, that's all I can say. Butter and flakes, too. Aw' ri', Bertie can take 'em round for you on 'is way 'ome."

"Much obliged," said Alice. "I've got to be off. Good-day, Mrs. Sims."

Thank goodness,' thought Alice, as she waited for the tram at the corner, 'I needn't be beholden to that woman any more.' For Mrs. Sims and her dirty little shop thrived on the unwillingness of the stores in Silver Street to give long credit. Inferior quality, high prices, long credit were Mrs. Sims's stock-in-trade, and she had a flair for collecting bad debts.

All the way in the tram, Alice tingled with returning pride. Of course, daily housemaid in a block of flats was just nothing at all when you thought of Everton Court in the old days, and the position a lady's maid took in every servants' hall all over England. Come to that, service of any kind was a come-down after the Ministry. Alice found it difficult to believe that she had ever worked in that long green room, with twenty girls under her, and had brought home six pounds a week. But there it was, you had to take what you could get in this life. Better a housemaid than a cleaner, any day. For just one minute, Alice let herself realise what a nightmare that cleaner's work had been ... the way the dirt oozed out of the cracked paving, the feel of the foul water as she wrung out her cloth, the weight of the bucket as she moved it over the interminable floors ... the bitter cold ...

'What's done's done,' thought Alice, I was lucky to get it. Better than housekeeping on the dole ...' She shook herself.

"Bottom of Silver Street, please," she said to the conductor, handing over her penny.

'A silly name for a street,' Alice thought as she snapped the catch of her purse. 'Half the folk in it haven't enough silver for cigarettes. Reckon we're all hard up these days,' she thought, 'whichever end of the road we live at.' The tram crossed the railway bridge and Alice rang the bell. Alfred House was a little way along on the left, just opposite 'The Silver Fox.'

It was one of a row of large Georgian houses which had been going steadily downhill ever since the railway had been built. Alfred House itself was so big that it was impossible to believe that it could have housed anyone humbler than a duke, though its pretentious architecture was beginning to crumble and the grey stucco was peeling from the cornices. The windows as far as the second floor were set between miniature Corinthian pillars and the door itself, under an immense portico, had elaborate stained glass behind a wrought-iron trellis. But the paint was flaking off and on either side were two rows of brass bells, some of them decorated with rather crumpled visiting cards.

The door was unlatched and swung open at Alice's touch. Apart from the mosaic tiled floor, the hall was not imposing, for most of it had been taken into the two ground-floor flats, and the landlord, ignoring the Grecian pillars by the front door, had painted it all hospital green with a brown border. The stairs, fortunately for him, were stone too and saved carpets. Alfred House had four floors and no lifts. According to the landlord, the flats were compact, the rents attractive and the view (over the railway) spacious.

Miss Snow's flat was number six, on the second floor. Alice rang the bell in case she were in; then, as there was no answer, she fitted the key into the lock. She had been a little discouraged by the entrance into Alfred House—the shabby building and the green paint—hardly any better than the Council flats. But Miss Snow's sitting-room was reassuring. It had mauve walls (a little faded) and white paint. Pink and mauve curtains fluttered at the windows and a big couch covered in the same chintz stood by the fireplace. The writing-desk under the window was mahogany and the candlesticks and photograph-frames on the mantelpiece were silver. The number of small china ornaments, enamel boxes and silver oddments standing on small fragile tables stamped Miss Snow, in Alice's view, as one of the gentry—the pre-war gentry whom she had known and served. It was comforting to touch such familiar objects—and they did need rubbing up, too.

Alice looked into the bedroom: pink and white paint, white net curtains shrouding the commonplace view, pink silk bedspread and a nightdress-case made like an over-blown rose. It was a very small room and most of it was blocked by a gigantic wardrobe which took up the whole of one wall and hid the fireplace. An equally gigantic dressing-table obscured the window. Alice's spirits rose again: it was clear that Miss Snow had been used to much bigger rooms. There was something solid and respectable

45

about all that mahogany—not to speak of the dressing-table fittings—all tortoiseshell and silver, the Madonna in a heavy gilt frame and the pile of good books on the small table by the bed. But that bed, thought Alice, shaking her head at it, would be a nuisance to make—it would have to be pulled out from the wall each time—a very awkward room to clean. Alice damped and laid a tentative finger on the dressing-table: it came away black with dust. Well, she'd just take a look round and take the thick of it off before she went.

She went down the passage again to the kitchen. It was a nice, prim little kitchen, with an enamelled table and a dresser with American cloth on the shelves. But it was not as tidy as the other rooms: the table was greasy, some milk had been spilt on the floor, a frying-pan and two or three saucepans cluttered up the sink, as though Miss Snow had tried to wash them and grown disheartened. And on the draining-board there was a tottering pile of plates and cups.

"Tut tut," said Alice, as she rolled up her sleeves and set to work. There would be time to wash up and lay the table and peel some potatoes.

She was just drying up the last dish as Miss Snow came up the stairs to her front door, her attaché case in one hand and a string bag with fish and matches and vegetables in the other. She was still wondering if she had been wise to give the key of her sanctuary to Alice Gedge.

The partitions in Alfred House were disguised to look solid, but they were remarkably thin. As Miss Snow got out her key, unmistakable sounds of china clinking against china percolated through from the kitchen. Someone was having a meal in that kitchen. "It all comes of being soft-hearted," whimpered Miss Snow, "and giving a key to a stranger." She was timid by nature, and her nerves magnified the small bustling sounds into the sort of clatter that a whole family of Gedges, engaged in raiding her kitchen, might be expected to make. For it was well known that thieves always ended up in the larder. Miss Snow beat upon the door that stood within two feet of her own, for perhaps Mr. Dean might be in. But he was not. And there was no porter at Alfred House, only a caretaker, three flights down in the basement and very probably out. So Miss Snow forced her key into the lock, but as she put it in upside down, it refused to turn. The front door shook on its frail hinges as Miss Snow wrenched at it, and Alice, rolling down her sleeves, prepared to deal harshly with errand boys.

"Now then," said Alice from the other side of the door, "what's all this? Why can't you ring the bell if you want an answer?"

"Oh, Mrs. Gedge," said Miss Snow in a panic.

"Good-evening, miss, I mean m'am," said Alice, too conscious of good intentions to be startled. "I've put the potatoes on and the soup's warming through. I hope I've done right ..."

But Miss Snow, still convinced of disaster, pushed wildly past her and scurried down the passage to the kitchen. It took her some seconds to believe that it was really empty. Then she saw that it shone with cleanliness, as though it were pleased at being polished. The shining pans winked at her and there was a pleasant smell of warm soup.

Miss Snow turned to Alice: "Oh, Mrs. Gedge," she said, "it's most thoughtful of you ..." But Alice, shy and suddenly tired, with a stinging feeling behind her eyes, pulled on her coat and ran. Miss Snow went across to the sitting-room and waved to her as she climbed on her tram.

Then, as she heard the key turn in the lock next door, she went along the passage and looked out.

Mr. Dean, young, fair-haired and absent-minded looking, turned to say good-evening.

"I've taken your advice," he said, "and sacked that sister of Mrs. Black's."

"I'm very glad you have," said Miss Snow warmly, "for I was just coming to tell you that I've found you a *Treasure*."

CHAPTER 4

I

ALFRED HOUSE - FLATS SIX AND SEVEN

IT was Miss Snow who arranged with Alice about the cleaning of Mr. Dean's flat: he was too shy, she explained, to discuss it and would probably never open his mouth to Alice at all. And in fact it was quite a month before he managed to do more than mutter a good-morning when Alice brought in his breakfast.

Yet Alice, with her experience of the best people at Everton Court, placed him at once: as nice a young man as you could wish and as incapable of looking after himself as a real gentleman should be. He was helplessly untidy; a trail of worn socks, discarded pyjamas, buttonless shirts, old letters, odd coppers, bills, receipts and bundles of manuscript marked his progress from bed to bath and bath to breakfast. His voice was quiet and smooth—Alice had heard many like it in country house drawing-rooms—and he had an endearing habit of getting up to open the door for her when she cleared the table. Yet Robert Dean was obviously hard up: he often got his own supper—bread and cheese most nights, but scrambled eggs occasionally. It took Alice all morning to clear up after scrambled eggs, and she could hardly ever save the saucepan. His cups and knives and forks and pots and pans all came from Woolworth's: his curtains and sheets were cheap and skimpy and his blankets worn to the thread. But his furniture was old and, from the polish, Alice knew that it had come from a good home. There was very little of it and the cleaning took her no time at all. Mr. Dean had no ornaments and only one silver-framed photograph, which he kept in his bedroom. Alice used to look at the plain, fattish, girl's face most mornings when she was dusting—an ordinary face, she thought—funny how easy some men were caught. The bedroom walls were smothered with school and college groups, but there were only two pictures in the sitting-room: one sombre etching of King's College, and the other a commonplace reproduction—a naked girl bathing coyly by moonlight. 'Poor innocent,' thought Alice the first time she noticed it.

Every morning, Alice arrived at seven-thirty to the minute, let herself in with the spare key, went along to the bedroom, knocked till she heard a grunt, put her head only round the door and said: "Bacon or eggs, sir?" Robert Dean shouted an answer from under the bedclothes, and Alice went along to fry in the kitchen. When Robert heard the kitchen door shut, he climbed reluctantly out of bed, wrapped a large dressing-gown very tightly round himself and tiptoed to the bathroom. He stayed there till he heard Alice laying the breakfast and then ran back to the bedroom to finish dressing. This modest manoeuvring took so much time that he was always late and usually forgot to brush his hair. But however late he was, Alice invariably waited till he had helped himself to what she considered an adequate meal and he invariably opened *The Times* and spread it as a screen between them. But Alice never tried to talk: once she was sure he was well and eating properly, she hurried across to Miss Snow's flat.

There she made tea and toast and laid the breakfast as decoratively as possible, setting the freshest bowl of flowers in the centre of the table, rubbing up the silver coffee-pot and butter-dish and toast-rack. She lit the fire and brought in the paper and the letters. If there were plenty of three-halfpenny things, she just said "good-morning " as Miss

Snow came in and then got ahead with the dusting and sweeping. But when there were very few letters, or none at all, she always stayed and talked.

For Miss Snow, who had to face a good many lonely, silent meals in a week, liked to talk, even at breakfast; and particularly she liked to talk about Robert Dean. Alice soon knew his whole history. He was the son of a doctor who was killed in the War, but he himself never got to the Front. "Just eighteen when the war ended," said Miss Snow. "Heartbroken, poor lad, that he never joined up." He was a barrister, beginning to scrape a practice together. "So promising—a brilliant boy," Miss Snow said, for the law, like medicine, was to her a mysterious and difficult profession and she had a superstitious admiration for any one who practised it. She told Alice that his mother had died a year ago and it was then that he had moved from lodgings to Alfred House. Alice told Thomas afterwards that it was easy to see that Miss Snow made a real pet of him, and, indeed, as Alice bustled between the two flats, Miss Snow would come pattering after her into Robert Dean's rooms to carry off a pair of socks to darn or a shirt that needed mending. Sometimes she put flowers in the sitting-room; but it was doubtful if Mr. Dean noticed. One Thursday, when Alice had been at Alfred House for about a month, *The Times* failed to arrive and Robert Dean had to face breakfast and Alice without it. When Alice asked if she should go out and get a copy, he said hurriedly: "Oh, no, no. I'll get one at the station. It's quite all right ... I wouldn't dream of bothering you ..."

"So long as it doesn't spoil your breakfast," said Alice amiably. "But there, you'd better have the daffies instead." She moved an earthenware jar full of pale and brilliant daffodils to the table.

"Match the sun, don't they?" she said.

Robert started and flushed.

"Oh Lord," he said, "oh good Lord, did Miss Snow ... I never noticed ..."

"There's two pairs of socks and an old coat in her basket this minute," said Alice.

Robert fidgeted with his knife and crumbled his bread. "She *will* do it," he said, "I've often thought ... since you've been here ... whether perhaps you wouldn't undertake ... it would be extra, of course ... save Miss Snow trouble ..."

"She doesn't want to be saved the trouble," said Alice. "Depend upon it, it fills the time if you've someone to be a trouble to you. Often she asks me if I reckon you get enough to eat."

"Oh, I know," said Robert, rumpling his hair. "She asks me too. Awfully good of her. D'you know," he added, "I don't even know your name."

"Alice," she said, never guessing that Robert did not even know her as Mrs. Gedge, but always thought and spoke of her as 'Miss Snow's Treasure.'

Robert flushed more than ever, but after that he always called her Alice, though it embarrassed him terribly at first.

Next morning, the paper was up to time, but Robert never bothered to open it. Instead, he glanced at his letters, pushed them aside and turned to Alice.

"Alice," he said, "I've been wondering ... Miss Snow, now, do you think she'd care to do a show or something? With me, I mean."

"If you ask me," said Alice, "I'd say she wouldn't half be pleased. Make a bit of a change for her."

Robert considered this while he poured out another cup of tea.

"And what sort of a show do you suppose Miss Snow would care to see?" he said anxiously.

"I don't know, I'm sure," said Alice. "I've never heard she was a great one for the theatre. But there, if you're set on it, I'll find out and tell you."

"Are you good at finding out things?" said Robert.

"Well, there's always ways," said Alice cautiously.

"Then I wish you'd find out who's taken the top flat," said Robert. "They'll be right over me ... the last chap used to throw the furniture about in the middle of the night."

"Fancy," said Alice. "S'matter of fact, I was talking to old Mrs. Tobias's housemaid from the first floor and she was telling me the number of bottles that went upstairs was something awful. But she says she's heard from the caretaker it's two young ladies who've taken it."

Robert groaned. "Gramophones!" he said. "Jazz and hen-parties!"

But Alice was looking at the clock. "Goodness!" she said, "Miss Snow'll be getting up already and me here."

On the landing between the two flats, she met Mrs. Barker, who was supposed, with her husband, to act as caretaker. One or other of them did in fact carry down the small dustbins that were put outside the flats each morning. They swept the stairs when an obtrusive amount of dirt had collected, and cleaned the steps when the weather was fine. But they were hardly ever seen, for Mr. Barker was nearly always lying-up with a bad leg—understood to be a legacy from the War—and his wife was a spiritualist and given to unexpected trances.

"I was jes' comin' upter ask yer if you'd be good enough to bring them bins from six and seven down with you on the way out," she said. "Me 'ubby's bad again. Can't put foot to ground. It's some-think cruel."

53

Alice looked at her severely. She was not prepossessing. Her short dark hair hung greasily round a fat grey face. She had large roaming black eyes, set in dark circles which owed something to paint and more to dirt. Evidently she was too proud to wear an apron, for the front of her green velveteen dress was covered with stains. She wore heelless felt slippers to ease her feet.

"And what's to hinder you from carrying them down yourself?" Alice asked.

"P'raps you wasn't aware that me 'eart is bad," said Mrs. Barker with dignity. "Being a seer is a great strain on the organs, in perticerler the 'eart."

"Well," said Alice grimly, "it's not my place to go carrying dustbins downstairs. Leave them be if you like. But I shall have to inform Miss Snow and Mr. Dean. I shouldn't wonder if they don't complain, him being a lawyer and all."

Mrs. Barker sighed. "Some people have no feelin's for others," she said, reluctantly picking up the two scrap-buckets. "Fair pestered, I am, what with them two young ladies what's comin' to number eight next week. In and out, they are ... all day long and half the night. Wantin' to borrow keys. It spoils the atmosphere."

"What sort of young ladies would they be?" asked Alice.

Mrs. Barker paused in her laborious progress downstairs.

"Flighty," she said, " 'and 'ard up. No good will come of them. Wood and Gray, their names is, if you want to know. A 'ostile influence, they are. I'm not speakin' lightly, mind. I've 'ad a warnin' from the Spirits."

"Fancy," said Alice politely, pushing open the door of Miss Snow's flat. "Her and her spirits," she said to herself as she went to the kitchen. "It's wonderful what some people get out of a bottle."

Ten minutes later, she was unloading the tray in the sitting-room.

"I'm that sorry I'm late, miss, I mean ma'am," she said. "But there's been trouble over those bins again. Mrs. Barker's been up ..."

"Oh, dear me," said Miss Snow, quite cheerfully, for the prospect of trouble swept away the slight irritation she always felt if breakfast were late. "You know, I don't trust Mrs. Barker, Mrs. Gedge."

"She gives me the creeps, ma'am, her and her spirits," said Alice.

"It's so unhealthy, all this spiritualism," said Miss Snow emphatically. She had never thought about it at all, but she felt sure that it must be unseemly for servants to go prying into the Unseen.

"What name did you say? Those girls, I mean, who're coming next week?"

"A Miss Wood and a Miss Gray," said Alice. "Mrs. Barker says they're no better than they should be."

"It doesn't do to judge harshly, Mrs. Gedge," said Miss Snow, pushing up her spectacles. "Besides, I do not trust Mrs. Barker."

"No'm," agreed Alice. "But they do say that Miss Martin on the ground floor—the one whose brother comes to stop so regular—they do say she hasn't got a brother."

"I don't think you should repeat idle gossip," said Miss Snow. "Personally, I've never seen the man. Is he like Miss Martin?"

"Not to notice," said Alice. "Always carries an umbrella and keeps his hat on. Never says good-morning. Mrs. Tobias's maid says it's always the same; he slinks in and out."

"Tchk, tchk," said Miss Snow, ripping open an envelope to discourage the conversation.

"Ever so pleased with the daffs, Mr. Dean was," said Mice, obediently proffering a new topic as she flicked a duster over the mantelpiece. ('The way she colours up,' she thought, 'if you so much as mention him. Poor soul.')

For Miss Snow had at once put down her letter and begun a discussion of Mr. Dean, his appetite, wardrobe, overwork and prospects, and was only reluctantly headed off by Alice on to actresses, their morals, abilities and clothes.

"Every one says," began Miss Snow at last, "how delightful dear Gladys Cooper is in MAGDA. Now there's a play I should like to see. I always admire her so. My sister was coming up to do the matinee with me next week, but she writes her household has influenza, so I suppose it must be a pleasure deferred. Dear, dear."

Miss Snow gathered up her letters and her paper and sat down at her writing desk to do some accounts. A little later when she had gone out to the Care Committee offices, Alice looked up the play in the paper and wrote a careful note:

"Miss S. keen to see MAGDA. A. Gedge (Alice)," and put it underneath Mr. Dean's collar-box, where he found it as he went to bed.

II

VERA AND BEATRIX

THE two girls called Wood and Gray arrived on the following Monday in a small van marked K. WEBSTER, PECKHAM, and a very battered yellow Rover filled with trunks and packing-cases and bundles done up in dust sheets. A fender, some fire-irons, a carpet-sweeper and an ironing board protruded from the back. More packing-cases arrived by Carter Paterson, a divan was delivered by the L.M.S., and the Southern Railway deposited a dresser. The elder young woman, helpfully identified by Mrs. Barker as Miss Wood, was on the doorstep all day. She was large and square, with straight fair hair cut in a bob and she wore a slouch hat with the brim turned down all the way round, a fawn coat and skirt, a vivid orange scarf and low-heeled shoes. Her voice was husky and loud, and when the Southern Railway banged one end of the dresser against the kerb both Mrs. Tobias's maid and Alice, who happened to be looking out, could hear her swearing quite distinctly.

Tchk-tchk," said Alice, disappointed, for she had hoped to add a little odd cleaning for the new tenants to her day's work. But she felt doubtful about working for people who swore: not that she wasn't used to a certain amount of language, what with Thomas and War Work. But it was one thing to be in charge of girls who occasionally swore and could be scolded for it, and quite another to take orders from a young lady who said 'damn' and 'blast' out loud, in the street.

But Mrs. Tobias's maid was more shaken by the van from Peckham and the Rover full of junk than by the language. Mrs. Tobias, now over eighty, had occupied the first floor of Alfred House for ten years, and during that time the other flats were constantly changing hands for better or worse. Mrs. Tobias's first question about incoming tenants was always: "Who moved them?" If it was Maples or Whiteleys or Harrods, she sent her maid up to offer the new-comers tea in the afternoon. If it was a less illustrious pantechnicon, her maid inspected the furniture very carefully and, provided it was sufficiently solid, Mrs. Tobias left a card within the week. Miss Snow's mahogany wardrobe, for instance, had earned a card, while Mr. Dean's belongings had not seemed likely to pass any test at all. However, it happened that the old lady was coming home from a drive just as his one good piece, a sideboard, was shot on to the pavement. She instantly diagnosed it as Chippendale and sent up her maid to offer tea.

K. Webster of Peckham and the peculiar assortment of chairs and tables belonging to Miss Wood and Miss Gray inspired no confidence at all, though their arrival provided Mrs. Tobias with a day's diversion. She sat in a carved armchair at her bow window, peering between the lace draperies, while Martha, the maid, on whom she relied for details, left the housework to come and answer questions, reporting Miss Wood's vocabulary accurately and with zest. Mrs. Tobias dismissed her contemptuously as a Modern Girl. She was not much interested in them and held that the Sunday papers devoted altogether too much space to their doings: she herself could remember far more sensational and costly entertainments in her own flamboyant youth.

About four o'clock, Martha brought in tea on an elaborate silver tray and laid it on the ebony table by the window. She stayed to remark that the other young lady had arrived, and that she was younger but just as peculiar. Vera Gray was, in fact, twenty to Beatrix Wood's twenty-three. She had sleek dark hair, waved round a small pointed face; her eyes were large and grey and her voice was soft and slurred. It did not carry at all. Usually she wore immaculate and carefully fashionable clothes, but at that moment she was dressed for a removal; she had no hat on, and her yellow jumper and pleated skirt were both cheap and shabby. While she was waiting for the last case to be unloaded, she lit a cigarette. Mrs. Tobias's maid sucked in her teeth and shook her head and put her down as Modern too—and probably painted as well.

If Vera had known that most of the tenants were watching her from behind their net curtains, she would certainly have been better dressed, for she believed in making her public appearances as effective as possible. Beatrix, on the other hand, would not have bothered about her looks at all, but she would probably have sworn like a parrot; for she believed in shocking the bourgeoisie as frequently and as effectively as possible.

When the L.M.S. and the Southern Railway had gone, their feelings soothed by a shilling tip, and when K. Webster had puffed up four flights with the last packing-case, accepted five shillings with secret elation and outward depression, cranked up his battered van and finally clattered off, Beatrix and Vera finished unloading the Rover. They were staggering upstairs with the fender, the ironing board and the bedclothes tied up in a dust-sheet when Miss Snow came in and overtook them. To her middle-aged eyes, they looked extremely young, innocent and tired. Beatrix's orange scarf was a little startling, but Vera's soft voice, in meek apology for blocking up the stairs, was entirely reassuring.

"You poor things," Miss Snow said, "I know what a removal is. You must be dying for your tea. There'll be a kettle on for mine at this moment, and you must put those things down and come and have some."

They were opposite Miss Snow's door at the time and when Vera, offering an incoherent medley of excuses and thanks, dropped her end of the fender by accident, Beatrix set hers down on purpose. And without intending to accept the invitation at all, they found that they had dumped their bundles on the landing and were following Miss Snow. Miss Snow looked back a little sadly at the clutter on her doorstep and instantly began to feel that her invitation had been rather rash; somehow she had not bargained for such prompt and literal acceptance.

Alice, on hearing of it, put two extra cups on the tray, feeling that she had somehow failed in her duty. She had intended to report that the young ladies were indeed proper minxes. And here they were invading the sitting-room and getting a free tea before they had been in the place five minutes. "Real nerve, I call it," said Alice, as she made the tea.

In the sitting-room, Miss Snow was asking questions. She wanted more than anything else to know who her visitors were (meaning what ancestors they had, if any). It took her less than five minutes to discover that Vera worked in a library and Beatrix did secretarial work for authors, that both of them were sick of digs and hostels were impossible for girls of spirit. All of which she set aside as uninteresting and unimportant. It was not until the end of tea that she had probed deeply enough to be certain that Vera'a people, at any rate, had a place in the country and were, in fact, some of the Wingfield Grays of Lincolnshire.

"My family don't like the idea of a flat for me at all," said Vera, obstinately shifting the conversation back from her people to herself. "They've been frightfully stuffy about it. Why, I could hardly get any furniture out of them at all. Except Great Aunt's dresser, which is absolutely my own ..."

Miss Snow clucked, in sympathy with Vera's parents rather than with Vera, and offered second cups of tea. Beatrix said little, remarking only that Miss Snow's flat was the same shape as theirs.

"Most convenient," said Miss Snow, focusing her curiosity on Beatrix. "I'm sure any parents—any parents would say it was a most suitable flat for two young girls. As far as any flat is really perhaps quite ... But this is so workable, you know, and of course the other tenants are all so nice ... it's all so ... so suitable."

Beatrix said nothing.

"Perhaps your parents know this neighbourhood," suggested Miss Snow.

"I haven't any," said Beatrix, so curtly that Miss Snow was quite disconcerted. "We took the flat," she went on, "because it was so cheap."

"Most central too," said Miss Snow. "Of course the outlook ... But there, curtains do such a lot." She shook her head at the thought of all the trams and railway lines outside but decently hidden from her sight behind double folds of net embroidered with mauve pansies.

"But I think the view is thrilling," said Beatrix, rising. "We aren't having any curtains at all. Come along, Vera, we simply must go and get that other bed up."

It was Vera who said thank you for both of them and whose smile so charmed Alice in the corridor that she came to the door and ultimately helped them upstairs with their burdens.

"Well, good-night, Miss. I'm sure I hope you settle in all right. Of course, if there's anything I can do ... well, I'm always round here in the mornings."

Vera said: "Oh, thanks most awfully. It is good of you."

And Alice said: "Pleasure, I'm sure." And they smiled at each other as though they knew already that they were intended to be friends.

"Oh, for goodness' sake, come along, Vera," said Beatrix, unlocking the front door. "What in the name of Heaven did you want to go into that awful woman's flat for?"

"I didn't. It was your fault. You planked all those damn bundles on her doorstep ..."

"Don't argue. I shall go mad. She was frightful."

"Which one?" said Vera. "Anyway, I don't agree. And I thought the maid was sweet."

"The old thing in that fearful flat," said Beatrix, "not the maid; I never noticed her."

"Oh, didn't you?" said Vera. "Now I thought she looked interesting ..."

"How could she be?" Beatrix fumbled with a knot. "No one with any guts could stand domestic service. Here, those are your blankets. Where are mine? Oh, over there? Why bother about any of them anyway. My God, I'm glad I don't have to live with lilac and pink chintzes. Come on, Vera, stop mooning and throw over the key of that trunk."

"There isn't one," said Vera. "You know that as well as I do. Here, let me do it—I told you it opened quite easily..."

"Oh, look," screamed Beatrix, who had gone exploring to the kitchen, "the men have put one divan in here."

"Well," said Vera, gloomily unresponsive to Beatrix's shrill laughter, "we shall have to go and lug it out."

The bumps and bangs vibrated through Mr. Dean's flat (he was fortunately out), and the ceiling of the first floor quivered indignantly. Mrs. Tobias, half-way through a stately dinner, looked up at it and shook her head. These Moderns were not only dull; they were mannerless as well.

III
ROBERT FINDS VERA

IT was only half-past seven on Tuesday morning, but both Vera and Beatrix had been up since daylight: the trains had kept them awake. They had wandered dismally in and out of each other's rooms, reminding each other that people got so used to the sound of trains that they could not sleep without it. But the screech of the early-morning trams and the clash of milk cans on stone in the Combined Dairies Depot was too hideous to be borne. Beatrix had got up first and started to tidy the kitchen, and then Vera had begun to wash the sitting-room floor.

"I suppose we shall get used to it," said Vera. She had already said this several times, hopefully at first, and then plaintively.

"Well," said Beatrix, "there are ten flats in this block, all let. So I suppose the tenants must get some sleep."

"I wonder how tired you have to be before you can begin to sleep through it," said Vera, as she filled her bucket and wandered into the sittingroom.

She sat back on her heels and looked dejectedly at the lino surround. It was disappointing, as so many fixtures and fittings turn out to be. When she and Beatrix had bought it from the departing tenants, the worst patches had been discreetly hidden behind furniture. But then the departing tenants had had a lot of furniture. Unfortunately, she and Beatrix planned to have very little. Perhaps if the floor were polished or stained ... anyway, it would have to be washed first. Vera considered the large crusted imprints of removers' feet and set to work with her floor cloth.

"Hi, Bee," she called presently, "I'm not going on with this. I simply can't get it clean. And I'm due at the Library in less than an hour." She pushed the bucket out of her way and got up.

Beatrix, in a red silk kimono, came in, coffee-pot in hand. "Keep calm. The coffee's done and so are the eggs. If you eat in the kitchen, you'll be off in time."

Vera shook a wave of hair out of her eyes.

"Yes," she said, looking at the floor again, "but we shall have to get this scrubbed."

"Well, I'd do it myself," said Beatrix, "but James just can't get on without me this morning. His book goes in next week."

"And the library can't do without me any morning," said Vera tartly. It was all very well for Beatrix—with only a half-time job with a temperamental author—to sound burdened with overwork. If she had to slave from nine to six, she wouldn't be able to dawdle in the mornings.

"I tell you we must get a woman in," said Vera again.

"And spend more than we can afford and find the silver gone when we get back, not to speak of the joint and the bacon and the bread ..."

But Vera, whose gentle voice disguised more tenacity than Beatrix as yet dreamed of, stuck to her point.

"I shall go and catch that Mrs. Barker as she collects the pig buckets," she said. "She'd probably do it herself."

As she spoke, there was a rattle at the front door across the passage; Vera swung it open, and Mrs. Barker herself promptly stepped in. She looked from Beatrix's scarlet kimono to Vera's pale blue pyjamas and pursed her lips.

"I jes' thought I'd look in to see you was all right," she said. "You're perhaps wantin' a bit of cleanin' up done?"

"Well, we're not straight yet, of course," said Vera, looking doubtfully at Mrs. Barker. The thin sunlight filtered into the passage and showed up the spots on the front of her dress and the dirt on her face.

"The new tenants requirin' cleanin' generally comes to me," said Mrs. Barker, eyeing Vera's pail and mop. "If unable to come up meself, I can always recommend ..."

"Very good of you indeed," said Vera brightly, "but at present we're hoping to manage by ourselves."

"Reelly?" said Mrs. Barker, taking advantage of a pause to step forward so that she could see right into the sitting-room. Then she screwed her head round and managed to catch a glimpse of a corner of the kitchen—full of litter.

"Reelly?" she said again. "Well, I might mention that Mr. Barker does not carry down the tenants' rubbish, other than wot is in the bins. Boxes and sacking and shavings tenants is expected to dispose of themselves."

"Good-morning," said Vera, suddenly stepping across the passage and blocking Mrs. Barker's view. Mrs. Barker was obliged to move and, as it was a very narrow passage, one step took her on to the landing. Vera shut the door.

"Well, really, Vera," Beatrix said, "I don't understand you. I thought you said . . ."

"Bee, we cannot have that woman inside this flat, that's certain," said Vera.

"She certainly does look much dirtier when you see her out of her basement," said Beatrix.

"She looks sinister," said Vera. She went through to her bedroom and began to dress. As she belted her short blue frock round her hips, she called to Beatrix who was clattering in the kitchen again.

"Bee, I've got it. I know what I'll do. I'll swallow an egg and then I'll look in at the flat below—what's the name, Snow?—and ask that maid if she knows of anyone ..."

"I leave it to you, darling," said Beatrix cheerfully. "It's your funeral. You want the floor scrubbed."

"Well, but look at the dirt ..."

"Wear off in time, darling," said Beatrix, with her mouth full.

It was just half-past eight when Vera came downstairs and Alice was going across from Miss Snow's flat to Mr. Dean's. Vera pounced on her.

"Oh, I was coming to look for you. I wonder if you could help us. You see our floor's in such a mess and I, we, want to find someone to scrub it. Only we don't know how to get hold of any one. You were so kind yesterday ... I thought perhaps you might know of someone ..."

"There's always Mrs. Barker," said Alice.

"Oh, I know. But ...Well, I don't think ... we don't think ..."

"That's all right then," said Alice. "I just thought I ought to mention it. But if you don't fancy her there's no reason why you should. Floors, is it?"

"It is," said Vera. "I always thought till this morning that scrubbing floors was simply hard work. Any one ought to be able to scrub. But I can't. I just seem to swish the dirt round with me."

"Scrubbin's an Art," said Alice, "believe me. But if you'd care for it, I'll come up myself. Only I can't get round to it before this afternoon."

"Oh, would you?" said Vera, " I never dreamed ... Are you sure it'll be all right?" Vera was overwhelmed, for Alice, spruced up in a white overall and grave with the responsibility of two households, did not look as if she could ever have scrubbed floors.

"That's all right," said Alice, "I'll be up this afternoon. Will I be able to get in?"

"I'll tell Miss Wood to expect you. She'll be in. It is nice of you ..."

"That's all right," said Alice again, as Vera's sleek apologetic head bobbed up round the corner of the stairs.

Beatrix took Vera's news calmly and celebrated by writing letters till she left for work at ten. It was a quarter to three when she came back to the flat again, and by then she was tired and hungry, for she had had no lunch. She gave one look at the dishevelled rooms, found the prospect unbearable on an empty stomach and went through to the kitchen to make coffee and cut some bread and cheese.

Worn to a thread, that was how she felt. Vera was quite wrong. Temperament was far more trying than routine. Vera didn't know how lucky she was, with a safe lunch hour at twelve and nothing to worry about. "She doesn't get in till six," thought Beatrix, "but at least she does come home fresh—not worn out with other people's tantrums like me. James and his fan mail and his moods and his ideas that won't work out ... as if I hadn't stuff of my own to write. I don't learn anything from typing his plots—they only get in my way."

She munched gloomily. A theme for a short story had blown into her mind and she wanted to hammer on the typewriter and dress it up in words and pin it down with commas and stops before it had time to turn into a phantom again and elude her altogether. For Beatrix spelt Writing with a capital and took her own efforts hard. But she knew that Vera would not think a short story a good excuse for scamping the cleaning that had to be done before the flat would be habitable. So she was quite relieved when Alice arrived at three, though she was, perhaps, a little absent-minded in her greeting.

Alice was relieved, too, to find Miss Wood busy with anything as commonplace as a typewriter. Typing was a nice, respectable occupation and the rattle and ping, penetrating into every room in the small flat, reminded her pleasantly of old times and the upstairs corridor in the Ministry where the secretaries worked. She wouldn't half like Dulcie to be a secretary when she grew up. Alice scrubbed and polished. But she could almost see herself sitting at the end of the big room, opposite the oblong window, under a green shaded light, checking up the morning's work. She savoured each remembered detail—the leather-edged blotter, the felt pen-wiper, the tray of pins, the burr of the telephone—till she was no longer sure whether she were seeing herself five years ago or Dulcie ten years hence.

With a vicious ping, Beatrix's typewriter stopped. Alice wrung out the floor cloth and sighed.

'Goodness only knows when they washed this floor last. Beats me how decent folk can leave their dirt behind for others to clean up. Queer, the things people like in a room.' She looked round, as she looked round every room she came to work in, for some clues to the owner of it. The walls were yellow and so was the paint. And the small square of carpet, still rolled up like a cocoon in the middle of the floor, looked as if it would be black. The curtains hanging over the armchair certainly were. There was a divan bed too. Not made yet. And a gate-legged table and a packing case. There was also one very peculiar picture leaning against the armchair. It was mainly brown and black and yellow, but there was one patch of scarlet and another of pure white. Alice recognised part of a musical instrument, a piece of newspaper and a loaf of bread in the foreground. She shook her head over it. It was beyond her and just as well. Then she went off to see if she could find some more polish to make a good job of the floor and, when she came back, Vera Gray had come in and was struggling up a step ladder with the curtains over her arm and calling for Beatrix.

"I think she'll be working, Miss," said Alice. And Vera, rather horrified to find Alice still there, said, "Oh, thank you," and went to rout Beatrix out and scold her for letting Mrs. Gedge stay so long. Vera was annoyed about it, partly because three and a half hours of cleaning would cost a good deal, and partly because she did not want to be under an obligation to Alice.

But Alice was so entirely at ease and so anxious to stay and help with the curtains that neither Vera nor Beatrix liked to send her away. Together they unwound curtains and one by one they toiled up the steps and tried to reach the pole. But the steps were unusually short and the rooms at Alfred House were, as the landlord said, lofty; for however much they were partitioned off, their original height was unimpaired.

"Bother," said Vera, as the third attempt was defeated, "I did want to get them up tonight."

"I suppose we shall have to get hold of a man," said Beatrix.

"Men do come in handy sometimes, don't they?" said Alice. "That reminds me, young Mr. Dean will be in now. He's coming back early to-night, that I do know. He'll come up and fix things in no time. I'll run down and ask him."

Neither Vera nor Beatrix had the energy to interfere: Vera wriggled down from the steps and Beatrix flopped on the floor.

"Who's Mr. Dean, Vera?" she asked. "Is he Mrs. Gedge's young man or the caretaker's brother?"

"I don't know and I don't care," said Vera, "as long as he gets the curtains up. Have you got a bob, Bee? Just in case. I'm down to sixpence."

Robert came in then, at Alice's heels, and Beatrix put away her bag and got up, for he was clearly not the sort of person for shillings, and her manners underwent a quite unconscious change for the better when pleasant young men were about. Vera, on whom young men had the reverse effect, remained in the background.

"Oh!" said Beatrix. "This is nice of you. I'm Beatrix Wood and this is Vera Gray. And we're absolutely in despair. We simply can't reach the curtain pole. A room looks so desolate, doesn't it, without curtains?"

"Oh, quite, quite," said Robert gruffly. He had only come upstairs because he wanted to oblige Alice. It was difficult to be ill-natured when someone took your kindness so absolutely for granted. "I daresay it won't take me a moment," he added. "That is, I mean, of course I'm only too pleased ..."

Alice handed him a curtain and gripped the step ladder.

"Mind the third tread, sir," she said, "it's got a crack in it."

Robert, who had been answering Beatrix and looking at Vera, immediately stepped on it. He lost his balance, wrenched at the steps, and sat down uncomfortably. He was up again immediately, inarticulate with confusion, and Alice dusted him down while Beatrix apologised. But there was a trace of smothered laughter in Vera's voice as she said softly that perhaps after all it would be better to leave the curtains and get a man in to-morrow.

"Not at all, not at all," said Robert. "It won't take me a minute. Really it won't." He clutched a curtain, avoided the third step, reached up for the curtain pole, wrestled with an obstinate ring and hook, and finally slid the rings along the pole and climbed down.

"I think they'll draw all right," he said.

"There! What did I tell you?" said Alice proudly. "Only taken Mr. Dean a minute."

"Marvellous!" said Vera.

"It is good of you," said Beatrix.

"Are there any more?" said Robert desperately, still watching Vera and thinking miserably of the step-ladder. He was not sure whether to go away and forget about it, or to stay and do the jobs these girls so obviously couldn't do for themselves. Beatrix settled it for him: she took him off to see about the green curtains in her room and the blue ones in Vera's; and Alice carried the step-ladder out after them, leaving Vera where she was, standing by the sitting-room window watching the trains, not caring, it seemed, about either curtains or young men. She did not move until Robert had shaken the last curtain into place.

"You have been kind," she said.

"It's nothing. I mean, it's a pleasure," said Robert.

"It's quite awful that we can't even offer you a drink," said Beatrix.

"Oh, please don't bother—I mean, it doesn't matter. I'm so glad I could be of use."

"What about a cigarette?" said Beatrix.

"I ought to be going ... it's getting on ..." said Robert. "But if there's anything you want hung up ... or hammered in ... I'm really quite good with a hammer. Any old time. Only too pleased ..."

"Splendid!" said Beatrix. "You must come and hang our pictures for us, and we'll see there's a drink next time."

"Shall I?" said Robert, edging towards the door. Vera's "Please do!" was drowned by Beatrix's exuberant "Rather!"

While Robert was upstairs hanging curtains, Miss Snow was anxiously looking out her evening frock and gilt slippers. For she found the idea of going out to dinner with Mr. Dean rather fluttering. Not that she wasn't used to dinner parties, but because it was important that Mr. Dean should not find her either dowdy or dull as a companion for the evening. And Robert, as he changed in more of a hurry than he liked, was wondering where he should take Miss Snow to dinner and whether the evening would be a strain. Miss Snow had been so kind—but an evening was different from brief and casual daily meetings and an occasional half-hour over tea.

In the end, he took her to the Magnificent and both the dinner and the play were a success. Robert had carefully thought out suitable topics for discussion; but he need not have worried. Miss Snow belonged to a generation which had been taught to make good conversation and had considered it a duty to keep dinner partners amused. It was like old times to her, except that, of course, in the old times a girl would hardly have gone out to dinner alone with a young man. And Robert, who was still young enough to be frightened of girls, found Miss Snow's talk entertaining and liked her reliance on his judgment. And he noticed her crisply waved hair, and the dress she wore—short enough to be smart and long enough to be becoming. She was in fact like the very nicest sort of aunt.

But as he helped her out of the taxi at the door of Alfred House, he wondered, quite suddenly, what the brown-haired girl in the top flat looked like in evening dress. He wondered whether the curtains pulled all right ... Miss Snow's thanks rippled round him and he smiled and pressed her hand. And Miss Snow thought what a dear boy he was—so young—and she was getting on, getting on ...

"Good-night, Mr. Dean, and thank you for such a very delightful evening. It has been a treat indeed."

"Good-night, Miss Snow ... kind of you to ... jolly ... must have another...." He rammed in his latch-key and fled into his flat. Miss Snow's door closed gently behind her. Robert's door slammed.

Girls ... it was a nuisance the new tenants were girls. But the dark one was all right, thought Robert. Pretty—such red lips. Perhaps it was lipstick? Now Joyce would never use the stuff. Robert picked up the photograph on his dressing-table. Joyce was not like most girls. Joyce was really a good sort. He must write to Joyce. Tomorrow.

CHAPTER 5

I

1924   TEA TIME : TUFFNEL ROAD

LEONARD pranced along Tuffnel Road, swinging his satchel against the iron railings. His dark hair, cropped prison-close according to school regulations, shone with grease and smelt of violets. He wore a vivid red-and-yellow pullover and he walked arrogantly alone. Three other Hubert Street boys—all bigger than himself—sauntered down the middle of the road, whistling and sniggering. Leonard might have walked home with them, for though he was small, he had a reputation as a 'card.' His stories circulated through the school, and he had a trick of scoring off boys and masters, and a knack of winning bets which made him notorious, though not popular. But Leonard could not be bothered with his peers: he ignored their overtures and swaggered on, sloshing his bag on the railings.

Dulcie followed him, but at a distance. On the whole, she was a docile sister, and in any case, Leonard was a grand enough brother to command admiration. He had said at the gate: "Come on, Dulce! Gotta bit of news for you." So she came; but he took no notice of her till he reached their own gate. Then the strap of his satchel caught on the hasp: he swore and dropped it, calling out to her to pick it up and bring it in. Without looking behind him, he ran on into the house to find his mother. But Alice had not come in. The kitchen was empty and there were slushing sounds from the scullery; then Thomas came through, carrying a dripping bundle. Every now and then, as there were already more men than jobs, he was stood off work for a day; and when this happened, Alice made him get on with the family washing. He was not very thorough, and quite useless with an iron; but he could get the copper going, boil up and wring out the clothes and put them through the mangle.

"Ho! There you are, you varmint!" said Thomas. "Look 'ere, d'yer think yer ma'll pass this? I can't get them marks out."

He unwound his flannel bundle and held up a wet, soap-sodden shirt.

"Looks fine to me, Pa," said Leonard carelessly "Where's Ma?"

"Extra cleaning for Miss Snow," said Thomas, peering at his work. "Left me to get on with the wash, she 'as. As if it was a man's job. What's women for, I'd like to know? Where's that sister of yours, eh? Hi, Dulce! You come 'ere and get these clothes 'ung out proper!" He dropped the shirt on the floor, sat down on the rocking-chair and put his feet up.

"Wot're you 'oppin' about for, me boy?"

"I dunno," said Leonard, swinging his toes and his heels in and out in a frantic Charleston. "Wish Ma would come in."

"Wot for?"

"Want me tea," temporised Leonard, who knew that his bit of news would not get the reception it deserved if his mother were not there.

"Then put the kettle on! An' tell your goodfor-nothin' sister to 'urry up and see to them clothes!"

"Coming, father," called Dulcie, who had been lingering in the bedroom, smoothing and re-plaiting her hair and tidying the books and papers which had escaped from Leonard's satchel and been blown over the front garden.

"Hi, Dulce!" said Leonard, still rocking from his toes to his heels, "Put the bloomin' kettle on, there's a sport!"

Dulcie picked up the wet shirt, flicked on the gas, lit it, filled the kettle and set it on the ring before she went through to the steamy wash-house. It was always the same when Pa said he'd do the washing. He never finished it and he swilled the soap-suds over on to the floor. It took so long to clean up that you might as well wash the things and get the credit for it. Dulcie, who tired easily in the hot weather, loathed the sight of the mangle: it grinned at her and dared her to leave the things lying for Alice to find. So she set to and fed it with heavy soaking sheets and thick shirts and pants and Leonard's shorts and her blouses and Alice's cotton frocks. Then she hung them on the line and mopped at the pools on the stone floor. Long before she had finished, the kettle boiled, and Leonard called out to her to come and make the tea.

"Get it yourself! I got more to do than slave after you," she snapped. Extreme fatigue spurred her to one of her rare defiances.

"Yer sister's tired," said Thomas, and Leonard agreed smugly.

As Thomas poured out, Alice's quick step sounded in the passage, and she came in, flushed with the heat but with a shadowy pallor about her eyes.

" 'Allo, Ma!" said Thomas proudly. I finished the wash for yer. 'Ave a drop of tea. Or shall Dulcie make yer some fresh?"

Alice shook her head. "This'll do. Good job you've finished so quickly, Thomas. Fit to drop I am. Where's Dulcie? Oh, there you are! That's a good girl!"

"Ma, I got a bit o' news for yer," said Leonard, edging nearer to her.

"Not in trouble again, are you?" asked Alice quickly.

Leonard wriggled and shook his head.

"Then what is it?"

"Ooh, Len! Come on an' tell us!" said Dulcie.

"Get it out, can't yer?" growled Thomas.

"Teacher says can I go in for Grammar School Entrance for a free place wot's goin'," said Leonard in one triumphant breath.

"An' wot may that be?" asked Thomas, who disapproved on principle of everything the school recommended.

"Sh!" commanded Alice, bridling with annoyance at Thomas and pride for her son.

"It's a bit of good news," said Leonard, feeling that his audience was not really appreciating him. "It means if I'm lucky an' get a place, I can leave Hubert Street and the kids and be educated proper and stay at school ever so long. There now! Ain't that a bit of orl right?"

"Well," said Alice, "I suppose it's a kind of scholarship. But I don't see that you've got it yet, have you, Len?"

"Got it!" said Leonard indignantly. " 'Ow can I till you've signed the paper fer me to go in fer it? I'll get it orl right, you'll see. Besides, there's only three boys in my standard wot's even good enough to go in fer it, and I betcher I can beat any of 'em, the silly swipes. Only teacher says I've got to 'ave parents' permission. See?"

"Well, of course you can try for it, Len, I'm sure," said Alice, stifling some of her gratification; it wouldn't do for Leonard to get conceited and not try hard enough and never get the place or whatever it might be. And it wouldn't do either to let Thomas see how pleased she was. "It'll be fine if you get it, son."

"Course I'll get it," said Leonard.

"Get it you may or you may not," said Thomas, "but you can't engage to stop at school when you're turned fourteen."

"But you don't 'ave to pay, Pa," screamed Leonard.

Thomas got up. "I went to work the day I was fourteen," he said, wagging a large finger at his son, "and wot was good enough fer me is good enough fer you, see?"

"Thomas," said Alice, "you're being foolish. You know very well you wouldn't stand in the boy's way."

"I know very well I ain't goin' to keep 'im once 'e's fourteen," said Thomas. "There's a law in this country wot says 'e can't go to work till 'e's fourteen; but I'm goin' to 'ave my rights, I am. I ain't goin' to keep 'im once 'e is fourteen. Nor 'er neither." He jerked a thumb at Dulcie, sat down again and choked on his tea.

"And if you won't work to keep Len, I won't work to keep you," said Alice quickly. "And then where'll you be? Don't be so silly, Thomas! You don't see further than your own nose. Give me that paper, Len! I'll sign it up for you."

"Teacher says will you go in and see 'im about it," said Leonard, triumphantly passing the slip of paper to his mother, but keeping a wary eye on his father.

"Next time I'm passing," said Alice, getting up to clear away the dishes and end the discussion. "You going out, Father? All right. And what are you up to, Len?"

Leonard, sidling towards the door, stopped and wriggled his shoulders. "Can't I go over to 'ave a look at 'Arry's gramo?"

"And come back late for supper, and too tired to do your sums properly?" said Alice. "Not if I know it, my lad."

"Oh, come on, Ma, be a sport! Wot's the 'arm in a gramo? Wish we 'ad one. Why can't we 'ave one?"

" 'Cause I'm not a millionaire," said Alice. "You be thankful you've got good boots and a good tea inside you!

It's more than Harry often has with his father buying up the shops on the Hire Purchase."

"Just this once, Ma!" Leonard flung his arms round her waist and Charlestoned violently across the room. Alice put the tray down on the dresser and sidled gallantly.

"Just this once, then," she said, as he let her go. "But what about that scholarship? Won't you have to start working real hard soon?"

"That's all right," said Leonard. "I'll start in and work to-morrow." He winked at Dulcie, kissed his mother and slid down the passage, already inventing excuses for his neglected preparation.

Dulcie said nothing. Leonard had got his say in first, as usual. Because he was a boy. It wasn't fair, Dulcie thought, that boys, who were no real use at all, should have all the chances. Boys! They didn't have to do scrubbing or cooking or have babies or even mind them. Who wouldn't be a boy ? And spend all the Saturdays and Sundays playing footer or hanging about garages or laying bets. Girls hadn't a look-in.

Dulcie dragged out her books and set to work. She did her sums grudgingly, and then grew happy because she enjoyed ruling red lines underneath them to make sure they were right. She pulled out a dog-eared history book and read about Richard the Lion-hearted. Girls had a dull time in those days, always sitting at home. But men appreciated them all right, singing ballads and fighting tourneys for them. Not like to-day ... Shut up in her own thoughts, Dulcie never heard her mother fetch in the dry clothes and lay them in piles ready for ironing. Even the swish of the tap, as Alice turned it on and washed-up, made no dint in her consciousness.

After she had finished, Alice went upstairs and had a chat with old Mrs. Watkins, and when she came down again Dulcie was still working. "You're a good girl, Dulcie," said Alice, suddenly stooping to lay a hand on the child's thin shoulder.

"Ma!" said Dulcie; instantly waking up and seizing her opportunity. "Ma, could I try for a free place, too?"

"Good gracious, Dulcie!" Alice was surprised. She had long ago made up her mind that Len was the clever one. But Dulcie was a quiet child and you could never go by looks.

"My teacher wants me to," said Dulcie, "though I'm younger than Len. Only it would be next year I'd go on to Grammar School. Not this year, like Len, if he's lucky."

"I don't know I'm sure," said Alice. "There's Len to think of and one thing and another. Two to keep at school all that time. I don't know what your father'd say. You'd better not mention it to him. Still, I won't say no. There's plenty of time, isn't there, if it's not immediate?"

"Teacher wants to know, 'cause I'll have to do extra lessons next term. She wants you to 'ave a talk, when you're passin' that way."

"Oh, does she now?" said Alice absently, looking at the clock. "Well, I'll think about it. But run out now, there's a good girl, and get me some fried fish for Len's supper! You know how he fancies it."

II
LEONARD TAKES HIS CHANCE

"OF COURSE, I don't know how you feel about it, Mrs. Gedge."

Mr. Perkins, Head of the Boys' Department, folded his arms across the pile of official forms on his blotter and smiled down at Alice in a friendly way. She was one of his most reasonable parents, and he was prepared to be gracious, though a little condescending.

Alice, who had come in on her way back from Alfred House, stood at the foot of the raised dais and looked up at him. It never occurred to either of them that she might be offered a chair. She glanced round the long brown hall hung with maps and portraits of Royalty and crude lithographs of tea-planting and lion-hunting in the Empire. The drone of lessons and the scraping of chairs, an occasional agonising squeak of chalk on blackboards, echoed through from the class-rooms opening off the hall. Alice turned to the master again.

"If Len's got brains," she said, "neither me nor his father will stand in his way."

"Oh, Leonard's got brains all right, up to a point. He's quite an intelligent lad. He should have no difficulty in getting one of these vacancies at the Grammar School for the autumn. But whether it's wise to encourage him ..."

Alice said again: "If Len's got brains—" and Mr. Perkins went on, tapping an impatient forefinger on the desk: "Of course I like to see a promising lad go on; but it means he'll have to stay at school till he's sixteen at least. Now can you manage that, Mrs. Gedge?"

"Have to," said Alice.

"You see, Mrs. Gedge," Leonard's headmaster smiled confidentially, "I spend my time trying to make my parents understand that extra schooling doesn't necessarily benefit a boy. It depends what you're going to do with him afterwards."

"Well," Alice said, "I've been thinking. If Len's all that bright, he might get a scholarship to stay on longer at the

Grammar School. P'raps he'd get one on to college … and take up school-mastering …"

"He might," Mr. Perkins sounded doubtful. "But I can't promise you he will. But if he couldn't get as far as that, he might get a post in a bank. Or there's the Post Office, or the Air Force, if he turned out mechanical. He'd have a very good chance …"

"Oh, he shall have his chance," said Alice. "I'm set on that. If he can get this free place, me and his father are willing for him to take it."

"In that case," said the master, "I'll put him down. You see, Mrs. Gedge," he added, "I don't want to over press you about Leonard, because I know how keen Miss James of the Girls' School is about your daughter's chances. There's so little difference in age … If you can only manage to keep one of them on at school, you might do well to consider the claims of the girl …"

"Oh, Dulcie …" said Alice. "Well, that's just it. She's only a girl. Boys come first in this world, don't they?"

"You'd better have a talk with Miss James," said Mr. Perkins. "The floor below. In the Central Hall."

"I suppose as I'm here …" said Alice. "But I'm decided about Len, you know."

"That's all right. I'll make a note of it. Thank you for looking in, Mrs. Gedge. Good-day!"

Mr. Perkins put a tick against the name of L. Gedge, and looked expectantly down the long hall. That Mrs. Davis ought to be here soon. He'd have to give it her straight about Jack. If parents couldn't back up the school it was a poor look-out. And there was young Clarke, sauntering along with his hands in his pockets! The magisterial ruler thudded on the desk and the boy jumped, removed his hands from his trouser pockets and broke into a run.

Downstairs Miss James began to talk to Alice about Dulcie's chances; but Alice was impervious either to praise of the child or sympathy with her own difficulties. She just reiterated that it would have to be one thing at a time, and Len must have his turn first. After that ... well, if Miss James still thought that Dulcie should go on too, she'd see.

"But there!" said Alice. "Dulcie's a real good girl. Only she can go out as a clerk without all this schooling. Come to that, I did pretty well at office work myself and I hadn't any training. It doesn't seem to me girls need it so much."

"Indeed they do," said Miss James briskly, for she spent her time arguing with parents, school managers, employment agencies and women's organisations about the need for girls to train and their right to good wages. "You've got to think of it this way, Mrs. Gedge. Dulcie will only get a job as a run-about or a matcher or a lift girl if she leaves school at fourteen. And she'll be too tired to spend much time at night schools. But if she stays at the Grammar School till she's sixteen, she can learn secretarial work in her last year and get quite a good post when she leaves. I see no reason why Dulcie shouldn't do very nicely."

"Well, it always seems Len's the brainy one," said Alice, "but I'll bear it in mind. I want to be fair to Dulcie, you understand. But there it is! Leonard's the boy, and he has first call to a chance like this, seeing that we mayn't be able to keep two at home so long."

"Dulcie's such a satisfactory pupil," said Miss James; but she knew it was useless to argue. Alice was already preparing to say good-bye.

Later on, Miss James and Mr. Perkins met in the Senior Staff Room for tea.

"Did you see Mrs. Gedge?" he asked.

Miss James nodded over the rim of her cup. "I did," she said, "and she's set on Leonard getting on. She's got some idea the boy's a genius. And of course she doesn't think the girl has any right to extra schooling unless the boy has it too."

The boy's all right," said Mr. Perkins, anxious to escape a discussion on Women's Work. But Miss James took him up at once.

"You've said yourself that he's got no moral stamina. I've heard you."

"He may turn out all right, if he isn't spoilt. He's too sharp, that's his trouble."

"Sister's worth two of him," said Miss James, nibbling a biscuit. "I hear a lot about that family one way and another. I've got a C.C. worker. Name of Snow."

"The elderly one? She's got more sense than most." Mr. Perkins helped himself to another cup of tea. It was no use expecting Miss James, with her ideas of equality, to pour it out for him.

"She's all right," said Miss James. "She knows her work and doesn't interfere with mine. She's known the Gedges for years ... the mother chars for her. She's crazy about the whole family ... says the children are bound to get on ..."

"I hear that a dozen times a term from parents and Infant School Teachers," said Mr. Perkins wearily, "and nothing ever comes of it."

"Well, I back Dulcie Gedge," said Miss James as the bell clanged.

III

AUGUST IN THE FLATS

IN Alfred House, Miss Snow walked cautiously through her burnished flat. It had just been thoroughly turned out, and it was so tidy that it seemed a shame to sit down in it. She wandered from room to room, thinking how polish improved the mahogany, how good the paint still looked when it was washed, how silver properly polished was always a credit; how well Alice Gedge kept things, and what a worker she was. And because it really did not seem right to rumple the sofa cushions or litter paper about, and because it was too thundery to walk round the shops or into the Park, she kept up her restless pacing until all the house-proud satisfaction had worn off and she was aware of a secret discontent. She began to wonder whether the laundry had sent back the embroidered tea-cloth from the week before last, and whether the butcher had refunded the two-and-fourpence charged for chops she had not had. But a glance in the linen cupboard confirmed the return of the teacloth, and the butcher's book showed a credit of twoand-fourpence. She paused in front of the gilt mirror. Her wave needed setting; but it would last another day or two and there was nothing else amiss. She had faced her plump, double-chinned, pink-and-white, middle-aged reflection too often to be in the least concerned by it. An invitation, now out of date, still tucked in the frame, caught her eye and she tore it up, thinking as she did so that July was always a lonely month, and August was worse.

That was it, thought Miss Snow. The beginning of August was always rather a dreary time. She picked up the *Memoirs* of Lady Fotheringay, that were causing such a pleasant sensation to so many people, deliberately ruffled the sofa cushions before she sat down and, glancing round the orderly room, began to recapture some of her satisfaction.

A sudden burst of laughter from the flat above made her start. These young people were such very noisy neighbours. Vera Gray must have got back early from work ... somebody else with her too. But she hadn't so many men friends ... unless perhaps Robert Dean had gone up. The Law Courts had risen, and his friends would be away too. Vera would be company for him in the solitary days of August. If it came to that, Robert was company for Miss Snow, too. Not that she had seen very much of him lately. But then, she had been very busy until this last week. And he had been overworking again, no doubt, and besides, it was natural that he should like young friends. 'An elderly woman like me,' thought Miss Snow, prodding at the thought as if it were an aching tooth. For she had not thought about her age for so long; and now it took her by surprise again. 'I don't mind growing old,' thought Miss Snow. 'It's being left out ... If I were his mother,' thought Miss Snow, 'he'd be telling me about things ... only they say that young people don't nowadays. So I daresay it's the same for all. We get left behind. And what's forty-eight, after all, in these days?'

She threw away her book and went into the kitchen, where she made a very delicious cream pudding that would do nicely for Robert's supper if he were in, and for her own if he were out.

And upstairs, Vera and Robert laughed again over Robert's best story of the Motorist in the Police Court. They had met by chance on the landing, for Robert had been looking at the empty flat next to Vera's, in case it might do for a friend of his. Vera, thoroughly bored with solitude, had pressed him to come in and have tea.

"It's true, too," said Robert. "I assure you it is." And Vera, sprawling on the divan, reached for a cigarette. Robert bent over her to light it and then perched on the edge of a wide, low stool.

"Ach!" said Vera, proudly blowing smoke rings, "I hate London in August."

"Then what do you stay for?" asked Robert.

"Work," said Vera.

"Work? But you can't make me believe that you really like working."

"Oh yes, I do. Really I do," said Vera with immense conviction. "It's enormous fun."

"Not for a girl like you," said Robert stubbornly.

"I'm through with all that old-fashioned rot," said Vera, flaring up at him. "You're so Victorian, Robert. No one would think you were living in 1924."

"A girl like you," went on Robert, more dogmatically than ever, "ought to be having a good time."

"So I do!" Vera retorted instantly. "I have a marvellous time, and a perfectly good career as well."

"It's not good enough," said Robert fiercely. "You can't burn your candle at both ends."

"Or eat my cake and have it, I suppose. Go on, Robert! You're talking exactly like my family."

"Well, no man would do it," said Robert argumentatively. "No man who wanted to get on, I mean."

"Nonsense! Everybody does it—except prigs," snapped Vera.

"You can't play every evening and work all day," persisted Robert, convinced that if his argument were trite, his case was good. "At least, you can't do it for long."

"Yes I can," Vera said obstinately.

"That's why I say," Robert went on, "that a girl like you oughtn't to talk this nonsense about careers ..."

Vera made a face and threw a cushion at him.

"... ought to get married," said Robert, fending it off, and realising at the same time that he was talking recklessly.

"Thank you!" said Vera tartly. "But I prefer to be independent. I can keep myself without turning into some boor's unpaid housekeeper."

Robert flushed and said nothing.

"Can't I make you believe that I really like working?" Vera asked, her temper rising. "You're just stupid and pig-headed and narrow-minded and out-of-date."

"If I've offended you ..." Robert flushed again.

"What's the use of trying to talk to a person like you who won't even try to understand?"

"But, Vera—I think you're magnificent. I didn't mean ... I daresay it is different for you ... I wish we didn't seem to—to—to disagree so much."

"Oh well," said Vera, more cheerfully, "it's better to be quarrelling with somebody than moping up here all alone. Three weeks more before I go off on holiday, and every single soul I know is out of town. It does give you the blues, you know, being by yourself every evening and not a soul to speak to ... except Alice, of course. Alice is divine. She knows all about everybody."

"I like Alice too," said Robert, thankful to find a safe topic. "She knows by instinct when you want conversation with your breakfast."

They chattered on, skimming over the surface of a dozen subjects, Robert suddenly and desperately aware of Vera's attraction; Vera, aggressively nonchalant, wondering uneasily if this strange faint tingling meant anything important.

At last she saw Robert out, refusing his invitation to let him take her out to supper, but taking the sting out of the refusal by half promising an evening later in the week.

Robert clumped gloomily downstairs, intending to go out to supper himself because it would be easier to stop thinking about Vera if he were away from Alfred House, where she was sitting by herself preferring the blues to his company. On the half-landing by his own front door he met Miss Snow. She asked him how he was and if he had much work, and if many of his friends were still in London, and Robert tried to collect his wits to answer her. But she knew he was thinking of someone else, so she did not ask him in to share the cream shape she had made. Instead she said: "I see you're just going out. You mustn't let me keep you." Robert hurried away, and Miss Snow waited by the open door of her flat till his footsteps ceased to echo through the stone entrance hall. Then she went back to her book, hoping that he was not unhappy.

But Robert, on the brink of loving Vera, was not unhappy. He was merely perplexed; for Vera was not his kind of girl. She was so unlike Joyce, whom he had always admired. There was nothing definite between Joyce and himself; but he had hoped for the last year that he would soon be able to propose to her. His income was going up steadily: soon there would be no reason why he should not ask some girl to marry him. Vera and Joyce—Joyce and Vera ... Robert ate a dull supper in a dreary A.B.C., and came back to the flat feeling that he ought to make some definite choice. But he could not. For Joyce was away in her country vicarage, and Vera's footsteps sounded, night and morning, overhead.

Before three weeks were up, Robert was sufficiently in love with Vera to admit it to himself and to try to convey it to her. But though Vera came gaily to cinemas and upper circles, Hampton Court and Kew, she would have nothing to do with making love. In fact, she refused to admit that she and Robert could even be friends for long.

"You see," she said on the last Sunday afternoon they spent at Kew, "we don't even like each other. I disagree with almost everything you say, and you disapprove of me."

"I don't," said Robert hotly, pulling up tufts of grass and sifting them through his fingers.

"Oh yes, you do," Vera said, wedging Robert's mackintosh more firmly between her shoulders and the tree against which she was leaning. "You disapprove of all the important things about me—my career, and socialism and not having a religion."

"I don't disapprove," contradicted Robert. "I just think differently. Opinions have got nothing to do with friendship. Why, my best friend is a Labour candidate."

"Yes, but he's a man," said Vera, and then wished she hadn't said anything so true and so reactionary. Robert pounced on it at once.

"What's that got to do with it? I thought you were always saying that women are as sensible as men, and all that."

"So they are," said Vera. "But a man like you always tries to convert a woman. That's the trouble. That's why this is just desert-island friendliness—London in August and everybody away."

But Robert wouldn't believe her, though he wisely gave up the argument and was so attentive an escort and so willing a listener that Vera, when she got home, hardly knew whether she believed it herself.

Long before Robert told Vera he loved her, Alice knew about it. In fact, she had known that it would happen when she first brought Mr. Dean to put up the curtains in the upstairs fiat and saw him watching Vera. At the time, she was sure that it was all for the best: it would do Mr. Dean good to have a really nice girl to set his heart on, someone brighter than the dull young lady on his dressing-table. It never occurred to Alice that Vera might not want to get married at all, and yet there was Mr. Dean, glum and irritable in the mornings, unresponsive to any gossip which did not concern number eight, and wildly partisan over any that did. And whenever she went upstairs to do a little cleaning, she was sure to find a square envelope addressed in his writing lying neglected on the hall lino. She always picked the notes up and set them carefully in front of the pile of postcards and bills on Vera's mantelpiece. Sometimes she was still there when Vera came in and found them, and Vera sighed and glowered as she read them and was excited and irritable afterwards, too.

But in Miss Snow's flat, Robert Dean had almost ceased to be a topic of conversation. She still darned his socks, but she no longer pattered in and out of his flat after Alice. Instead she talked a great deal to Alice about old Mrs. Tobias and the new tenants who were coming to the flat upstairs— friends of Mr. Dean's, she had heard. A Mr. Howard Kennedy was the name.

"A bachelor?" asked Miss Snow.

"Yes and no, mum," said Alice. "That's to say, he is single at the moment, but when the lease is signed he'll be married."

"But I don't see," said Miss Snow, "what signing a lease has to do with marriage."

"Why, mum," said Alice, "even the gentry goes short of houses these days, if they're not made of money. And what's marriage without a home? There's a lot of good sense in waiting to put the banns up till you can get a home."

Miss Snow agreed that there was indeed, and hoped that the new tenants would be a nice addition. The wife would perhaps be company—especially for Miss Gray next door. Alice said that she had only set eyes on the young lady once, and, come to that, a married woman would hardly have much in common with Miss Gray, would she? And Miss Snow looked up from her darning and said perhaps not, but she supposed Miss Gray was a thoroughly nice girl, wasn't she?

Alice agreed, went on with her work, and thought that it was a pity for Robert to have fallen for Miss Gray. Three people's feelings were being hurt and no good was coming of it. And somehow it was hard on Miss Snow. "If Miss Gray and Mr. Dean was to make a match of it," said Alice to herself, "it'd be only right and natural, and Miss Snow could dote on the pair of them. But the way it is, Mr. Dean hasn't a thought in his head except Miss Gray."

As for Vera herself; she perplexed Alice. For Vera had always been her nicest self in the kitchen, an eager, gay learner, quick to admire Alice's skill with pots and pans and scrubbing-brushes. While Beatrix was on holiday, Vera kept at Alice's heels whenever she was in the flat, grateful for conversation and vividly interested in the entire Gedge family. With other people she was either consciously charming or purposely casual: she flaunted her independence and was persistently though unobtrusively selfish. But Alice knew by instinct that Vera's kitchen manners were the important ones.

IV
SECOND BEST

VERA left for her holiday without saying good-bye to Robert, and Robert was hurt. He was so hurt that he began to compare Vera and Joyce in his mind, a thing he had not done for weeks. But as usual the comparison did no good, because though he knew he ought to admire Joyce, he could not escape from being in love with Vera.

The day after Vera travelled to Southsea, Beatrix came back, grudgingly because it was still August and fine, while her holiday had been mostly wet. She had very little to do, though she went every day to her novelist's house and tidied up the correspondence and tore up or forwarded letters. In the afternoons she lounged about the flat, driving Alice crazy because she had theories about domestic science, and when Beatrix had a theory she forced it on everybody in the vicinity.

She spent most of her spare time working on the novel she had just begun. It was all about life in a women's college, and by luridly exaggerating every minor detail she had found it possible to make the setting sensational. In the intervals of writing she rang up the few friends who were marooned in London and asked them round to drink cocktails. I t was some days before she remembered Robert Dean's existence; but when the supply of friends had run out she thought of him and rang him up to suggest a drink before dinner.

Then she went out and bought a bottle of gin and another of vermouth across the road at 'The Silver Fox,' which conveniently had an off' licence. Mrs. Tobias's Martha saw her coming home with the bottles under her arm, and Mrs.

Tobias was profoundly shocked. She had nothing against good drink for man or woman; but she did feel that any girl who had not only to provide her own but actually to carry it home must be strangely lacking in social flair. Miss Snow also saw her, and thought kindly of Vera Gray for the first time in a fortnight. And Alice, when she found the bottles next morning, merely thought again that such behaviour was only what might be expected from a girl who swore out loud in the streets. Alice, in spite of street corner socialism, war work and Thomas's increasing contempt for his betters, still thought it was the duty of the gentry to behave themselves, and when they did not, she felt as though a personal friend had let her down.

But Beatrix, mixing and tasting and listening for Robert's knock, was happily unaware that Robert was coming to see her merely for news of Vera. So she was surprised when his first words, after a rather embarrassed greeting, were: "How's Vera?"

"Vera?" said Beatrix. "All right, I suppose. She's at Southsea with an aunt."

"Oh!" said Robert, wondering if he dared ask for the address.

"Foul place, Southsea," said Beatrix cheerfully, thinking that Robert was even shyer than she remembered. "I can't think why Vera should go there. Parades and bathing-machines and trips round the 'Victory'—not my idea of a holiday." She broke off to light a cigarette and Robert shifted to the other foot.

"For God's sake sit down!" said Beatrix. "Here! Take that stool thing, if you like!" But Robert avoided the stool; it reminded him of Vera. He sank reluctantly on to the divan. Beatrix refilled her glass and flopped down beside him. As he seemed to have nothing to say, she went on: "When I go away I like to get away, right off the beaten track, you know. I must have space and I must have quiet."

"Quite!" said Robert. And Beatrix's talk surged on. When she drew breath, Robert tugged his mind back from memories of Vera and said: "Where'd you go?"

"Cornwall," said Beatrix. Robert looked surprised.

"But Cornwall's awfully popular," he said. "I mean, there're always plenty of people there."

"The right sort of people," said Beatrix. "At least, on the whole. If you avoid the towns and keep to the small coves."

"Must be grand," said Robert, setting down his glass, which Beatrix automatically refilled, still talking of the artists and writers she had met, of long evening bathes from the rocky shore, of sunsets and the rising moon, and finally of wet weather and Cornish cream.

Robert, encouraged by Beatrix's fiery mixture, agreed with all she said and tried to keep to the subject of holidays in the hope that Southsea would crop up again. But Beatrix, who found holidays far too impersonal a topic, turned to face him and talked of the loneliness of London in August, and finally of her writing. Even Robert, his wits numbed by shyness, over-concentration on Vera and Beatrix's cocktails, had the perspicacity to see that this was an important topic and demanded comment.

He said: "Must be extraordinarily interesting work, writing."

"It is," said Beatrix solemnly.

"Must take a lot out of you," said Robert, rising to the occasion with determination. "Creative effort, and all that."

"It does," said Beatrix. "One must live every episode, be every character one creates."

"Needs tremendous concentration, I should say," said Robert.

"People won't realise," said Beatrix, warming to the subject, "that one's writing is work. At least, not till one can afford a secretary or two and a country house. And yet writing is work, frightfully hard work, far harder than scrubbing, for instance."

"Would you say that?" Robert was doubtful.

"Of course," said Beatrix. "It's both a physical and an emotional strain. There's no emotional strain about scrubbing."

"No, but—" said Robert slowly. He disliked the comparison, which seemed to him inexact, and he had a lawyer's love of precision. But Beatrix did not allow him to finish his sentence.

"I know what you're going to say," she said. "You're going to say that nothing is worse than physical fatigue. But there is something worse, and that's nervous exhaustion. No cleaner has nervous exhaustion."

"Quite," said Robert, baffled.

"But on the other hand," said Beatrix, "one's writing has its compensations. Think of the richness of a writer's life! Every incident has meaning, every experience is significant, doesn't matter what it is—riches, poverty, illness, work, love."

"Marriage?" asked Robert.

"Well, yes, I daresay even marriage," Beatrix said. "Not that I consider that marriage and love are at all synonymous."

It was some time before Robert could escape from Beatrix's views on marriage; but at last he got up, thanked his hostess, and made for the door. Beatrix was talking hopefully of plays and cinemas and long evenings, and Robert felt that good manners compelled him to make some return for such a lavish supply of cocktails. So he suggested dinner, and Beatrix immediately pulled a diary out of her bag and fixed a date. Robert went downstairs sadly, wishing that Vera had been as ready to go out with him, wishing that Vera, if she had to have a career, had chosen writing, since it interfered neither with love nor marriage.

And Beatrix, typing rather confusedly, felt sure that the entertainment had been a success.

She had fixed a Sunday evening for her dinner with Robert, because she had two complimentary tickets for a Sunday Dramatic League performance, and it seemed a pity not to take a man with her when she could. For in 1924, many people still found it difficult to get men to partner women, and it was worst of all for women of Beatrix's age, since there seemed to be so few men between seventeen and fifty. So Beatrix felt that it would do her good to be seen about with Robert.

Meanwhile, she stimulated the friendship by lending Robert books (which he never read), and she met him, apparently by accident, in the hall, on the stairs, by his own door, as often as she could arrange it. But Robert began to feel a little persecuted: he did not admire Beatrix's type. Bobbed hair and beads had never appealed to him, and he was distrustful of all obviously clever women. Besides, he thought that Beatrix must be self-centred, too, for she did not seem to know Vera's address or to care whether she had news of her or not.

But as he was pledged to it, Robert came back early from a tennis party at Richmond that Sunday. He changed into a blue suit because he had gathered that a dinner jacket would not be acceptable, and wondered where he should take Beatrix to dinner. Finally, he chose Soho, and the Blue Cock, because he knew that he could get a respectable *prix fixe* meal, and they could drink Chianti. Robert was not really mean, but merely cautious; and he did not feel that Beatrix was the kind of girl who deserved an expensive setting. Beatrix met him, wearing a plain long-waisted red silk dress, the full skirt of which fell, surprisingly for 1924, nearly to her ankles. She had on amber ear-rings, and a chain of milky yellow beads dangled to her waist.

She accepted Soho with resignation, but she wished that Robert had chosen a more conventional and luxurious milieu, for she felt sure that he did not really know his Soho. The Blue Cock confirmed her fears; but though she condemned it mentally as utterly bourgeois and unworthy of her, she did not quarrel with Robert, for the Chianti proved a sufficiently cheering wine. She began to talk again about her writing, the play they were going to see, and psycho-analysis, which was just then causing one of its periodic sensations, and Robert blushed over psycho-analysis as Beatrix had intended he should. He hurried over the dinner as much as possible, so that they reached the theatre a good deal too early. They went up through a disappointingly empty entrance hall to seats at the back of the dress circle. A few people were wandering about the stalls, and Beatrix's attention was immediately diverted from Robert. She kept bobbing up and down, hoping to catch glimpses of the few celebrities known to be in London and likely to be lured to a Sunday Dramatic League performance. Soon, the theatre began to fill with men and women in every degree of evening dress, from tails to smoking jackets, and from short dance dresses to trailing picture frocks or satin jumpers over pleated skirts.

Beatrix waved a good deal to various people whom she knew or imagined she knew, and displayed Robert as much as she could. But Robert did not know anyone, and would not have waved if he had. He was bored by the play, which was a laboured satire on party politics, and he was able to agree with Beatrix when she condemned it as cheap and unintelligent. So Beatrix felt she could introduce Robert to some of her friends in the foyer; and he compared so favourably in appearance with them that Beatrix felt his political views did not matter. On the way home, however, she did her best to convert him; but he was not very responsive.

"It's been a splendid evening," said Beatrix at last, as they reached Robert's landing.

"Yes, indeed!" said Robert absently. "Er—by the way, when does Vera come back?"

But Beatrix had flounced off upstairs.

CHAPTER 6

I

1924   SUSAN'S HUSBAND

A DRY September followed that damp August, and by the end of it Alfred House had settled down for the autumn. Vera was back, and after a sharp quarrel with Beatrix on Robert's account, she took as much pains in avoiding him as Beatrix did in pursuing him. Alice was annoyed with both of them, but she was more annoyed with Beatrix, because she thought her behaviour unladylike. Miss Snow, too, had been away and come back the better for it, while old Mrs. Tobias had been carefully transported to Littlehampton and safely returned to her armchair in the window.

And in Tuffnel Road, Leonard, who had won his free place with the narrowest possible margin and was bottom of the list of successful candidates, swanked about in the blue knickers, grey jersey and red and blue cap required by the Grammar School.

"There now, ma!" Len said when the results came out. "Wot did I tell yer? I done it easy." Alice, who had not seen the lists, believed him and was more lenient over evenings wasted with Harry; while Dulcie who had, never undeceived her, though she twitted Len about it in private. Thomas grumbled about Len's success every day for a fortnight, and then forgot it. He had a new grievance: he was stood off work every Monday, and Alice made him do the washing regularly. Her own capacity for work was boundless, especially now that Len needed so many more boots and clothes for school. So she offered her services to the future tenants of the top flat next to Vera Gray, and Howard Kennedy's fiancée, Susan, engaged her at once.

The Kennedys' furniture came in (some of it from Maple's) ten days before they were married, so that Mrs. Tobias was obliged to postpone her offer of hospitality. The furniture certainly warranted it, but it would have been made in any case, for Mrs. Tobias took a ghoulish pleasure in newly-married young women. Susan came round once or twice, and she and Alice and Mr. Barker, whose leg was having a good spell, pushed and pulled cupboards and tables into place. Once Howard Kennedy came too and did a little pushing and pulling and a great deal of talking. He was very hearty in his manner to Alice, and affectionately possessive to Susan—"a affable man, without a doubt," as Mr. Barker remarked.

Susan left them to shift a wardrobe and slipped through to the kitchen, where trunks of linen and blankets still waited to be unpacked. She flushed as she asked Alice to make up the bed on October 25th with the best embroidered sheets and to do what she could about airing them. Alice said she would pack them up in blue paper and a cardboard box and take them home to warm by her own kitchen fire, and she wondered how anyone so young and gentle had come to choose such a hearty, affable man. "For they give you no peace, that kind, and that's a fact," said Alice, as she re-folded the sheets between layers of tissue paper.

And now it was October 25th, and a wet day, and Susan and Howard Kennedy, married for one week were on their way from Torquay to Alfred House.

Alice had set three dinners going on three separate stoves and commanded their owners to take them off at such and such a time, for she herself would be too taken up with settling in Miss Susan (as Alice still thought protectively of the childish, red-haired creature who was now Mrs. Kennedy) to give them another thought. A chicken with fruit pie to follow they were having, and all Alice's employers, as well as Mrs. Tobias, Martha and the Barkers, knew about the menu and hoped Alice would have luck with the pastry.

"You need something tasty to cheer you up, coming to a new place, and that's a fact," Alice said to Vera Gray.

"What?" said Vera ironically. "Even when you've a husband with you?"

"That's got nothing to do with it," said Alice. And this seemed strange to Vera, who still believed that if one married one must be in love, and that to be in love was automatically to be happy.

The Kennedys did not arrive till after six, and when Alice opened the door of the flat, a slight altercation was going on with a taxi-man who held that sixpence was an inadequate tip for carrying a heavy trunk up three flights. Howard Kennedy paid no attention to his argument, he picked up the suitcases and strode over the threshold. But Susan fumbled in her bag and gave the man a shilling with some vague idea of propitiating fate. Then she went in search of Howard and found him in the kitchen, being affable, while Alice watched him curiously.

He was fattish and short, a bare two inches taller than his wife, with the bristling dignity of five foot seven, a high colour, and a dark, well-trimmed moustache. Who'd have expected him to take Miss Susan's fancy? But there, you never could tell.

"Well now, Mrs. Gedge, glad to see you, I'm sure. Fine little place. Looks good to me. Bit of luck striking it, what? Here, Susan, where are you? Come and tell me what you think of your new home."

Susan allowed herself to be kissed and then shook hands with Alice. Alice thought she looked tired and pale—but then so many young brides did. Now Mr. Kennedy seemed happy enough, going from room to room, looking the furniture up and down and choosing places for his favourite pictures. Well, she'd better be dishing up.

And Susan went quietly into her new bedroom—so new and strange with nothing of her own in it to welcome her. She took off her hat and tidied her hair, seeing her face for the first time in the oval mirror. She fingered the stiff silk cover on the broad bed in which nobody had ever slept, and pulled open an empty drawer which still smelt of the workshop. Then she rubbed a little colour into her cheeks and leaned out of the window, sniffing the smells of London—the reek of smoke from the railway, petrol fumes, a whiff of warm oil, and a heavy, stuffy, musty smell of dust and beer and other people's dinners. And suddenly out of her memory came the sweet, sharp smell of a cold country evening. She turned quickly from the window, almost as if she were going to open the door and run out of the flat, down the stone stairs, into the street. But she checked herself and came back to the window again, twisting the wedding ring on her finger. Then she went slowly across the narrow hall into the kitchen, where Alice was setting forks and knives on a red and white checked cloth. For the Kennedys had decided to eat all meals except breakfast in the kitchen and have their food hot from the oven, with the sink handy (though behind a screen) for thrusting plates and forks into hot water before the fat congealed.

"I'll do that while you dish up, Mrs. Gedge," said Susan, straightening the salt-cellars. Alice opened the oven door and brought out the chicken, setting it on the table proudly, with a vegetable dish on each side of it.

"The tart's in the oven, miss ... ma'am, I should say," said Alice. "P'raps you could get it out when you're ready, so's it keeps hot."

Howard came in, rubbing his hands together. "Ah, ha, chicken." He opened the oven door and sniffed. "And pie. I was always a great one for pie. Here, Susan, give me the carver." He flourished the knife and plunged it awkwardly into the fowl, shaving off a minute fragment of breast for Susan. "This is extravagance, this is," he said. "But there, our first night in the new home. Here's to it."

"I'm sure I wish you luck, madam," said Alice primly, as she put on her hat and coat.

"Thank you very much, Mrs. Gedge," said Susan.

As the door closed behind Alice, Howard patted his wife's hand and pulled his chair closer to hers so that their knees touched. Susan looked away, round the unfamiliar room, gay with its yellow and red paint, and out of the uncurtained panes down a long lane of lighted windows. At home the curtains would be drawn; at home her family were probably eating chicken too, eating it off familiar plates, against a familiar background of faded wallpaper and blue chintz, saying the things they always said. Susan had come to think her family boring and their background dull. But that evening at Alfred House she hunched her shoulders against a cold, relentless gust of homesickness. There, in the Wiltshire manor house, was the life she knew and loved; the life that was safe and wholesome and comforting. She looked up as Howard patted her hand again and saw with dismay that he was a stranger. And she was suddenly appallingly afraid of being alone and ill and poor and growing old.

1925   Mrs. Tobias Gives a Party

EVERY year Mrs. Tobias celebrated her birthday: nothing was allowed to interfere with the festival, not even the deaths of near relations. And 1925 was a special occasion, for Mrs. Tobias was eighty-one, or, as she preferred to put it, "eighteen the wrong way round."

The parties were always rather assorted, for Mrs. Tobias invited every one on whom she had bestowed cups of tea during the year, including all her descendants and other relatives. Sometimes mere acquaintances refused, but no relation ever dared to do so. They appeared punctually at half-past four, in their best clothes, with presents as lavish as their expectations. Every year, the number of contemporaries dwindled and great-nieces, or great-nephews, supplanted them. Every year Mrs. Tobias asked the tenants of Alfred House on whom she had called, and on this particular 18th of January, she stretched a point and asked everybody, even Vera and Beatrix and the Kennedys. She also engaged Alice to help with the coats and washing-up.

Beatrix said she supposed she would have to go for the sake of copy. Vera said that as a working woman she had no time for frivolity, but she would look in on her way back to Alfred House if the party was still going on. And this cheered Robert, whose good nature compelled him to go. But he decided to be rather late and arrive in time for cocktails with Vera. As for Susan, she felt that any party which would bring her friends among the other tenants was worth going to. For she was lonely during the long days:

her neighbours in Alfred House did not like to intrude on a bride still almost on her honeymoon.

Miss Snow, pursing her lips over Mrs. Tobias's florid At Home card, gave Alice gentle but unmistakable warnings about Mrs. Tobias and what she expected from her staff. Having warned Alice, she went upstairs to give a hint to the new tenants, for, as she said to herself; how could they know? And if they didn't know they'd never think—especially being young.

Beatrix, on the point of setting out for Hampstead, received Miss Snow with rather obvious hostility. She did not ask her in, for it was not one of Alice's cleaning mornings, so the beds were not made and the sitting-room was littered with papers and cigarette ash. Miss Snow disliked being kept on doorsteps. She flushed and said curtly that in case Miss Wood and Miss Gray were going to tea with Mrs. Tobias they might care to know the old custom.

"It's the same every year," said Miss Snow. "We always accept, you know, and, well, we all bring some little token. Poor old lady—so delighted always—so disappointed if any of us forget. And so I thought, perhaps—but it doesn't matter."

"Good Lord," said Beatrix with a giggle. "D'you mean I've got to take a present, as if it was a kids' party? Well I'm damned!"

"I only felt," said Miss Snow, retreating, "that as one of the older residents I ought to let you know the custom."

"Oh, quite," said Beatrix. "No present—no tea. I'll toss for it. Thank you for telling me." And she slammed the door shut. Miss Snow rattled the knocker of the Kennedys' flat, braced to encounter another snub and vowing that Beatrix Wood should never enter her flat as long as she lived.

But Susan was so delighted to find that Miss Snow was not a tradesman that she asked her in and brought her

Bovril. And Miss Snow sat down in a new and shiny leather armchair and warmed her toes at the gas fire while Susan removed the mop, the carpet-sweeper, two dusters and a brush and dustpan from various corners of the room. Quite a man's room, too, thought Miss Snow, what with the leather chairs and coats of arms and piperacks. One thing about being single was that you could have your rooms as you liked them, when you came to think of it.

"Do forgive me," said Susan, still tidying, "but Alice doesn't come till this afternoon, and I'm so bad at housework. Only it seems so awful to sit down and read a book in the mornings, and if I don't have something to do the days go so slowly."

"Yes, don't they," said Miss Snow. "But I should have thought there must be plenty to do when you're just married. New friends, you know, and lots of shopping."

"Not in London, somehow," said Susan. "Friends to come about the place, I mean. And shopping—well, it seems to depend on what you've got to spend. I can't make a morning's occupation out of buying a pound of butter and some herrings. It's my own fault, I know. It's because I'm a bad housekeeper and no good at bargaining."

"Oh dear, neither am I," said Miss Snow. "I'm no good at all at marketing. I gave up trying long ago."

"But what do you find to do with your mornings?" Susan said. "I do so want to find out what other people do with their spare time. I just waste mine."

Miss Snow was surprised. This was not the sort of conversation she expected from a bride. Brides, happy brides, were traditionally content to potter about their new homes, day-dreaming till their husbands came back.

"Well," she said, rather guardedly, "I'm a very busy person. I do a great deal of social work. But then you see, I've got no husband with claims on my time."

Susan, interested and eager, did not notice the change of tone. "Couldn't I do something like that?" she asked. "Would it be any use my trying? Could you tell me how to find out about it?"

Miss Snow said: "There's always plenty of work for those who can do it. But it needs the gift. Some people have a real gift for that sort of work and there are never enough of them to go round. I'm afraid I don't know you well enough to say ... But there," she added, at the sight of Susan's drooping mouth, "I daresay you may have. You're young and energetic and kind. Probably we could find you something to do. If your husband approved, that's to say. We must consider his feelings, mustn't we?"

"Yes," said Susan. "Oh yes. Of course. But my mornings are my own, aren't they?"

"Er—yes," said Miss Snow. "But that wasn't what I came here to talk about. I really want to ask you whether you and your husband are going to Mrs. Tobias's party. Because, if so ..."

"Oh yes," said Susan. "Rather. Indeed we are."

Miss Snow explained that she'd thought Mrs. Kennedy would like to know that custom required each guest to bring a little gift. "Eighty-one, she is," said Miss Snow. "And kindness itself at heart. And she is so pleased to be remembered."

"Of course," said Susan. "The poor old dear. Will flowers do?"

Miss Snow said that they would do nicely, and went away wondering what Mr. Kennedy was really like, and vaguely shocked to find a newly-married young woman hoping for interests which she could not share with her husband. It seemed all wrong, and she felt she ought not to encourage it unless the husband himself approved. And Susan got out her brushes and dustpan and dusters again and swept and dusted rather absently, thinking that if only those mornings could be filled, life would be bearable again.

At breakfast on the morning of Mrs. Tobias's party she mentioned the flowers to her husband.

"What nonsense!" said Howard. "Why should we have to take the old dame a present? Never even met her."

"Well, but you said you wanted to go to her party," objected Susan.

"So I do. Daresay she knows plenty of useful people. Never know who you might meet. She's rich enough, by all accounts," said Howard, crackling the morning paper.

"Then would you give me some money, Howard? It's the end of the week, and by the time I've paid the books I shan't have a penny."

Howard lowered the newspaper and speared a piece of sausage. "Haven't you got any of your own dress money left?" he said judicially.

"Not very much."

"Well, you don't want very much, do you?" said Howard. "And after all, that sort of thing's always left to the woman, isn't it?"

He gulped down his coffee, folded his newspaper and went out into the little hall, where he floundered into his coat.

"You might come and help your husband into his coat, I do think," he grumbled from the doorway. "Get a clothes-brush, my dear, and brush me down. And a clean handkerchief; too, there's a good sort. Must look after your husband, you know, little girl. Been married to him four months now."

He came back into the sitting-room and waited there with his hat on till Susan had got his handkerchief, his gloves and his stick. Then she opened the door and kissed him, stiffening her lips against his moustache. She watched him go down the stairs and then went back to the window to wave, as he wished her to do. She looked down on him as he crossed the wide road towards the Tube station and wished that he didn't walk on the backs of his heels. Then she went out and bought a bunch of jonquils for Mrs. Tobias.

The party began promptly. Susan went downstairs to it, feeling shy and conscious that her bunch of flowers was a small one. She had put on her best trousseau dress, a plain blue crepe-de-chine with a broad velvet sash and a blue velvet hat which made her hair a vivid bracken gold. From the landing window she saw large cars rolling up to Alfred House, and Mr. Barker, in the unusual glory of a faded green uniform, parading on the pavement ready to fling open saloon doors or to produce an umbrella if it should begin to rain.

A temporary butler opened the door of Mrs. Tobias's flat, but Susan was comforted by the sight of Alice, busy helping people out of their coats in the background. Susan had meant to keep hers on, but she let Alice take it.   "My word," whispered Alice, "you have got some lovely flowers, Miss. I'd sooner have them than any of these hot-house things."

Mrs. Tobias, in maroon satin and black lace, was receiving her guests at the drawing-room door, with her only surviving brother at her elbow. She was feeling pleased with herself because he was bowed with rheumatism and lived on hot water and charcoal biscuits since he had trouble with his digestion, while she could still stand with Victorian uprightness to greet her guests and sit down to a good tea afterwards.

"Ah, ha, I know who you are," she said, wagging a knotted finger at Susan. "You're the little bride from the top flat. But what have you done with your husband, my dear?"

Susan said he was afraid he would be a little late, and proffered her jonquils.

"I call that too bad—letting a bride go out to her first party in Alfred House without him. My husband would never—what's this, eh? For me? My dear child! William, these flowers are delicious—what a pretty thought! Spring flowers for an old lady—eighteen the wrong way round. You and I must have some long talks, me dear. Some long talks ..."

She peered at Susan (pride forbade her to wear spectacles at a birthday party) and then, with a regal inclination of her head, dismissed her and turned to greet a relation. Susan wandered on. The room was oppressively ugly, with its heavy, ornate furniture and imitation panelling, its plush curtains and useless little tables; but the walls were banked with flowers—mostly sent by relations—as though the party were a wedding reception. In the far corner Susan saw Miss Snow talking to a young man whose hooked nose and darting eyes proclaimed his relationship with Mrs. Tobias. He was actually a grand-nephew, and as Miss Snow introduced him, he looked most appraisingly at Susan.

"Meet Miss Snow here regularly once a year," he said. "Never see her again. Always come to Auntie's parties for the pleasure, eh? Come to dinner, too, sometimes. Must do it, you know. Awful old sport, Auntie. You don't know her? Ah well, you'll find she's a good sort. These parties are a bit of a strain, don't you know. But Auntie always has some pretty girls about, I'll say that for her. Cocktail for you? Or tea?"

"Tea please," said Susan.

"Ah well, no accounting for tastes," said young Mr. Tobias. He went away and fetched a cup of tea and another young man who admired Susan too, and for some time she was kept busy greeting the younger male relations. Pricked with success, she began to chatter happily.

Mrs. Tobias, now seated in a place of honour, noticed the group. "That's right," she said. "I like to hear 'em enjoying themselves. Who've the boys got over there? Me eyes aren't what they were, William. Ho, the little bride from upstairs? That serves the husband right. Husbands with pretty little wives have no business to send 'em out alone."

Just then the butler reappeared in the doorway.

"Mr. Dean and Miss Gray: Mr. Kennedy and Miss Wood," he announced, rearranging the new arrivals as he thought best.

Mrs. Tobias was gracious to Robert and Vera (whom she immediately married off) and curt to Beatrix whose type she disliked. Then she plucked at Howard's sleeve.

"Goin' to give you a scoldin', young man," she said. "What d'you mean by it, leavin' a pretty little wife like that to go out by herself?"

Howard was annoyed. The unexpected attack interfered with the speech of congratulation which he had prepared on the way home, and he began to shout excuses for his late arrival down Mrs. Tobias's ear.

"I'm not deaf, young man, I'm not deaf!" she said indignantly. "Eighty-one I may be, but not infirm, thank God."

"Growing younger every day," interpolated a relation.

"Good for another twenty years," sighed another.

"Eighteen the wrong way round," murmured young Mr. Tobias.

"Congratulations, my heartiest congratulations," said Howard, as soon as he could make himself heard.

But Mrs. Tobias was not listening. "Over there, your little wife," she chuckled, with a pointing forefinger. "And won't the boys hate you when you take her away!"

Howard edged out of the group, noticing with annoyance that Susan was indeed surrounded by young men.

"Too bad," murmured Beatrix at his elbow. "But old people are all alike."

Howard looked down at her. She wasn't at all bad-looking, he thought, and there was a very proper hint of admiration in her dark eyes.

"You must meet my wife," he said heartily, "I know she'd be delighted."

"Rather," said Beatrix. "I believe in knowing my neighbours."

"So do I." said Howard. "You must come in and see us. Fix it with my wife." He ploughed through the press of people towards Susan, who turned as he came near her.

"I must introduce my husband," she said. "Howard, do come and meet ..."

"Susan, my dear, come here," said Howard, planting himself firmly just out of greeting distance, "I want you to meet Miss Wood."

Susan sketched an apologetic gesture round her circle and came up to her husband. They stood and talked haltingly until Beatrix, seeing Vera and Robert, moved across to them. Robert was talking quickly and anxiously. Beatrix could see that from the far side of the room. And Vera was fiddling with the stem of her glass. Robert was trying to arrange something and Vera was undecided. Beatrix edged determinedly through the crowd. But just before she was near enough to speak she saw Vera look up and smile and nod, and knew she was too late. But she persevered. She brought Susan and Howard and introduced them, and Howard began to talk in his rather high voice about all the celebrities he knew. Susan and Vera exchanged banalities and Beatrix noticed again that Robert's attention kept wandering. If only she knew what Vera was up to!

Miss Snow, from the corner of the room where she was listening to a female cousin of Mrs. Tobias, also wished she knew what Vera was about. For she could see clearly how much Robert loved her, from the way he kept turning to look at her, and his nervous protective movements in the crush. And there was that Mr. Kennedy not bothering at all about his wife—just talking much too loudly down his nose, though anybody could tell that Robert Dean was hardly listening to a word.

And Alice, now that the party was thinning, came in and out to clear away glasses and remove cups before they were broken. Martha, on the same errand, spent most of her time following Alice round and hissing instructions to be careful and to hurry up. For Alice, slowly clearing up the relics of an accident, could not help watching her ladies and gentlemen. There they all were, Miss Snow rather out of things again, and Miss Gray and Mr. Dean looking happier than they had for weeks, and poor Miss Susan ... her fun spoilt by Mr. Kennedy, who never noticed nobody but himself, but had to have his audience as usual. Rather like Miss Wood he was, come to think of it, only a man. And of course in men you couldn't look for much unselfishness ...

And as she picked up the last fragment of china, with Martha tut-tutting in her ear as though she had been the one to knock it over, Alice found herself wondering how much trouble these people were going to make for one another.

III

PENNY WISDOM

ONE morning about a week after Mrs. Tobias's party, Howard set down his knife and fork and said to Susan:

"What's happened to the potatoes I left last night?"

Susan looked up in surprise from a letter from her family. "I really don't know, dear. Why?"

Alice was in the passage just then, and Howard's voice was perfectly audible. She cocked her head at the sitting-room door, set down her mop, wiped her hands on her apron and went through to the kitchen. There she took the lid off the pig-bucket and removed two greasy potatoes from a pile of cabbage stalks.

She had just laid them in a clean saucer when Howard came through, still chewing a shred of bacon and with a table-napkin in his hand. He looked put out at the sight of Alice and swallowed the bacon quickly. He said:

"By the way, Mrs—er—Gedge, do you happen to know what is happening to the potatoes I leave over every night?"

"I'm sure I don't know what happens to scraps, sir," said Alice. "There's some potato on that saucer if you require it."

"Who put it there?" said Howard.

"Mrs. Kennedy as like as not. Excuse me, sir, but catering is not my duty and never was. The catering is usually left to the mistress ... sir."

Howard picked up the saucer and considered Alice; but she was placidly scraping saucepans in a perfectly respectful way.

He cleared his throat. "Quite—ah—quite," he said. "But I dislike waste, Mrs. Gedge, and I trust you will remind my wife if she should appear to forget. Potatoes left over from supper should be fried for breakfast—regularly."

"If you think I come and carry your scraps home in my bag—" said Alice.

Howard held up a deprecatory hand. "No, no, I'm sure. I only want economy and care ..."

"What you leave, sir," Alice said, with some heat, "isn't worth the taking, even if I'd a mind to. And that I've never had and never will." She picked up the frying-pan from the sink, tipped in some rather doubtful dripping that she had been going to throw away, and reached over to take the saucer out of Howard's hand. The gas popped into flame and the dripping sizzled as the potatoes fell into it, slice by slice.

'Better to ignore the woman perhaps,' thought Howard, and he stood with uneasy dignity in the middle of the floor till Alice had finished scooping the crumbling, greasy mess on to the saucer again. Then he stodged back importantly into the sittingroom.

"My word," grumbled Alice at the sink, "I hope they taste like what they smelt! Funny how some people have no use of their noses. Men, men! Once let a man into your kitchen and peace flies out of the window!"

In the sitting-room Susan was still at the table, sipping coffee and trying to pretend that she and Howard had never had a sordid encounter about potatoes. But large, round, childish tears kept trickling slowly down the curve of her cheeks, until they splashed into her cup. She tried to wink them back—it would be so undignified to wipe them away.

Howard looked sulkily at her. It seemed unreasonable for a grown woman to cry over such a trifle. If he couldn't speak his mind occasionally to his own wife or get his way about fried potatoes it was a poor show.

"Mrs. Gedge cooked these for me," he said. "She told me you'd saved them up, so that's all right."

Susan looked at him, wrinkling her nose at the thought of the pig-bucket, and twitched away a smile at the idea of Alice's cleverness. If Howard were fool enough to eat potatoes that smelt like that ... Susan was surprised to catch herself wishing that the beastly things would make him sick.

"Ah, by the way," said Howard, clearing his throat again: "You shouldn't let Mrs. Gedge forget her place. She was most impertinent to me just now. But I chose to overlook it."

"Oh, Howard," said Susan, "for goodness' sake stop worrying about Mrs. Gedge. Any good servant hates being interfered with by the man of the house, Mother says."

"My dear," said Howard, "you must try to remember that you're not in your mother's house now. You've married a poor man, my dear—at least, comparatively speaking. Try to think of that and not waste good food." He opened the paper and turned to the financial news, only to be irritated by reading that some shares of his had fallen again. He threw the paper into a corner.

"And while I think of it," he said, "it would be most inconsiderate of you to take on that work you were talking about yesterday."

"Oh, Howard, why?" Susan leant across the oval table, pushing aside the coffee-pot and the hyacinth in its blue bowl. "Oh, Howard, it's not as if it were taking up time that I could spend with you. It's only the mornings. And not even every morning either."

"What's the sense?" said Howard. "There's no pay."

"But it's useful, Howard, and, besides, the days are so dismal with you out all the time, and everything new. I haven't many friends in London."

"Well, Susan, you're not a very good housekeeper, are you?" said Howard. "If you were, you'd know that there's always plenty to do in a home—even a small home. Especially for a newly-married wife."

Susan slid her hands back across the cloth, set the coffee-pot and the flowers neatly in the centre of the table again and went across to the window. The Cornish Express was roaring past, trailing grey smoke that rose slowly upwards, engulfing bridges and blotting out the tall houses on the other side of the line. It had begun to rain.

"Now then, Susan my dear!" Howard strode across the room and set his hands on her shoulders. "Now then, Susan, you do your duty to your husband, little woman, and never mind about anything else."

He kissed her moistly and firmly. "Get me my coat," he said, "there's a good girl."

When Susan had gone through the ritual of seeing Howard off, she went into the kitchen to see Alice, half afraid that she would give notice on the spot.

"Mr. Kennedy says will you please save what scraps you can …" she began, and at the sight of Alice's kind face could go no further. She blinked, clenching her hands.

"That's all right, Miss Susan," said Alice. "Never you mind. Men are all alike. You don't have to take any notice of them half the time. You leave it to me."

"I wish you'd show me how to be more economical," said Susan. "After all, we are awfully badly off, I suppose. And I know I'm not a good housekeeper."

"If I was you," said Alice, "I'd let Mr. Kennedy order the meals for a bit and have a good lunch in the middle of the day yourself; instead of just those snacks."

"But if we're poor …" said Susan.

"When people are real downright poor," said Alice, "they don't make this song about economy. They eat what they can get while they can get it and go without when they have to. Believe me, Miss, I know. I didn't marry Thomas Gedge for nothing. You've got to stand up to men in this life," said Alice, wringing out the dish-cloth with immense vigour. Then she draped it over the edge of the sink and rolled up the blue apron she put on over her overall for the rough work.

"Fancy," she said. "There's the half-hour. And me with Mr. Dean and Miss Snow to wash-up yet."

Susan did not stay in the flat very long. She went from room to room with a duster at first, thinking of what Alice had said. Stand up for yourself ... Well, Alice probably knew. 'It isn't as if Howard wants me to be unhappy. It's just that he doesn't know what it's like. After all, he doesn't know me very well yet,' thought Susan, who was beginning to get used to the idea of not knowing someone you had married. If he did, he would realise that I'd be better-tempered with something to do. He'd like me to be better-tempered, too. He'd really be pleased if he knew that was why I wanted to work. And, anyway'—Susan's chin came forward in a way that Howard would not have recognised—'and anyway, my mornings are my own.'

So she went downstairs to Miss Snow, and arranged to try Care Committee work, and told her that she had discussed it very thoroughly with her husband and she had decided that it would be excellent to have some occupation in the mornings. Miss Snow hesitated a little; for Susan was so very guarded and her sentences were so well thought out, and her eyes so strained. As a Care Committee worker, Miss Snow had learned to recognise prevarication when she saw it. But, against her better judgment, she arranged for Susan to go round to the office and sign on as a part-time voluntary worker, under her own direct supervision.

IV
DULCIE MAKES HER CHANCE

AFTERNOON school was just over: the forty girls in Dulcie's class were grabbing at their satchels and stuffing them with text books and pencil boxes and exercise books and all the odds and ends of pencil sharpeners, photographs of film stars and actors that they were constantly borrowing and trading. Dulcie hung back. Inside her satchel was the form teacher had given her yesterday—the form which her mother or her father must sign if she were, like Len, to try for a free place and go on to the Grammar School next term. But the form was still blank. She had not produced it at home. Dulcie took it out and looked at it. Teacher was still at her desk with a cluster of girls about her, for she was young and popular, and they were all too absorbed to notice Dulcie at the far end of the big room.

"Miss, need I do all of it again? Please, Miss ..."

"Miss, what d'you think? I saw Doug and Mary last night at the Blue Hall. Coo, Miss, Doug's grand!"

"Here, 'oo're you shoving, Daisy Atkins? I got 'ere first, didn't I?"

"I say, girls, teacher thinks ..."

"Oo, Miss, do let me look. I'll be ever so careful, cross me heart I will; thanks ever so, Miss."

Dulcie sat down at her desk. It seemed such a pity to give in the form back like that, quite blank. But there, Mother had as good as said she wasn't to be bothered any more with Dulcie and her scholarships and her school. One at the Grammar was more than enough, Mother said. That Leonard wanted something new every week, and goodness only knew where the money was coming from. This term it was proper football boots and a new pair of shorts. It made Dad mad all right. Mother might think different—probably if it came to that Mother would like it if Dulcie did get on to Grammar School. But Dad would make trouble. If it just happened, sort of, Mother wouldn't let you down. It was all this filling up forms and signing things and deciding ... it put people off when they were busy like Mother. It was a worry, that was what it was. But why should Mother have to worry, why shouldn't Dulcie go in for the exam and get a place if she could? If she did Mother would be as pleased as pleased. If only the horrid old form was signed up good and proper she would have her chance. She ought to have a chance ... Leonard had a chance ... everybody had a chance.

Dulcie looked up at teacher again. She was still talking to the girls round her. There was nobody rise in the class-room. Dulcie picked up the pen that lay beside the ink-well and cautiously dipped it in the ink. She filled in her own name, her age and the date of her birth, her place in school. Then her address. That was easy. There, the form was ready now. It would only take Mother a minute to sign it. But would she? ... Why not save her the trouble? She dipped the pen again, and curling her tongue round her upper lip, she wrote 'A. Gedge' laboriously and firmly on the dotted line left for 'Parent's Signature.' Then she folded up the form again, picked up her satchel of books and went quietly across to the outskirts of the group round teacher. Teacher was getting tired of them.

"Get along now, girls. It's long past tea-time."

Reluctantly they scattered.

"Why, Dulcie Gedge," said teacher, "I didn't notice you. And that reminds me, are you going to bring me back that form or are you not? It must be in by to-morrow or you can't go in. I shouldn't have thought you'd find it so difficult to remember if you'd set your mind on it."

"Please, Miss, it's signed up all right," Dulcie said, colouring. "I can't think how I came to forget to put it on your desk. It's here."

"That's right, Dulcie." Teacher took the form, and Dulcie's heart seemed to block her throat. But she clipped the paper to the other forms without a second glance, and Dulcie's heart plopped back into its place.

"That's all, then," said the harassed young mistress. "Get along with you, Dulcie Gedge. I want my tea."

And Dulcie ran down the passage to the cloakroom, snatched her things from her peg, and dashed away through the playground and across the tram-lines towards Tuffnel Road.

All the entrance forms went through Miss James's hands, and she sat at her desk in the Main Hall of the Girls' Department after school and sorted them out. There were only a dozen entries from the Girls' Side this term, and among them she was pleased to see the name of Dulcie Gedge. It was surprising that Mrs. Gedge had come round. She had been so obstinate. Miss James read the form through again, just to make sure that Mrs. Gedge had really filled in everything. She did not want any disqualification here, and parents were so careless. Then something incongruous in the signature caught her attention. She fumbled uneasily in her drawer where there should still be the note that Mrs. Gedge had sent her last week when Dulcie was away with a feverish cold. Mrs. Gedge was better about sending notes than the other parents: writing wasn't the weary labour to her that it was to most of them. Miss James found it and pulled it out. There was the signature, 'A. Gedge,' and there was a line underneath it. Still, Mrs. Gedge might have left it out for once if she had signed in a hurry. Miss James laid the form and the letter side by side. The signature at the foot of the letter had a boldly Edwardian pointed A with twirls. But the A on the form was in the new round script that modern children use.

Miss James took off her horn-rimmed spectacles and ran her fingers through her short grey hair. This was a nuisance. It was more than a nuisance. It was a disaster. Miss James was surprised to find that she was more exasperated at the loss of a good scholarship pupil than indignant with Dulcie. For of course, when this came out, there would be trouble all round. Forging a parent's signature—why, it was the sort of crime that ranked with theft. Dulcie would be disgraced: the entire Gedge family would be disgraced. Miss James began to run over the measures that would be taken with a child who committed forgery. Well, it would serve Mrs. Gedge right. This was what came of sacrificing girls to boys. That unpleasant little Leonard Gedge was handed every chance, so that his unfortunate sister was forced to steal hers. What a pity Dulcie hadn't been a little more careful. If it hadn't been found out ... 'After all, wasn't it the merest accident that I noticed,' thought Miss James. 'The merest accident ... I don't believe that Mrs. Gedge would have stood in her way for one moment if she had come out well in the examinations,' said Miss James to herself. But now that it had been found out ... Miss James sighed and shook her head. There was no doubt about her duty in the matter. No doubt at all.

But it was another injustice to women. Miss James sat back and squared her shoulders. It was hard that she should be the one to thwart a girl's ambition. And after all, was it any business of hers to quibble over parents' signatures? If

Dulcie won her place and Mrs. Gedge made trouble—well. what of it? Time enough for making trouble when the child had had a chance to prove what she could do. Very deliberately Miss James tore up the note from Alice Gedge and clipped the entrance form among the others again. Then she put them all into her battered case and went off to leave them at the office, glowing with the satisfaction that used to belong to firing pillar-boxes before the War.

In due course, Dulcie sat for the examination. She had not worried about the entrance form at all until she found herself in the Main Hall, at a desk placed well apart from its neighbours and facing a text: "Thou God Seest Me." She read it uncomfortably as the papers were being given out. Had God seen her write her mother's name on that form? It had been a sin, like stealing, when you came to think of it. And perhaps God would punish her now. Perhaps He would make someone find out. She would be found out for certain if she got her free place. That was it. She had stolen her chance, and if she won she would be punished. The only way was to fail. Dulcie bit her lips to keep herself from crying: "Please God," she prayed desperately: "Please God forgive us our trespasses and let me fail."

But God did not let Dulcie fail. For Dulcie, in blind faith, wrote her papers with an abandon that gave her usually tame, correct answers a touch of brilliance. In fact, Dulcie Gedge came out top.

The results were announced one day about a month after the examination, and when Dulcie heard them she buried her face in her hands and howled, to the amazement of the admiring class. But her teacher put Dulcie's hysteria down to overwork and spent five minutes in comforting her. And Dulcie, coherent at last, gulped down a glass of water and pushed her teacher aside. Then she broke through the crowd of girls round her desk to run wildly to Miss James.

Miss James saw her coming and held out her hand with a smile: "Congratulations, Dulcie Gedge," she said, and Dulcie burst into tears again.

"There's something I ought to tell you," she said, between sobs.

But Miss James put her fingers in her ears. "There is not," she said firmly. "Tell your mother anything you like. But there's no need to tell me."

That afternoon Alice came up to the school. She seemed a little fretted, but she listened to Miss James's congratulations with obvious pride.

At last she said, looking down at her gloves: "Oh, while we're on the subject of Dulcie, Miss James, she tells me there's some trouble about the form she sent in not being signed up proper. But I don't really see how that can be, seeing I put my name to it myself."

"That's all right, Mrs. Gedge," said Miss James warmly. "It's quite in order. And I'm really glad, Mrs. Gedge, that you've decided to let Dulcie keep her chance."

CHAPTER 7

I

1926   EAT, DRINK AND BE MERRY

THAT Autumn, Dulcie went to the Grammar School and Thomas was irritated nearly out of his judgment by the sight of her in the new regulation tunic, felt hat and long reefer coat, even though he had not paid for these ceremonial garments. Alice had been saving all the summer for them, but two days before term began she was still seven-and-six short. Susan discovered it by accident; she had been sorting out old stockings and shoes and jerseys, and Alice, crimson and nervous, had suddenly asked if she might have them. It was so unlike her to ask for anything that Susan sensed the urgent need behind the unexpected request.

At last Alice told her; Dulcie, it seemed, was at home in tears; she had a hat, a coat, but only half the money for a tunic and no tidy shoes and stockings. And Alice had not got seven-and-six or anything she could pawn without Thomas noticing it. So Susan and Miss Snow banded together and bullied Alice into letting them provide the rest of Dulcie's outfit.

For Susan and Miss Snow were allies now. While Miss Snow padded conscientiously from Medical Inspections to After-Care Committees, Susan trudged round the back streets of the district, collecting money for spectacles, compelling the unwilling to have their teeth seen to, and arranging free dinners, free milk or free cod-liver oil for the undernourished and rickety children of the unemployed. She did not tell Howard about this until the plan had proved

125

a success, and when he heard, he merely shrugged and said that he preferred to believe that charity began at home. There were two pairs of his socks with holes in them and he supposed it would be weeks before they were darned.

But Susan just laughed and went to rout out the socks and mend them. She found it easier to keep her sense of proportion about Howard now that for one afternoon and three mornings a week she concerned herself with other people's lives instead of her own. To Miss Snow's gratification, she had become a thoroughly efficient worker who could be trusted to be sympathetic and understanding without wasting time and who never failed to turn up when she was expected. Yet Susan could never cross the railway bridge to the poorer end of Silver Street without an ache of pity: it always hurt her to look down the noisy crowded dusty road or turn off into one of the narrow side streets. Silver Street was her road, where she lived, fortunate and married, in comparative comfort; and so the misery and poverty and dirt she encountered were in some way hers too. She felt guilty about them, as she might have done if she had had a dirty bug-riddled room in her own house. At first she dreaded the hours she spent there but in time she grew accustomed to standing on draughty doorsteps listening to long tales of unemployment or consumption or drink or bugs. She was often invited proudly into stuffy parlours crowded with ornate furniture—but always with a bed or two squeezed in. She climbed, in spite of the tenants' protests, to cold attics out of which everything had been sold except the bed and the cracked basin which caught the drips from the leaking roof. And though she never grew really hardened, she learned in time to distinguish between endurance and shiftlessness and dealt suitably with both.

Without Alice, she would have been slower to learn. But Alice saved her from constantly breaking the conventions of the poor. Certain streets were bad class, said Alice: it did nobody any good to be seen going down them. The people there were that used to interference they didn't mind what was asked so long as they got something for nothing at the end of it. But other roads were good middle-class, like Tuffnel Road. "Why," said Alice, "there's plenty of people living along here that only eat English meat." And though Susan laughed afterwards at the distinction, she found that the people with these standards did indeed need different handling. Meddling would not be tolerated, and if they refused stubbornly to send their children to the school clinics, it was only because they preferred to pay their own doctor or to rely on the chemist round the corner whose 'bottle' they bought uncomplainingly.

So the autumn went its uneventful way. People left for Christmas and came back again, and Mrs. Tobias celebrated her birthday, and in a couple of months she was talking of being eighty-three next January.

"And then eighty-four, eighty-five, eighty-six," said Vera lightly. "Why shouldn't she live for ever?" She flicked her gloves along the twisted knobs that ornamented the hand-rail up the stairs and smiled over her shoulder at Robert, who had caught her up on the doorstep that spring evening.

"I've hardly seen you since her party," said Robert glumly.

"Oh, that's nonsense," said Vera. "You're always seeing me."

"Out of the window," said Robert, and Vera's laughter echoed up the staircase.

"You're not dashing enough, Robert," she said. "Girls wait till they're asked ..."

"All right. I'm asking you now. Come out with me to-night."

"If you like ..." said Vera, flashing her excited pleasure at him.

"Done," said Robert, elated. "We'll eat drink and be merry for to-morrow we ..."

"Oh, shut up, Robert. Or I won't come ..." Vera's voice quavered, for it was the last day of April, 1926, and though few people really believed that there would be a general strike on the first of May, there was an undercurrent of madness and crisis and drama into which people like Vera and Robert were irresistibly swept.

"I'll dash up and change," said Vera the next instant. But Robert came up behind her three steps at a time and gripped her elbow. "Once you go upstairs, how am I to know that you'll come down again?" he said. "Out we go."

"But Bee," began Vera.

"Bother Bee ..." said Robert. "My supper's on the stove this minute ... But who cares?"

Vera shrugged and laughed and let him persuade her. They went down the stone stairs again and Robert held her elbow firmly all the way. To her surprise he called a taxi and they went to the Piccadilly Grill.

"Damn expense," said Robert. "We probably shan't be able to spend a penny to-morrow, let alone get a good meal. What'll you drink, my dear? Cocktail first?"

"Robert," said Vera, suddenly grave, "what do you think will happen? ... If there's a strike to-morrow mayn't there be a revolution the day after ..."

"Oh, hardly," said Robert. "Rioting, perhaps. But England ..." Vera was not listening. She sat with her small blunt chin cupped in her hands silently watching the shifting, changing crowd of well dressed women and attentive men.

"Funny to think," she said at last, "that all this sort of thing may be ended to-night. Just like that." She snapped her fingers.

"That's just why you ought to marry me," said Robert, seizing his chance. "Then there'd be something left we could be sure of. Besides, I could look after you. And besides, I love you. I keep telling you that." The broad brim of Vera's hat hid her eyes; but she slid her hand across the table into Robert's. For this was different; this was a crisis; it changed Robert's loyalty and affection from a tiresome everyday affair into romance in the midst of danger.

They went home, walking part of the way hand in hand. Robert kissed her hopefully under a plane tree in an empty Bayswater square, and went up with her to the flat where Beatrix was gloomily laying out glasses in which to drink to the downfall of capitalism—"or any other damn thing you like," she said.

And indeed it did seem as if the whole course of life might be altered. That night all hope of a peaceful settlement between the Government and the T.U.C. was lost. Howard Kennedy, who always seemed to think that he was the only one with a wireless, went round all the flats with the news.

Miss Snow was really badly fluttered at first, and convinced that this was the Revolution which a palmist had prophesied for her, and Howard spent some time explaining why the English character made violence impossible. Mrs. Tobias had already heard the news when he arrived; but she gave him a whisky and soda, and listened to him for five or ten minutes while she went on sorting out her jewels and silver. Then she told him briskly that his place was with his wife and called for Martha, to sew the best silver into the mattress of her double bed. "I can only lie on one side at a time, can't I?" she said. "Then do as I tell you, and you can stuff the jewels in the bolster. I'll sleep easier that way."

Upstairs in Vera's flat, Robert was sitting on the divan with Vera on his knee singing *God Save the King*, while Beatrix mixed cocktails and intoned the *Red Flag*. Howard fetched Susan and they all had more drinks and sang *God Save the King* against Beatrix and the *Red Flag*, until Susan went over to Beatrix's side to make things more even. The party did not break up until Mrs. Tobias's Martha came up with a message to remind them that the rules of the house prohibited disturbances of any kind after 11.30 p.m.

Vera went to bed elated. But she woke up next morning with a twinge of disappointment. For supposing there were no crisis after all and nobody's career was broken and there were no perils to be faced—then in a humdrum world did she really want to marry Robert, to give up the adventure of working and settle down?

But that morning a heavy ominous silence lay over London. Alice crept out into it and walked to work. Hardly anyone was about, but just as she reached the corner by Alfred House, she saw something which set her heart thudding as she ran for shelter to the porch and pounded upstairs, scrabbling with her latch key at the door of Miss Snow's flat.

"Oh Ma'am," said Alice, gasping, "It's—begun. Look! The Barricades are up!"

Miss Snow trotted to the window and peered cautiously between the net curtains. Sure enough, there in the distance the road was blocked with timber and two red flags were flapping disconsolately.

Miss Snow and Alice looked at each other—white and frightened. They spoke in whispers. But Miss Snow was quite startled by the sudden thrill that set her pulses racing.

It might have been 1914 over again. In 1914 the country had needed Isabel Snow: it had given her a uniform and a job. And once a W.A.A.C. always a W.A.A.C. Perhaps ... But Alice was nearly in tears. In Tuffnel Road nearly every household had brothers, sons or fathers among the strikers. For weeks there had been a demo at the street corner every night, watched by groups of impassive police. She could think only of the death and ruin and bloodshed that might come again; she remembered the thud of the guns in the war, and she wondered what guns would sound like close to, in the next street ... when the fighting began.

Then Miss Snow drew herself up. "The first thing to do," she said, "is to fetch as many of the other tenants as possible. Not Mrs. Tobias ... we must spare her as long as we can. You might put on some coffee as you go. I've always found that so helpful."

Soon Miss Snow's room was crowded. Vera and Beatrix were giggling hysterically in a corner, Susan was preoccupied with trying to be brave, but Howard elbowed his way to a sheltered corner of the window and produced field glasses, while Robert, the last arrival, came down in his dressing gown with his hair on end. He waved to Vera but went straight to Miss Snow.

"What's all this?" he asked, "and who's talking of barricades? Why should anyone want to waste time barricading Worcester Terrace anyway?"

"Never mind about that, my boy," said Howard. "They have. It's a fact. There's undoubtedly an obstruction placed across the public roadway with two red flags on it. But it's not Worcester Terrace, you're wrong there. It's Silver Street itself."

Robert began to laugh. Howard turned heavily on him, saying that as far as he could see, it was no laughing matter.

Miss Snow expostulated and Vera rounded on Howard. "Shut up," she said, "and let Robert speak."

Robert stopped laughing. "Howard, old man," he said, with deliberate parody, "never mind about that. It may be Worcester Terrace or it may be Silver Street if you like. But those barricades, as you call them, were there last night. Road Under Repair, the notice at the other end says. Only as the Strike's on to-day, it probably won't get done."

He turned to Alice, now crimson and sniffing. "Don't take on, Alice," he said. "I can understand your being upset. I bet you've lived within earshot of some pretty nasty threats for these last weeks, up at your end of Silver Street."

Miss Snow began rather hurriedly to give everyone coffee, and Vera and Beatrix ate a great deal of bread and butter with it to save the trouble of cooking breakfast in their own flat. Howard, laughing loudly but wryly, took Susan off upstairs and Alice went and cried a little in the kitchen. Robert made Vera promise that she would not start for the library, which was gallantly carrying on, until he was ready to come with her. And when they had all gone Miss Snow told Alice not to worry, put on an old navy blue coat and skirt and went out to volunteer for any work that might be going.

For ten dramatic days she managed a canteen, while Vera and Robert were hardly out of each other's sight. With extreme forethought, Robert had hired two bicycles the week before the strike was declared, and he and Vera cycled wildly through the streets to the envy of pedestrians and the admiration of amateur lorry drivers. And sometimes for a change they left these precious machines at home and went on foot, cadging lifts in Rolls Royces or clinging frenziedly to the footboards of a lorry or van.

"This is fun," Vera would say, and Robert would reply enthusiastically that it was indeed. But he only meant that careering about with Vera was fun. About the strike he felt differently, and without Vera's knowledge he enrolled as a special constable, so that he often played with Vera by day and trudged a beat at night.

All that time, Vera was recklessly happy and dizzy with excitement. When she saw convoys of food coming slowly from the docks with armed guards, or went near the immense emergency organisation of Hyde Park, met patrols of Special Constables or buses with broken windscreens and buckled mudguards driven by young men in plus fours, she was delirious with pride and terror. She clung to Robert, producing wild schemes for immediate marriage, or for a flat together without marriage, or for anything that meant having Robert beside her continuously, to play with her, run risks with her or protect her. Robert, short of sleep and apprehensive, was bewildered and happy at first. But, as the days went on, he began to mistrust her enthusiasm. He gave her a sapphire ring and asked her to wait till the strike was over and his practice should improve.

And then all the excitement suddenly subsided. The strike ended as amazingly as it had begun. Life jolted back to normal. Vera was promoted to be head of a small section in her library and began to take her career seriously again. But Robert was distressed to find his practice shrinking. Everybody knew that the country had lost millions, and people hesitated to spend anything on litigation. Employers began to talk about wage cuts, and there was less money for everybody. Sometimes Robert remembered the crazy ten days during which Vera had implored him to marry her and wondered if he would ever have such an opportunity again.

II
SUMMER IN LONDON

THROUGHOUT the hot summer that followed Robert and Vera alternately made love and squabbled, Beatrix toiled over her book and Susan and Miss Snow went quietly on with their medical inspections and their round of visits.

For Howard said that he could not afford to take a proper holiday; he preferred to take his leave in odd days, at week-ends when he could get away to stay with friends without very much expense. But Susan, being country bred, found no comfort in these hurried visits to seaside bungalows or good golfing centres where organised amusements occupied the entire days and dragged on into the summer evenings. Nor had she much in common with Howard's friends: some of them were rich and some were poor but all of them were noisy. The loneliness of London in August was almost a relief, and Susan, keeping a careful eye on her slum families, spent a good deal of time in the park with a book, sitting propped against a tree on the sooty, faded grass. Once she lay down on it, pressing her face into the turf and catching, in spite of petrol fumes and smoke, a faint smell of summer that turned her faint for want of country fields. For the first time in her life she was glad when the summer was over and the drab autumn rains reminded her less poignantly of home.

The rest of the year was unmarked by the people who lived in Alfred House, except perhaps by Mrs. Tobias and Miss Snow, for whom the passing of time was in itself momentous. Then it was 1927, and spring again. And by April Howard was congratulating himself that Susan had settled down at last—though my word she'd taken some handling—and that his life was ordered to his liking. But Susan herself suddenly began to realise that she was no longer either well or pretty. Her colour had gone, her hair hung limp and lank about her face, her head ached all the time and, whenever she walked, her legs ached too.

There was no excuse for it either, Susan told herself. Her days were filled—some of them with quite useful work. She had friends in Beatrix and Vera and Miss Snow, and even in old Mrs. Tobias, who was the first to notice that she looked peaked.

"You're not as rosy as a young married woman should be," she said, one day when Susan went in to tea. "I wonder your husband hasn't complained of it." She picked up the enormous silver tea pot with both her frail hands and poured her tea into fragile Wedgwood cups.

"I don't think Howard notices how I look," Susan said. "He's not the sort of person who does."

"Lives by his stomach, I daresay," said Mrs. Tobias acidly. "Now when I was a young gel, husbands put looks first and cookery second—at least in the upper classes."

Susan, thoroughly embarrassed, tried to turn the conversation back to the days when Mrs. Tobias was a young gel, for the old lady generally took a delight in gloating over the despairs and jealousies and triumphs of fifty years ago.

But Mrs. Tobias was not to be turned. She got out the spectacles in which she rarely allowed herself to be seen and looked at Susan more closely. Then she said:

"Have you begun to be sick yet?"

Susan, sinkingly aware that she often felt sick, muttered non-committally. Mrs. Tobias squeezed her hand. "I might've known," she said cordially, "what you were in for when I set eyes on you. Is yer husband pleased? I'll warrant he is. That type of man has always a peculiar pride in it."

Susan's eyes grew rounder and rounder. "But I'm not ... I mean I don't want ... I'm quite sure it's not that ... It couldn't be ..." she said despairingly.

But Mrs. Tobias would take no denial.

"Pull your chair closer, me dear," she said, "and I'll tell you a thing or two worth knowing, eh?"

Reluctantly Susan drew nearer and listened to tales of births, deaths and the conjugal habits of men. And Mrs. Tobias, her eyes on Susan's waist, gave her bawdy hints and tips she could not understand. "And if you really don't want it, me child, now's your chance. You just ..." she cupped her hands round her blue lips and hissed appalling expedients down Susan's ear. When at last she could escape Susan ran upstairs, snatched a hat and coat, seized the telephone, made an appointment with Dr. Hawkes, and almost ran from Alfred House to her surgery.

Dr. Hawkes, her slow and careful examination finished, leant back in her leather chair and considered Susan. She had met her occasionally over Care Committee work for nearly two years and had summed her up as a capable and cheerful person, though possibly over-imaginative.

"Now look here, Mrs. Kennedy," she said decidedly, "I can find absolutely nothing wrong with you and you don't need me to tell you that you're not pregnant. You're run down, and you need a holiday. Country people like you don't take kindly to town, especially if they're there for two or three years on end. I can give you a tonic that'll put a bit more go into you. But if you've something on your mind, medicines won't help."

"Oh, but I haven't," said Susan, firmly. "Why should I have? I've got a home and friends and plenty of work ... and a husband."

Dr. Hawkes put away her stethoscope, wrote a prescription, pushed her horn-rimmed glasses up on to her forehead and then looked up at Susan again.

"Not short of money?" she hazarded. "Not trying to hide anything from your family or your husband? Not that you need tell me if you don't want to. But it sometimes helps to tell a person like me who is a professional keeper of secrets."

But Susan looked back at her, wrinkling her forehead in obvious perplexity.

"Well, then, Mrs. Kennedy, you can't do more than take your tonic and try and get away into the country for a bit," said Dr. Hawkes. "Come and see me again when you get back. By the way," she added as Susan pulled on her hat, "I suppose you do love that husband of yours?"

"Of course I do," Susan answered indignantly, promptly and convincingly. Dr. Hawkes said good-bye, and watched her walk away down the road, with a curious immature, offended dignity.

In Alfred House, Alice was hurriedly circling between her dinners for the Kennedys, Miss Snow and Mr. Dean. In the end, she had just put all three lots of vegetables on the Kennedys' gas stove. "It's all right, Miss Susan," she explained, as Susan came in, whipping off her hat and coat and throwing them over a chair. "Mr. Kennedy'll not notice, and even if he does, we must remember our cabbages were cooked on Mr. Dean's stove last week, and the Sunday roast went in with Miss Snow's bit of a pie. So all's fair, as they say, and my legs saved into the bargain."

Susan agreed. The system of communal cooking had gradually crept into Alfred House under Alice's supervision, and the crockery and utensils of the households she served were almost interchangeable. When Vera and Beatrix had last had a party, Alice and Susan had their doubts as to whether their glasses should be loaned out for the occasion, but it was an understood thing that if Miss Snow or Mr. Dean, or even Mrs. Kennedy herself, went short of a little plate or china for a celebration of some sort, Alice just took a basket round the flats with her and collected such goods as came up to the standard of the household that required them.

So Alice, dividing the vegetables into their proper portions, began to tell Susan of Miss Snow's Hoover—which might possibly be loaned for spring cleaning. But Susan, tired of domestic strategy, sat on the window sill, fidgeting with the blind cord, and asked Alice about her family.

Alice put some plates up to warm and said that Thomas was as usual and the children well. "But," she added, "I'm bothered, and that's a fact. I've come back just this evening from that precious school of Len's and it doesn't seem as if Len was going to do so well after all."

"I'm sorry about that," Susan said. "But Len's only fourteen, surely. Quite a little boy, yet ..."

"Fourteen's a good age in our class, Miss—I mean Ma'am," Alice said. "Come to that, Len's fifteen. Ought to stay on at school another full year, though. The Post Office his father and me had in mind for him. But it seems his work isn't all it should be."

"But I thought he was such a clever boy." Susan was sympathetic and puzzled.

"Cute, Len is. Not clever so much. That's what I've come to think. Of course, I did have my ideas for him once. When he got that scholarship ... well, I thought Len would go right ahead then. But there it is. Seems as if Len wouldn't do much after all, and there's Dulcie, that I thought could quite well do without schooling, gone on to Grammar school and top of her form."

Susan began to tell Alice that bookish cleverness didn't always get very far and how she was sure that Len had wits enough to make a fortune.

"Yes," said Alice with sudden vision. "If the same wits don't run away with him."

Then Susan said she had always thought that Dulcie was really the cleverer of the two and there were lots of careers in front of girls nowadays after all.

"If they don't throw them away for a man," interrupted Alice. And Susan knew that no balm she could provide would really soothe the pain that every one of Leonard's shortcomings caused her.

III
ROBERT SPEAKS HIS MIND

WHILE Alice was talking to Susan and separating Mr. Dean's share of the cabbages she had cooked, Robert himself was standing in Vera's sitting-room, feet apart, hands locked behind him, his face red and his fair hair on end. He bristled, thought Vera, like an angry wire-haired terrier.

Vera herself; still in her blue working dress, lay curled on the yellow divan listening with relief to Beatrix's footsteps receding down the passage. 'Thank goodness,' Vera thought, 'she's gone to have a bath. That'll take half an hour; I'll be through by then.' She switched her attention back to Robert and lay listening to his stormy voice and twisting the small sapphire ring he had given her. Her face was so pale with temper that the faint touches of rouge stood out in red circles on her cheek bones.

"My good Robert," Vera said as he paused for breath. "Talk sense. You know perfectly well that I said I'd marry you ages ago—in the Strike."

"That's what I say," Robert went on with dogmatic, pitiless, infuriating logic. "You did promise to marry me ..."

"Then what are you complaining about?"

"Because I don't believe you mean to keep your promise."

"You wouldn't marry me last year," raged Vera, propping herself on her elbow. "Rushing into things, you called it then, I seem to remember. You said you didn't know where the next penny was coming from and your practice was probably going to blazes and you couldn't ask me to risk it. You said that, you know you did."

"Of course I said it. Because I loved you. Because I'd some sense of responsibility about you. I wouldn't marry you or anyone else unless I could keep you. And now I can. I've pulled through and I want to marry you ..."

"You wouldn't marry me when I wanted it," interrupted Vera sullenly. "The least you can do now is to wait until I'm ready. And I'm not ready."

"If you cared," Robert said, "you would be ready. You'd be glad you could marry me now."

"Yes, and be like Susan Kennedy, trotting round scraping and saving and warming her great husband's slippers. Not me. If you loved me, you'd want to offer me something better than that." Vera dragged out a green enamel case and lit a cigarette with an affectation which would have enraged Robert if he had not seen that her hand was shaking so much that she could hardly steady the match.

"Vera," he said more gently. "Vera darling, don't let's quarrel like this. I'd hate you to turn into a drudge. I want to make a home for you to stay in. I don't pretend I like the idea of my wife working from nine to six. But if you must have work to make you happy, well, then go on working."

Vera wriggled. Soon there would be no excuse for not marrying Robert. And yet marriage with him would be so much more commonplace than anything she had ever dreamed of for herself. Either a brilliant marriage or a brilliant career, thought Vera. But Robert gave her neither. Only, it would be silly to lose him altogether ...

She looked up at him with her most enchanting smile, threw away her cigarette, and held out her arms:

"Robert, darling," she said. "Of course we won't quarrel. Only don't rush me, angel. Let's leave things as they are till next year and then talk about it."

But Robert did not catch her hands and kiss her as he had always done at the end of other storms. Instead he backed away to the door. "I won't leave things as they are any longer," he said. "I'm tired of this." He paused to run his tongue along dry lips; then he went on, his voice thick with anger and not entirely under control:

"You're nothing but a callous, selfish little flirt. I may suit you all right as a sort of tame dancing partner, to take you out and pet you when you want it. But you don't want to risk giving up a single thing for me. Four years you've had me hanging round after you, but if you think you're going to get away with it as long as you please you're wrong."

Vera let her hands fall and then buried her face in them.

"And this finishes it." He opened the door, and Vera, struggling for dignity, sprang up and faced him defiantly, tugging at the sapphire ring.

"Take that, you beast," she shouted. But the ring she meant to hurl in his face stuck obstinately at her knuckle and Robert shut the door behind him.

As the latch clicked Beatrix leaped out of her bath and, half draped in a towel, padded damply along to the sitting-room.

"My God, Vera, what has been happening?" she said. And Vera, crying loudly and childishly with rage, unclenched

141

her left hand and thrust it at Beatrix. The fourth finger, scratched and swollen, still mocked her with Robert's ring.

"For God's sake get a file or a chisel and take it of. Robert's gone, gone, I tell you!"

"Well, what about it?" said Beatrix placidly. "I'll get you a drink. I daresay we can soak the beastly thing off in hot water. And as for Robert, he'll come back all right. He always does, my dear."

IV

ROBERT PACKS UP

BUT Beatrix was wrong. Robert lurched miserably downstairs, and before he had reached his own door, he had decided to leave Alfred House. So he did it immediately, leaving the chop and cabbage that Alice had set out for him untouched. He wrote briefly to the landlord giving a quarter's notice and suggesting that he should find a tenant to whom the flat could be sublet. He had a short interview with Mrs. Barker, to whom he explained that the sudden death of a near relative compelled him to leave at once and that he did not quite know when he would be back. Mrs. Barker looked at him unbelievingly out of her vague, dirt-rimmed eyes and subsequently telephoned to the landlord to ask if the rent was all right. Robert packed a suitcase, strapped some of his most treasured possessions together, enclosed two weeks' wages in an envelope for Alice with a kind but definite note, called a taxi and went. Only Mrs. Barker watched him go.

She was so startled by the proceedings that she got up unusually early next morning and did the steps before breakfast, so as to be sure of waylaying Alice.

"Your young man's gorn," she said, gloomily acknowledging Alice's distant good-morning with a nod.

"My young man? What d'you mean?" said Alice indignantly.

"Fact," said Mrs. Barker. "In trouble too, I bet. Told me a relative had died unexpected. But I've heard that one before. Besides, I had a séance last night and we tried ever so to get into touch with 'is relative on the Other Side. But there wasn't no new spirit floating around for 'im."

"Fancy!" said Alice with contempt. "I only wish I knew who you're talking about."

"Your Mr. Dean. Left last night in a taxi."

"Well, and why shouldn't Mr. Dean go off in a taxi if he's a mind to?"

"Gone permanent." Mrs. Barker sniffed.

"Well, last time I saw him," asserted Alice, with conviction, "he said, 'Chops for dinner, Alice, and kidneys for breakfast.' So I don't see how you can be right."

"And why should you that's only a daily woman set yourself up to know more about the tenants than Mr. Barker and me wot's responsible for 'em and always on the premises? Besides I saw 'im go off."

"So might anyone've done. That doesn't prove anything." Alice was firm.

Mrs. Barker dropped her scrubbing brush into the pail with a plop, wiped her hands on her apron and took Alice's arm.

"You may well ask, 'Ow do I know. But I do know. SEE? Mark my words, Mr. Dean'll never set foot in this place again. For I never yet seen a gent take 'is trouser press with 'im unless 'e was leaving for good."

"Well, I never," said Alice, confronted with this irrefutable logic. "Well, I won't keep you, I'm sure." She shook herself free of Mrs. Barker's detaining hand and swept upstairs. Mrs. Barker, her mission accomplished, left the steps unfinished and returned to tea, kippers and Mr. Barker in the basement.

Alice went straight to Mr. Dean's flat. The note told her nothing—the chaos in his room and the absence of the trouser press confirmed Mrs. Barker's story, and all Alice's doubts on the subject disappeared when she was at last free to step up to the top flat and saw Vera's red eyes and Beatrix's bad temper. Alice eyed both of them with cold disapproval. For the Vera who teased and laughed in the kitchen, she had an almost protective affection, but for the Vera who played fast and loose with her Mr. Dean she had nothing but contempt. So now she faced the second Vera, demanding money for the butcher's book and saying coldly:

"Sad about Mr. Dean's uncle, isn't it, Miss?"

Vera looked at her blankly.

"Dying so sudden," Alice went on. "I thought perhaps Mr. Dean might've told you."

"Oh, but he didn't. When was it?"

"Oh, I thought everybody knew, Miss. They're all talking about it, upstairs and down, it seems," said Alice deliberately, watching the colour creep over Vera's face and neck.

"Last night, it was, I suppose," said Alice. "You've given me two shillings too much, Miss. Six and ten the butcher, and three shillings the milk. That's the cream, that extra is. Anyway, it was last night that Mr. Dean left."

"Left? Left? Oh, for the funeral or something, I suppose you mean. He might have let me know." Vera's shrill voice quivered on the last word. She bit her lip and kept turning the two shilling piece over and over in her hand.

"Will that be all, then, Miss, for to-day?" said Alice.

"Yes, no. Oh, yes, I suppose so ... D'you know when he's coming back, Alice?"

"Gone for good, Mrs. Barker says and she may be right for once. He's taken a lot of luggage and his trouser press."

But Vera hardly heard; she brushed past her and stumbled through to the bathroom where Beatrix was noisily washing her teeth.

From the sitting-room, Alice could hear their voices, Vera's blurred with sobs and Beatrix's with a bitter edge to it as she answered her:

"Gone, has he? Well, now I suppose you've got what you wanted, blast you."

CHAPTER 8

I

1927   JOHN TAKES A FLAT

FOR some weeks after he had left, Robert's departure was the main topic of conversation in Alfred House. And though Alice, loyal to her Mr. Dean, could never be persuaded to discuss the matter, everybody assumed that he had gone because of the girl upstairs—jilted by the hussy in number eight, as Mrs. Tobias said. Most people forgot him over the summer holidays, but Howard Kennedy seemed never to tire of the subject and Susan was continually fending off his questions. She herself was not squeamish about gossip, but there was a certain way of probing into people's lives that she found distasteful.

"Threw him over, didn't she, the spitfire?" Howard would say, lounging on the sofa after dinner. "Come on, Susan, you ought to know. Was that it?"

"Everybody seems to think so, so I suppose it's true," Susan would reply, elaborately casual, and switching on the wireless clumsily so that it screeched and Howard was distracted. For Susan had indeed heard the story from Beatrix, turned confidential in her anger over Vera's stupidity in throwing away a man she didn't want without considering anyone else's feelings or convenience. But she had no intention of repeating it.

However, no amount of tact could keep Howard away from the topic for long. He was continually wondering where young Dean had gone off to, what he was doing about letting the flat, whether that girl would stay on and if it was a fact that the other one had really been after him the whole time, too?

"I say, Susan. That girl and young Dean? Exactly how far did they go? You know what I mean. You're a friend of theirs, you ought to know," he said one evening when the paper was unusually dull.

But Susan just turned mulish and walked out. Locked in the bathroom—the only room with a key—she suddenly considered Dr. Hawke's surprising question. Did she love Howard? Howard who flopped on the sofa after dinner, kicking off his shoes to warm his feet better. Howard, grinning lasciviously, and urging her to reveal other people's intimacies before importuning her for intimacies with himself? She was bewildered, sure only that she could never have fallen in love with Howard as he was now. When had he changed?

'Oh heavens,' thought Susan as she powdered her nose and went slowly back to the sitting room, 'I must have loved him when I married him. I mean, I must love him because I married him. But is it me who's made him like this?'

In the sitting room, Howard was writing a letter, sitting with tolerant but clearly injured dignity at Susan's desk.

"Oh, there you are," he said. "Can't understand you, Susan, being such a prude. Not as if you were a *girl*." He began to recite one of the many limericks which he saved from the club smoking room for the teasing of Susan. But this one fell flat; for Susan said nothing; she merely picked up the paper and sat down by the window.

"I'm just writing to young Dean, to condole, don't you know," Howard went on. "And anyhow he must want to let that place of his. He's not a rich man ... scratching a bit of a practice together at the Bar can't be much of a joke." He picked out an envelope, addressed it to Robert with a flourish and a final line interrupted by two dots, and borrowed one of Susan's stamps.

"Funny thing, you know," he said amiably, "but I met a fellow in the club the other day I hadn't seen for the best part of ten years—A Civil Servant too—got quite a high-up job—all luck of course— But he'd be just the man to take Dean's flat. Think I'll write to him to-night as well. Last time I saw him, he was roaring drunk. And so was I by Gad. Drunk as a lord. Armistice day, that was. 1918 you know. Good fellow, John Abbot. With me at Liège. I remember once in an *estaminet* ..." and Howard started another of his stories, till Susan began to pray that John Abbot might be run over by a bus before he had time to take Robert Dean's flat, for two men like Howard about the place would be more than she could bear.

Two days later, Robert Dean got Howard's letter, and though he was profoundly irritated by Howard's sympathy, he did accept the suggestion that Mr. Abbot should be introduced to Number 7, Alfred House. And in fact, John Abbot, who had just lost rather more money than he could afford on the Stock Exchange, was glad to take Robert's cheap, unpretentious and fairly comfortable flat. Directly the agreement was signed Robert himself wrote and asked him to take on the services of Alice Gedge if he wanted someone reliable to look after him.

Howard was pleased. He took some trouble to speed up all the formalities so that John Abbot could take possession immediately, sent Susan down to supervise the cleaning of the flat and told her to be sure and ask Mr. Abbot in to tea on the day he arrived.

"Even if I'm not in myself, Susan," he explained, "I think you should ask him up. It would be only friendly. And mind you, though John Abbot's not in the same department as I am myself, still, he's a man who's got on, and there's no knowing when he might not be useful."

Susan reluctantly helped Alice with the cleaning of number seven and even more reluctantly went down to meet John Abbot on the day he moved in. She expected to find someone as hearty as Howard, but John Abbot was a pale quiet person, rather younger than her husband. He was dressed in shabby grey tweeds and carried a picture wrapped up in an old blue curtain under his arm. He followed Susan meekly into the sitting room and put the bundle on a chair. The curtain slipped off one corner of the frame; Susan stared at it and then tweaked off the remaining folds. "Oh," she said. "Why, it's beautiful. But I didn't mean to rootle round your things ..."

"Rembrandt," said John Abbot, who had been checking up his possessions by a pencilled list. "Glad you like it. It ought to hang over there, don't you think? No use putting it up yet, though, because there's some more furniture to come."

"But do let's put it somewhere safe," Susan said imploringly. "Or all the rest of your things will get dumped on top of it. Besides, Howard said you'd be sure to be glad of tea. It's ready in our flat. You'll come up, won't you?"

John said that he certainly would; he wrapped the Rembrandt up very carefully, tucked it under his arm again and followed Susan upstairs. There Susan made him unwind the curtain and prop the etching on a chair so that she could see it while she poured out tea. As she gave him advice about flats and food, and listened for Howard's returning footsteps, she tried to imagine John Abbot roaring drunk or blustering in smoking rooms. And she failed.

II
THE GEDGES KEEP CHRISTMAS

JOHN ABBOT was grateful to Howard and found plenty to say to Susan on his occasional visits to their flat, but he did not respond to the curiosity of the other tenants. Mrs. Tobias asked him to tea on sight and complained that he never opened his mouth, and Alice, beyond saying that he was a pleasant gentleman but no talker, was so uncommunicative that no one was able to find out much about him.

So Christmas came round again, among the usual rumours of industrial trouble. Miss Snow, remembering Robert, cut Vera pointedly on the stairs and omitted her from her Christmas lists. The other tenants exchanged cards and calendars and went away one by one, Miss Snow early in December, Mr. Abbot the week before Christmas, Susan and Howard three days before and Beatrix and Vera on Christmas Eve itself.

Mrs. Tobias did not go away but prepared for celebrations on a large scale, hoping to sit down ten at least to Christmas dinner. And Alice counted up the money and gifts from Alfred House and thought that everyone had been very kind, but that Christmas wasn't much now the children were nearly grown up. Susan had given her a large turkey, Howard (ignorant of this) contributed five shillings, Miss Snow had given her a whole pound. Beatrix had presented a rather brilliant bag and Vera, in a moment of extravagant contrition, bought her a charming satin blouse. Alice reckoned that the last two would do nicely for Dulcie. She spent the five shillings on crackers and fruit, set aside ten shillings for Len and bought a new hat for herself and a tin of tobacco for Thomas out of the balance. Shopping in the warm companionable bustle of Silver Street did her good and she finally let herself into the Tuffnel Road house feeling that there was something about Christmas, after all.

A blaring, rasping jazz tune told her that Len was in. Alice wished for the twentieth time that she knew how he had come by that gramo. Thomas said he'd take his oath the lad had been betting at shove 'alfpenny—and don't blame 'im neither when 'e wins. Len said he'd been doing odd jobs and the thing was dirt cheap anyhow, so why worry?

He was sprawling in the kitchen rocking-chair, a gasper between his teeth, tapping out the tune with his feet and fingering a ukulele he had bought for next to nothing too. Len was nearly sixteen now; his dark hair was sleeked down and he wore his Sunday trousers—dull purple and the real Oxford width—to mark his emancipation from school. For Leonard had just left: there was no sense in keeping him on, for he'd never make a scholar; and his headmaster had found him a job with a firm of brokers in the city. As office boy. Alice comforted herself by remembering all the wellknown men who were proud to acknowledge similar beginnings.

"There you are, Len," Alice said, putting her parcels down. "Where're the others?"

"Dunno about Pa. Playing snooker, I expect. Dulcie's gone shopping down to Woolworth's. Pa gave her a bob to buy a bit of Christmas with. Come on, Ma, here's a tune for you." He jumped up and twirled Alice round the room just as he used to do as a small boy. And Alice, irritated though she always was by his Sunday trousers which offended her trained taste in clothes, clung to him proudly as he sidestepped and bobbed and dipped.

"And now p'raps you'll let me take off my hat and coat and get a bit of supper ready," she said; then stepping back and surveying his legs, she added: "My word, Len, it's a good thing you're going to Blenkinsop's in January. Maybe you'll learn not to wear those disgusting trousers when you've seen a few real gentlemen close to."

"Coo, Ma, you're all out of date, that's all. Everybody's wearing them now. Jolly good pair of bags these—and cheap too. Do for a toff they would."

A staccato tattoo on the front door sent Len scurrying off down the passage, to let in Dulcie, back from Woolworth's, with a bundle of coloured streamers, some silver balls and a little holly.

Len examined her purchases critically. "You've forgotten the mistletoe," he said gloomily.

"My word, what next?" said Alice. "What do you children want to be doing with mistletoe? You can kiss each other or your father and me any time without that."

"Well, all I say is Dulcie's wasting her chances," Len said. "There's that Reggie Baxter who's gone on her coming round to-morrow."

"I wouldn't kiss Reggie Baxter, mistletoe or no mistletoe," said Dulcie, bridling. "And as for you and your girls, Len, you don't wait for it."

"Now children, stop your nonsense, please," said Alice. "Here's your father back from his game of billiards and wanting a little peace and quiet."

Thomas pushed his battered cap to the back of his head as he came in, kissed Alice without removing the pipe from the corner of his mouth and cuffed Len in passing.

"For Gawd's sake, boy, turn off that row," he said, waving his pipe at the gramophone which was slowly grinding and moaning its way to the end of the record. "Anybody's think you owned the 'ole 'ouse. Come on, Alice, dish out the supper. If these kids want to sling them flags and things about they can do it when I'm fed, can't they?"

Supper, like most meals in the Gedge family, was eaten in silence. Thomas and Leonard concentrated entirely on their food, and Dulcie on the table manners she had acquired from her mother, while Alice as usual was content to watch her children. Here was Dulcie, growing up, with boy friends already in the offing, doing well it seemed and looking good enough for anything in her Sunday frock—one of Miss Gray's—with her fair bobbed hair curling round her pretty pink and white face. A good girl too. And Len—well, there was just no knowing. It was too late to plan and scheme for him ... you just had to make the best of it ... She laid down her knife and fork and stared at Thomas, who had raised his glass of beer and was waving it above his head.

" 'Ere, Ma, wake up. This 'ere is Christmas Eve, isn't it? And I votes we all have a drink. There's a drop o' port I bought for you, ole girl, over there in the medicine bottle. You an' Dulcie can 'ave some o' that and I'm blowed if I won't give ole Len 'ere a swig o' beer. Get out yer glasses. Now then. We're all set. 'Ere's to us and all of us and may we want nowt, none of us nor me neither. That's a good one, that is. Steady, Dulce, with that drop o' port, 'cause you won't get no more, you know. And 'ere's another: Merry Christmas. Merry Christmas and a 'appy New Year. What price Nineteen Twenty-Eight?" Thomas tipped back his glass. "Drink up, Ma," he said.

Alice smiled at him, so amiable he was when he could take life easy. Well, perhaps he could now. Perhaps they'd shake down together a bit better once the children were launched on their careers and she didn't have to watch every penny.

Thomas was filling up his glass again.

"Come on, now everybody, if you've a drop left. 'Ere's a last toast for you. 'Ere's to Len: good ole Leonard Gedge, h'Office Boy."

Len choked. "Junior Clerk, Pa," he spluttered. But Alice got up and leaned across the table to clink her glass against his. "Just you wait, Thomas. Here's to your New Year, Len," she said proudly.

III

BEATRIX IS CLEVER AND LEONARD TOO CLEVER BY HALF

IT was an arctic January: all the pipes burst in Tuffnel Road. Len, his Sunday trousers now in daily use, spent his days at Blenkinsop's and his evenings with an odd collection of new friends, 'fellers in business like meself,' he explained. He talked knowingly of stocks and shares and referred to his job as Something in the City. But he found it very much harder to get up in time to be at the office at 8.45 than to saunter into the Grammar School at nine. Nor did he take kindly to the exacting regulations of office life; for senior clerks had even firmer views on wasting time than schoolmasters. And to a person of Leonard's ingenuity routine work was foolish drudgery. He shirked it as much as he could and spent most of his time staring drearily round his murky cubby hole, tilting his stool on to its hind legs, fiddling with his tie, tapping a pencil against his teeth, making smudgy calculations on scraps of paper and fabricating a future in which he suddenly acquired wealth and fame. Even the telephone, with its ten extensions, palled after the first few days; he loathed turning the handle of the duplicating machine for an hour or so at a time; he revolted from the mere thought of addressing envelopes and the postage book, at first sight, conveyed no possibilities beyond an infuriating number of sums in halfpennies. During his month's trial, he just sat hunched up on his stool till somebody's buzzer summoned him to run an errand. But even these interludes did not give him much scope, for he had to be back on time or some bloke in a stiff collar would want to know the reason why.

Thomas, too, found a particular pleasure in teasing him, dragging him out of bed unnecessarily at six because he himself had always risen at five. And at supper he would pull out the evening paper and ask Len's advice about fictitious investments or tell him to be sure and find out the price of shares in some preposterous gold mine. "Leastways, if you ain't too busy filling other people's ink-wells, me boy."

Len bore it sullenly and kept a discreet silence about his work, merely remarking that it was all right or sometimes that it might be worse. In private, however, he told both Alice and Dulcie that there 'wasn't much scope for a chap with ideas in that sort of bum job.' He got no sympathy from Alice, who merely told him that he didn't recognise a good chance when he saw one, though she was faintly disturbed because he did not seem either so well or so happy as he had been at school. He looked peaked, and she guessed that he missed the games in the fresh air. But it was only a vague uneasiness and so she thankfully told her own neighbours and Susan and Miss Snow that Len had got in with a real good firm and had the chance of a lifetime.

It was an uneventful year at Alfred House. Mr. Abbot emerged very slowly from his habitual reserve. Vera and Beatrix did once succeed in persuading him to drink a cocktail with them, but nothing came of it. Howard took Susan to Brighton at Easter and Llandudno in August to celebrate a rise in salary. And in October Dulcie quietly put her name down for the Commercial Training class which taught shorthand and typing and book-keeping and business letters in French. In November Beatrix's novel came back for the third time. She put it into a new folder and sent it indomitably out again without telling Vera.

Towards the end of the year, too, Leonard seemed to settle down in his job, and Alice was downright glad to see something of his old slapstick swagger and conceit again. But he was very little in the house these days: he was always off to see a chap about a deal. It never occurred to Alice to connect this with his new and rather furtive interest in the racing news and the unusual respect with which he listened to Thomas, who liked to come back to the embers in the kitchen grate after an evening at 'The Feathers' and tell his son a thing or two about form.

When 1929 came in Alice was extra busy again, with everyone back at Alfred House and talking of spring-cleaning already. There was Miss Snow, for instance, just arrived back from Ealing, where she had spent a couple of months with an ailing great-aunt who had been forced by hard times to live there in a draughty half-timbered villa with only one maid and a canary. Alice had never known Miss Snow so fussy ... she came down on you for three specks of dust behind a photo frame. Sometimes she would stand peering round the kitchen, chiding Alice for an unscoured saucepan and wondering uncertainly what she would have for dinner. 'She's getting older,' thought Alice suddenly, as Miss Snow stood hesitatingly in the February sunlight. 'She usen't to stoop so much before.' And Miss Snow seemed to catch the thought, for she said:

"Dear me, Mrs. Gedge. Time does run on, doesn't it? Just fancy-1929, and February here. Don't you sometimes feel quite old with your great big children? Leonard grown up and in an office —why, it seems only the other day that I came to see you about the little fellow's glasses!"

"Well, you can't flatter yourself you're staying young if you've children outstripping you, that's a fact, Miss," said Alice. "But you haven't changed," she added defiantly, "not a mite, since the day I first knew you."

"Well, well, we elderly people don't change so much, I think," said Miss Snow, remembering the old aunt at Ealing who had seemed so very old for such a long time. Better, thought Miss Snow, to have young people about the place to keep one in touch with youth and take one's thoughts off the changes in oneself till one grew old suddenly at the end, than to change into dead wood before one's time.

"I wonder," she said, "if Mrs. Kennedy would care to come down for supper, if Mr. Kennedy is out." For Susan was the kind of young person it did one good to have round: she asked advice and set a premium on experience.

"Well now, I know Mrs. Kennedy expected to be in alone. It's Mr. Kennedy's night at his club," said Alice. "I'll ask when I go up, shall I, and let you know." She whisked a dish mop round the bowl, set it on end, untied her apron, gave Miss Snow the morning paper to keep her occupied and went upstairs. On the top landing, she was startled to find Miss Wood dancing about in red pyjamas waving a letter in front of Mrs. Kennedy.

Susan was being suitably enthusiastic and Vera kept slapping Beatrix mechanically on the back, while Howard, who disliked women in pyjamas, was trying to propel his way through the group with his elbows and an umbrella.

"Oh Howard, don't look so glum," Susan said. "Bee's book is going to be published. It's tremendous."

Howard hooked his umbrella over his arm and held out a stiff hand. "Congratulations, heartiest congratulations," he said, thinking what a fuss girls made over trifles.

"It's marvellous," said Vera, with more enthusiasm than she had shown before. "Simply marvellous. My dear, it'll be a best seller. I know it will."

Beatrix denied this in an unbelieving tone, stepped out of Howard's way and pulled Susan back into her flat. "And Alice must come in too," she said. "Because I shall have to give a party at once and we must count the glasses and things and then Alice must go and snaffle what we need from the old Snow and that queer man Susan's so fond of."

Alice reluctantly followed her into the flat; it was hardly worth while giving Mrs. Kennedy Miss Snow's message now with Miss Wood so set on getting her own way always. But perhaps if she had to have a party, she'd ask Miss Snow to come up too, since she wanted her glasses. So Alice began to clear away the breakfast things with Susan while Beatrix rang up her author and said in a voice that excitement conveniently changed into a stranger's that she was sorry to say that Miss Wood was down with flu. Then she spent the morning with the telephone collecting people to come and drink to the book, while Alice and Susan toiled furiously, setting out glasses, cutting sandwiches, arranging flowers, putting away Beatrix's litter of clothes and papers, sweeping up the sitting-room, polishing the table, straightening cushions, till the whole flat looked a different place. Dowdily respectable, Beatrix called it.

And both Miss Snow and Mr. Abbot were invited because Beatrix could not do without Miss Snow's glasses and knives, or Mr. Abbot's cocktail shaker. Miss Snow, who loved a party and felt that perhaps she had misjudged Vera, said she would certainly come. So did John Abbot, because Susan had been made to invite him. "You ask him: you know him better than anyone else," screamed Beatrix from the landing below on her way out to buy drinks.

By six o'clock, people began to drop in to congratulate Beatrix and wish her luck in strange mixtures of gin and vermouths. Alice was still busy setting out glasses and opening bottles, for excitement had quite incapacitated Beatrix and Vera was only just back from work.

She was coming into the sitting room with a heavy tray when the dark young woman talking to Beatrix looked up and met her eye and quickly looked away again, flushing a little and turning her shoulder towards Alice and her tray.

And Alice put the tray down without looking in her direction again. Then she went back to the kitchen. As Vera pattered in behind her, Alice said:

"Excuse me mentioning it, Miss, but is that dark young lady talking to Miss Wood a Miss Drew, Miss Joan Drew, by any chance?"

"Why yes. She's a great friend of Miss Wood's."

"There now," Alice said. "I knew her at once."

"But why, how—where could you have seen her? Oh, you worked for her, I suppose. How funny," Vera said absently.

"Not exactly," said Alice. "She was one of my junior clerks in the Ministry as a matter of fact."

"Good gracious, how priceless," said Vera, swinging round on her. "Was she really?"

"I can see her now," Alice went on, " dancing down the office table with all the baskets flying. Armistice Day that was, in 1918. Used to dust my desk every morning, now I come to think of it. There you are. That's life, that is." She wiped a glass and set it with the others.

"Best be careful of that lot, Miss," she said. "They're not ours. Some of Mrs. Kennedy's best. And there's the bell again."

"All right," said Vera, "I'll see to it." She scurried away: it was fun about the Drew woman. Perhaps Bee wouldn't be so infatuated with her when she heard she was just one of Alice's ex-clerks and mannerless enough to cut her too. "Give me Alice any day," said Vera and flung open the door to let in a swarm of Beatrix's guests.

The flat was crowded with people and vibrating with noise. Beatrix, too excited to sit down, was prancing about in the middle of the room, rattling John's cocktail shaker. Howard had brought his wireless in and dumped it in a corner where it brayed unheeded. Someone else had found a gramophone and set that going too. The party overflowed into the passage and bedrooms and even the kitchen was hazed with cigarette smoke.

In the sitting-room it was so stifling that Susan unobtrusively opened a window, but the thunder of buses and trams and trains could not compete with the racket of talk inside.

Howard stood on the edge of the admiring crowd round Beatrix; people came up and waved glasses at her and slipped away with empty ones and found others and came back.

"I say," he shouted, leaning towards her, "I must say, Beatrix, m'dear, I don't know what your book's like, but anyway you aren't stingy with the gin, what?"

Beatrix mazily waved back at him and winked.

In the corner near the door, John Abbot was urging Susan to have another drink and she was explaining that she simply daren't.

"It's not my legs I'm afraid of: it's my tongue," she explained with a vague owlish gravity. "I say too much."

"Who cares," said John softly. "I'll look after you. Besides, I'd like you to say too much. Forget you're Caesar's wife."

"Caesar's wife?" said Susan blankly.

"Never mind, my dear. Never mind. Say whatever you like. I'll listen to every word of it and forget it all the next minute. I've a wonderful memory; there's nothing it can't forget."

Susan began to laugh as he filled her glass. It wasn't often that cocktails made her so happy.

Then she set her glass down on the red lacquer table. "What was that?" she said.

"The door, I think," said John. "Late arrivals. I suppose they can squeeze in? I'll go and see, shall I?"

He dodged behind a large lady dressed in chintz. Susan could just catch the sound of his voice from the passage.

"What d'you want?" he said. Then he came back and beckoned to Susan. "Your Beatrix is far too happy to be bothered," he said, "and I can't see the dark girl. But there's a boy out there who says he wants his mother and she's here."

"Oh, it's a Gedge child, I expect," said Susan. "That's who it'll be. All right. I'll see about it. Mrs. Gedge belongs to all of us." She pulled the front door open again. Outside on the landing Leonard Gedge was standing, huddled in his coat. He looked so much smaller than usual that Susan hardly recognised him.

"It's you, Len, is it," she said, "come to call for your mother?"

"Bin waiting outside an hour, Miss."

"Oh, didn't you know she'd be late? There's a party."

"She's wanted urgent," Len said.

"Well, I don't know that she can be spared yet. What is it? Dulcie's not ill, is she? Or your Father?"

Len shook his head. " 'S'urgent," he muttered. His voice was thick—he might almost have been drinking—For a moment Susan hesitated. Then she said: "Oh well, go along quickly to the kitchen. You can always stay and help her with the glasses."

Leonard cringed past her along the passage.

"My goodness, Len," said Alice as he came in. "Whatever are you doing? Come to take me home, have you? Well, there's plenty of clearing up you can do first.... There's nothing wrong, Len?"

Susan came to the door. "Miss Gray says ..." she began. But neither Leonard nor Alice heard her.

"What is it, Len?" Alice said again.

Leonard looked quickly up at her and then down at the swagger pointed shoes he had bought with his first week's wages.

"Got the sack."

Alice caught his arm. "What for, Len, what for?"

" 'Cause the post book was wrong." He gulped an unmanly sob and with a desperate attempt at defiance said: "It's a shyme. They 'ad no business to look at it to-day. To-day's only Thursday. Fridays they see the book. And to-morrow it would've been all right."

Half an hour later Alice made an excuse to Vera and took Leonard home. In the tram he said nothing, but as they went down Silver Street he grew garrulous. Up and down they walked, for Leonard dared not go in till he had made an ally of his mother. But Alice groped vainly among his wordy explanation for some reassurance against her own forebodings; she found none. At last she took him roughly by the elbow and brought him to a standstill by a street lamp.

"Tell me again, Len," she said, "exactly what you did do."

"I keep telling you. It was a Thursday and the head clerk …"

"Not the head clerk. You. What did you do?"

"I only borrowed a few stamps …"

"How many?"

"I dunno …"

"How much?"

"Quid or so. I tell you, mother, it'd've been all right to-morrow …"

"Why would it have been all right to-morrow?"

" 'Cause to-morrow I should've 'ad the cash to put it back with."

Alice dropped his arm and pushed him away from her.

"Stealing …" she said. "You've been stealing." She turned away and walked quickly ahead of him to her own gate. She let it clang behind her as though she did not know he was at her heels. She opened the front door with her latch key without waiting for him and in sheer panic he ran up the path and caught it as it swung to.

As he closed the front door behind him, he could hear his father's loud and cheerful voice and smell his usual shag. The passage was empty. Leonard crept along it to the kitchen door. His father was still talking to Dulcie, but his mother was not there. He slid back again to the bedroom door, but he shuffled away from it and stood hesitating. Where should he go? Into the kitchen and face his father's blustering anger, into the bedroom in search of his mother? Or outside to fend for himself in the cold hostile streets peopled with the other men and boys who were down on their luck?

As he pulled back the latch, the bedroom door opened. Alice stood on the threshold with her hands crossed on her breast. Her face was greenish white. Drops of sweat shone on her forehead.

"Leonard," she said in a dry, sick voice. "I'm going to bed. You must go by yourself to tell your father. No lies ... no lies."

Then she went back and lay down dressed as she was on her bed. And the pain which twisted her mind was so great that it seemed as if Leonard were being born again.

CHAPTER 9

I
1929 THE TRUTH, THE WHOLE TRUTH....

THOMAS did not take Leonard's failure so seriously: he said that boys would be boys and Leonard was a fool for being found out. But he'd go and see the Manager and get it put right. The Manager did not pay much attention to Thomas: he said that dishonest office boys were as common as gooseberries and what was needed was an example. He proposed to make one of Leonard.

Dishonest office boys turn into dishonest clerks, if they're not checked," he said. "And believe me, Mr. Gedge, it's a whole lot better for your boy to learn his lesson now while he's only a lad, than when he's a man and liable to see the inside of a prison."

Thomas reckoned that Len had learned his lesson, and what was more, he himself would gladly pay up for every stamp Len had been foolish enough to ...

But the Manager stopped him. Mr. Gedge had not understood the position. He felt compelled for the good of the community and the good of Leonard Gedge, to prosecute.

Thomas protested, raged, pleaded: he begged the Manager to let Len off for his mother's sake. But the Manager merely pressed the buzzer and a new office boy came in to show Mr. Gedge out.

When Thomas got home and found that the police had been there and that Len had actually been charged at the Station and would come before the Magistrates in due course, he became obsessed with the enormity of Leonard's crime. He washed his hands of the boy, refused to speak to him and when the Summons was served ordering Leonard to attend at the Court on the second Monday in February he swore by every oath he knew that he would not go with him.

So it was left to Alice to bolster up Leonard's courage and attend the Court. And Alice found an unexpected comfort in standing by Leonard. Her own bitter sense of failure was appeased now that there was something she could do. Her misery had been for Leonard and what he had done—his punishment and their disgrace were relatively unimportant.

On the appointed day she took Leonard to the Police Courts. As he was not quite seventeen, his case was heard in the Children's Court and to Leonard this was the bitterest humiliation of all. Thanks to Thomas he still looked on his appropriation of the stamps as a business deal which had not come off: it was a man's crime, not a childish escapade. Since he had been charged, he had comforted himself with dramatic visions of the trial, with judges and warders and policemen and a handsome young prisoner in the dock. Probably they would let him off, too.

But the Children's Court was not dramatic at all. The proceedings were held in a long, musty, ordinary room, where spring sunshine filtered through dusty panes with the cheerful clipper-clop of horses' hoofs and the heavy traffic noises from the busy street outside. There was no dock; the magistrates did not look at all regal; they were just two grey-haired, tired looking men and one fat and fussy woman. They sat at a green baize table. At right angles to it was a desk covered with papers and a small wiry Clerk of the Court sat behind it and took charge of the procedure. Even the policemen did not look majestic, for of all their regalia they only retained their blue trousers and heavy boots. Over these they wore shabby tweed jackets and coloured shirts.

In front of the Magistrates' table stood a row of hard chairs. As Alice and Leonard came in, the elderly magistrate in the chairman's seat rose and asked Alice, quite kindly, to sit down. But he left Leonard to stand drearily on her right, by the window. The charge was read out ... a long list of words that seemed to mean nothing at all.

"Now, Leonard Gedge," said the Magistrate. "You've heard the charge. Do you plead guilty or not? That means: do you admit that you stole the goods or do you not?"

"I didn't steal 'em ..."

"Sir," rapped the Clerk.

"Sir," mumbled Leonard.

"Very well, he pleads not guilty ..."

"Oh Len," said Alice, half rising.

"D'you want to advise your boy, Mrs. Gedge? You can do that, you know, but you mustn't make any statement to us yet ..."

"Len, what's the use," said Alice desperately. "You know you took them ... we all know you ..."

"Now, Mrs. Gedge, you mustn't say that sort of thing, you know. We've had no evidence as yet. If your son wants to plead not guilty ..."

"I didn't steal them," said Len stubbornly. What was the use of trying to explain to these people. He wasn't a kid ... he ...

"He says he didn't do it. All right. He pleads not guilty," said the Magistrate. "Call your witnesses, will you?"

The head clerk of Blenkinsop's came in and stood beside the Clerk of the Court. He took the Bible and stood back to read the Oath from the printed notice over the mantelpiece. Then one of the Magistrates noticed that he had the book in his left hand. The Clerk took it from him in consternation and after an exchange of apologies the witness took the Oath again. He gave his name and address and was asked to identify Leonard.

"This boy was in charge of your stamps?" asked the Clerk of the Court.

"He was. All our office boys have charge of the post book. We give out stamps once a fortnight, to the value of about five pounds. At the end of the period, the boy's book must balance. In the case of newcomers, the books are inspected every few days, and then every week, until we are sure they are competent."

"This was the first time that any stamps had been missing while Leonard Gedge was employed at Blenkinsop's?"

"The first time it was noticed."

Leonard listened to the rattle of question and answer. It all seemed to be quite off the point. How could a fellow be a thief if he only borrowed ... all business men borrowed.

"Any questions, Leonard?" asked the Chairman.

Leonard pulled himself together.

"Please, Sir, I'd like to ask him why he came round and looked at the books on a Thursday when he wasn't due till Friday?"

"To make sure you weren't up to any monkey tricks."

"It ain't fair, Sir," said Leonard. "They would have been put back on Friday."

"Now, Leonard," said the Magistrate, masking a smile, "you've practically admitted now that you took the stamps ... Hadn't you better tell us about it?"

"It doesn't pay to be obstinate, you know," said the J.P.

Leonard mumbled.

"Speak up now, speak up, boy," said the woman again. "You can talk louder than that, I know. You make plenty of noise when you're playing in the streets." Leonard winced, and the Chairman silenced her with a quick gesture.

"Well, we'll call the next witness, then," he said, and the Manager of Blenkinsop's was brought in and sworn. Leonard looked at him in surprise: he seemed so much shorter and more ordinary when he was not sitting behind the big desk in the inner office. Mr. Blenkinsop added a little to the head clerk's story and made a short speech, saying that he bore Leonard Gedge no ill-will and attached little importance to the value of the theft. But he felt that it was for Leonard's own good as well as for the good of the community that he should be prosecuted ... The woman Magistrate murmured: "very proper, very proper, I'm sure," and the Clerk wrote all the evidence down most deliberately with a scratching pen.

"Any questions, Leonard?" said the Chairman.

"I want to ask him if me father didn't go and tell him I could pay it all back?"

"He certainly did."

"Well then!" said Leonard in triumph.

"Why do you think that makes any difference, Leonard?" asked the Chairman patiently.

"How can it be stealing if you pay back, sir?" said Lonard, twitching with exasperation. "Pay him back," he added, pulling a dirty wad of notes out of his pocket, "of course I can pay him back. Four times over. Firefly won the three-thirty at seven to one."

The Chairman waved the witness away. The Clerk of the Court leaned back in his chair. Alice twisted her gloves. The woman Magistrate said "Tcha." The two men put their heads together. Then the Chairman asked Aiice if there was anything she wanted to ask. She shook her head and he turned to Leonard again.

"Now, Leonard Gedge, all the evidence shows, and you yourself practically admit, that you took £1 worth of stamps from the postage book while you were at Messrs. Blenkinsop's. In other words you stole those stamps, and from what you say, I gather that you laid bets with them. Now you say that you did not steal—you merely borrowed. Prisons are full of people who think they can borrow other people's money without asking their consent. This is your first offence and we're prepared to deal leniently with you. But you're almost seventeen and you should have learnt some sense by now. Will you let this court deal with the matter summarily, or do you want to be tried all over again by another court...?"

Leonard shook his head: he'd had enough of trials.

"Very well, we will deal with the matter. Now, Mrs. Gedge, is there anything you can tell us about your boy? Just stand up, will you, please."

"He's a good boy," said Alice dully.

"Often have to punish him? All boys have to be punished sometimes, you know."

"Not often. He's a good son." Alice fumbled with her gloves. What could she tell these people of Len? Len, whom she saw as a baby, as a toddler, as a small perky schoolboy winning scholarships ... as a young man starting off to Blenkinsop's to make a fortune and carrying all her hopes.

The Chairman screwed up his eyes at her and nodded. "Sit down, Mrs. Gedge. Let you down badly, has he? Thought he'd do well, did you? Still, don't take on too much. May be the making of him, this. All right. Now let me see the school reports ... h'm, yes ... they're goodish. Had a splendid education, this boy, and not made the best of it. Hmph. Well." The three magisterial heads came together again.

"We're all agreed," said the Chairman at last, "that the best course would be to bind this boy over for a period of two years. His mother to stand surety in the sum of forty shillings. Do you understand that, Mrs. Gedge?"

Alice shook her head. "But I'll do anything you say," she added hastily.

"Well, it means that Leonard undertakes to behave himself and that you undertake to see that he does. If he is brought here again during that time, you will lose your forty shillings and Leonard will be dealt with severely. And I think that he should be placed under the Probation Officer, to report to him as and when directed. It seems to us that the Probation Officer may be able to do a lot for Leonard. Evidently Leonard is a smart boy, but his ideas of life are still quite childish. Well, it's not too late to put that right. Now, Leonard, you see I am not punishing you. I am merely making it more difficult for you to do wrong again. In fact, we're giving you a new start and we hope that you will make good with it. That's all. If you and your mother will go over to the Clerk, he'll see that you sign the necessary forms ..."

Leonard stood dumbly. Alice had to take his arm and urge him towards the Clerk's table, where they signed.

"This way if you please," said one of the policemen, opening the door into the corridor.

In the room they had left Alice could hear the Chairman's tired voice: "Where are the papers for the next case?"

II

FLINT AND STEEL

THE spring dragged on. Leonard stayed at home, doing odd jobs and seeing the Probation Officer as seldom as possible.

Then influenza broke out as usual. Dulcie Gedge gave it to Thomas, and Leonard caught it too, so that all the family's plans for him were upset. Alice did not own to having it, because she said there was no time for her to lay up. In Alfred House, old Mrs. Tobias had it and looked like dying of it, though she struggled through and went to Bognor to recuperate. Vera and Beatrix had it, but slightly and at the same time, so that for them it was a welcome interlude. Howard Kennedy caught it, and a few days later John Abbot went to bed. Susan nursed Howard and sent down soup and chicken jelly to John, but, just as Howard was up and able to get out again, her own head began to buzz, she ached all over and in spite of her determination to be as brave as Alice over casual ailments, she collapsed weakly one morning with Howard's breakfast tray and went to bed with a temperature of 103.

"Most unfortunate, of course," Howard said, bending over her with impatient sympathy. "Just as I've got to go back to the office."

Susan felt too ill to mind where Howard was, but that evening, feverish and wretched, she began to dread the thought of another day alone in the flat. For Alice, with three invalids at home, could hardly do more than look in on Susan in the mornings. But Howard said that it would be a pity for him to take longer leave now and not be able to get a few days off later for golf when the weather improved. "It's just flu," he said. "It's not serious, my dear. And if you did want anything, you've got the telephone, haven't you? You could get Mrs. Barker to come up."

So Susan curled herself under the bedclothes and spent two dreary days shivering and sneezing by herself. She kept her eyes shut most of the time because she disliked the look of the room so much. Her table was covered with cough mixtures and aspirins and gargles and eucalyptus and lozenges and the fireplace was cluttered with kettles and saucepans and dirty cups and empty milk bottles and ovaltine and tea. Whenever she managed to get really warm with a newly filled hot water bottle and a hot drink, the door bell rang and up she had to get to fetch in meat for Howard's supper or bread or milk or groceries.

Three days after Susan caught flu and Howard went back to work, John Abbot, convalescing more leisurely than Howard, came up to call on the Kennedys with violets and snowdrops to cheer Susan up.

Susan had lit the gas fire in the sitting-room that afternoon and left the bedroom to air while she rolled herself in rugs on the sofa. When she heard his knock she pulled a coat on over her dressing-gown, pushed her hair out of her eyes, and dragged down the passage to open the door.

"Oh," she said when she saw him, "I thought you were the fish."

"Can't I come in," said John. "Even if I'm not? I came up to see how the other invalids were getting on. Don't tell me Howard's still in bed."

"Howard's back at work," Susan said. "But he isn't really fit."

"Nor are you," said John. "You oughtn't to be up and opening doors. Back you go, to bed or wherever you came from." He waved his violets at her.

"For me?" said Susan.

"Of course. Howard would prefer beer, I know. And if only you'll let me in so that I can send you back to bed and put these in water, I promise I'll come up this evening with a bottle of Bass and listen to him for hours."

"Well, you see," said Susan, retreating from the door, "I'm only sort of half up ... and the place is in a muddle because

Alice's family has flu and she can't get round more than once a day. And it's so surprising the way mess accumulates in an afternoon." John agreed. He said his own flat was in a state of chaos and he doubted if he had a clean cup or saucer left in it. But if Susan had any, he would like to make some tea.

So Susan let John into the untidy sitting-room. And John found a bowl for the violets and set it on the chair by Susan's sofa so that she could keep on sniffing at them. "Because," he said, "when you do begin to smell things again, it's so awful only to have vapex and Lysol."

Then he made tea, and insisted on taking Susan's temperature. He pottered round the room while the thermometer was in her mouth, straightening a pile of Care Committee Case papers and laughing at her reports. Susan laughed too, as soon as she could. She began to tell him about the good class people in Tuffnel Road who only ate English meat and the large lady in a disreputable basement, who wore a man's cap on back to front over curl pins and invited her in to talk about Duchesses and Royalty and asked what she thought of the Prince of Wales. "Then," said Susan, "she told me that she was simply a rabid Conservative, my dear, and couldn't pay for Alec's specs not having a cent in the 'ouse but would be glad if I'd drop in whenever passing."

John sucked Susan's lozenges because he could not smoke, and listened and laughed and listened again.

When at last he had to go, Susan sat in the dusk, waiting for Howard. He was late and cross and tired and said his throat was still sore, so she fussed about with gargle and scrambled eggs for his supper as the fish had not come, and Howard refused to rest or put his feet up, but went over to the desk to write letters.

"Your absurd papers are all over the place again. Wish to goodness you'd give up this work, Susan. Can't see the fun in it." Susan tidied up, pulled the curtains and told him that John was coming up that evening.

"Very nice of him. Should've thought he wouldn't want to waste leave either, hanging about at home instead of doing a little work. Still, it's good of him to look in. Always enjoy a yarn with old John. You'd better get off to bed, Susan, I don't suppose you're really fit to be up."

So Susan went away to run the bath, and as she soaked in the comforting hot water she found herself thinking how odd it was that you never knew you'd been lonely till you found someone to talk to.

John Abbot did not go back to work that week. He said he did not feel too good and that it was always uneconomic for people to try to work before they were fit. Meanwhile he enjoyed keeping an eye on Susan. He came up several times to see her, bringing flowers and books, and when she was really able to be up and out, he took her for her first walk in the thin morning sunshine and asked her to come to tea with him that afternoon.

III
THE KINDLING SPARK

SUSAN did not take much trouble with her dressing as she got ready for tea. She would have missed John very much if he had stopped coming to see her; but she did not yet know that she only came to life when he was there. So she went down to his flat in an old grey dress with a green jersey over it to keep her warm. Her face looked small and pale and her nose was still red and her eyes watered. When John saw her come in he suddenly felt humble and tender—as though he had found a small and half-fledged bird or a new and helpless animal. He made her sit in the corner of his couch and piled cushions behind her and turned the fire up, looking at her shyly and touching her with quick gentle movements.

Then he tried to turn their talk to safe banalities, asking after Howard—with little interest—and demanding news of the Gedge family.

"I wish I were like Alice," Susan said, "nursing three of them and having flu on her feet and not minding. Instead of crocking up like this."

"Well, you're not as strong as Alice," said John ..."my dear...."

Susan looked at him and turned her head away.

"You need to be strong, though, even if you're only a little poor," she said.

John came and sat at her feet and took her hand. "You're cold, still," he said.

Susan shook her head and put her other warmer hand over John's. John moved closer to her and they sat for a while not speaking, looking into the hard brilliance of the gas fire. And at first the room seemed to turn to mist and then every piece of furniture stood out brilliantly against the cream walls. And Susan noticed the smudge on the wall by the electric light switch—the mark of John's hand—and the ink stain on the carpet by John's desk, and the patent automatic calendar—John's new toy—that said it was the day after to-morrow. But John only noticed how red Susan's hair looked against his blue chintz, how thin her shoulders were against the shabby cushions. His hand slipped up her arm to her shoulder, he kissed her hand that lay on his knee. He looked up till his glance met her glance. Slowly, gently, relentlessly, their faces were drawn down to each other till

Susan's lashes touched John's cheek. Then John kissed her. He put his arms round her and held her soft and unresisting against his rigid body.

Susan closed her eyes, and behind them flickered a memory—a car driven recklessly along a wild moorland road, taking a corner broadside on, swinging helplessly from side to side and turning over and over in a bog at the bottom of a hill. Out of control. And as her spirit swung upwards into unbearable happiness, she felt her body slipping down, now taut, now limp, into intolerable pleasure.

It was John who broke the enchantment. He drew away, unloosed her hands and let Susan lean back against the corner of the couch again, her arms across her face. He stood there, quite still, looking at her in silence. Then he bent down and pushed back a loose strand of her hair. Susan did not move. He could hear her quick troubled breathing but he dared not touch her again.

When he moved away from her at last, he sought wildly for some way to bridge this dreadful return to normality. What could he get Susan—brandy ... there was none, whisky, sherry ... or perhaps just a glass of water. John started for the kitchen, and the soft reassuring whistle of a boiling kettle greeted him. That was it, tea ... that would warm Susan up, calm his own nerves, give them both something ordinary to do. But was it really only half an hour since he had set that kettle on a low flame for a sane bread-and-butter and cream-cake tea? He made it now, trying to think of nothing at all. He set out plates and cups and cakes and brought in the tray. Susan was still sitting as he had left her.

But when she heard the chink of china, she turned and looked at him and a small, happy smile lightened her eyes.

For though her body was cheated and wretched, all her mind was drenched in happiness.

"Susan," John said. "Susan, my dear, my sweet ...?"

"It's all right, John," Susan said. "It's just that I never knew...."

John waited.

"I never knew things could feel like that." But John, whose happiness was already clouded with perplexity, stroked her hair gently and pulled up a chair for himself. Neither of them spoke again of what had happened until Susan went. As she stood in the dark passage by the door, John said: "Susan, if you want to forget, I can forget this too." Susan looked up at him and though it was nearly dark, he saw such terror in her eyes that he caught her hands in his and said: "Susan, my sweet—I'd rather remember." And Susan lifted her face to his.

But when Susan had gone, John walked, fretted and feverish, from room to room. He knew now that lately his whole life had centred round Susan. He knew that he hated Howard, that fine blustering battle companion, that admirable teller of smoke room tales, because he possessed and would undoubtedly break her. And he, John, who loved her, would probably break her too. For he could see ahead to the inevitable sordid squabbles with Howard, to the interminable delays of the Divorce Court. And he wondered if either he or Susan would ever dare to face it out, or would ever survive it unchanged if they did. Perhaps if he had stolen Susan completely, seized her away from Howard then and there. But all John's principles, all his upbringing had conspired against it. And now perhaps it was too late.

IV
MAUDLIN MIDNIGHT

ONE evening, a few months later, Mrs. Barker dragged herself out of her sagging armchair in her basement den. It was past twelve. Time some people came back home. Too much noise there had been lately ... sounded like some people had had a drop over the eight. Might be worth while having a peep round ... funny the things you happened on that way.

She wrapped a black shawl over her green velveteen dress and stodged upstairs. The hall and stairs were dark, for the lights went off at 11.30 though there was one switch that late-corners could turn on. Mrs. Barker hardly paused by the ground floor flats; she knew all about them. They kept themselves to themselves and if one of them had a brother to stay frequent, what did it matter? He mightn't be a brother, but it wasn't for Mrs. Barker to doubt the word of a lady that tipped good and often. No, if there was trouble at all, it was farther up than that. She climbed. breathing heavily, past Mrs. Tobias's door, to the next landing. That Mr. Abbot now, he was a close one. Worth keeping an eye on ... you never knew what trifle you mightn't find in a gent's rooms that he'd be glad to get back and give you something for your pains.

She went on, nodding her head thoughtfully, to the top landing. There was no sound from the Kennedys' flat and no light under the door: they weren't the rowdy kind. But the wife was a pretty little piece, a cut above her husband. You never knew with that sort. Well, that was neither here nor there and she had nothing to go on at present after all.

But there was a light below the door of number eight. "Somebody's not in yet, I'll be bound," said Mrs. Barker, under her breath. She never had taken to them two young ladies from the first ... not at all surprised, she wasn't, when Mrs. Tobias's Martha happened to say just in passing that the young lady from number eight hadn't any consideration for others when she came in late ... Arguing with young men in taxis at the top of her voice, and running upstairs like a regiment ... Well, she'd just see for herself. Better go down now, perhaps. She could always get a nice view of the hall from the turn of the basement stairs and come up again if need be.

As she turned to go down, there was a clatter in the hall below. She heard Miss Gray's shrill laugh and a man's deep one, a slamming of doors, and then the quick patter of steps on the stairs ... One person or two? Difficult to say for sure with the echo. Mrs. Barker stayed where she was—after all she was only doing her duty. But she leaned back against the wall in the darkest corner of the landing. Like enough the girl wouldn't put on the light.

But on the top step Vera stopped abruptly, catching at the banister.

"What's that?" she said. "Who's there?" She stretched out her hand for the light switch and clicked it on. "Mrs. Barker! What on earth...?" Vera drew herself up. "Is there anything wrong?"

Mrs. Barker looked at her suspiciously. She was flushed and her eyes sparkled, and as she stood there, her hand still on the switch, Mrs. Barker sensed the deliberate effort she was making for coherence. In fact, to Mrs. Barker's knowing eye, Vera looked as if she were just prettily tipsy.

"I got me duty to do," said Mrs. Barker righteously.

"I can't really see," said Vera, "why it should be your duty to go prowling round my landing in the middle of the night." She fumbled in her bag for her latch key.

"It's not only the *time,*" Mrs. Barker said. Her voice had a sinister note in it.

Vera coaxed her key into the lock. "The time I come home has nothing to do with you," she said loftily.

"No, Miss, I'm sure. Still, as I said, it's not only the *time.* When I 'ear things, Miss, sich things as disturbing others and scenes on doorsteps, I likes to see for meself ..."

"I don't know what you're talking about," said Vera, twisting her stubborn key in the latch. "Will you kindly go away?"

"Very pertikler the landlords are," Mrs. Barker went on, edging past Vera to the stairs, "about the tenants 'ere. And it's me they rely on. Mrs. Barker, they say, we've 'eard so and so and so and so. And what do you think? *You* know ... you're on the spot. There's some people say gentlemen friends is always welcome in certain flats ... and there's some complains about the noise ... or meeting other people on the stairs who's had a drop ..."

Vera spun round. "Get off this landing before I get Mr. Kennedy out of bed to throw you off it."

"I don't advise you to be 'asty, Miss," said Mrs. Barker. "Duty is duty. In my walk of life. Besides, why should you take on? Namin' no names, was I? Namin' no names." She heaved herself slowly down the stairs. "But wot I always say is them as the cap fits ..." Her voice droned on and the stairs echoed with the heavy plod of her retreating footsteps.

Vera wrenched open the door of the flat and charged down the passage, knocking over a small table. Her silver cloak caught on the latch of the sitting-room door, but heedless of the frenzied crackling tear, she raced on to Beatrix's room.

"Bee," she screamed, "did you know that that old devil from the basement was on our landing? Spying ... on *us*."

Beatrix was sitting up in bed reading. She had had a dull evening, and it followed on a succession of dull evenings. She disliked being shouted at, and there was Vera, out night after night and coming back half tipsy clamouring for sympathy.

"D'you hear me, Bee?" Vera said. "Spying on us. Do you know what the old hag said?"

Beatrix shut her book and answered with aggravating flippancy:

"I suppose she thinks you're no better than you should be and wants you to dig out a quid or two to make her hold her tongue. Got her living to earn, hasn't she?"

"Blast you, can't you take anything seriously?" Vera raged round the room, upsetting a pile of books and letters, brushing two pairs of newly washed stockings off the chair and a dressing-gown from the bed and churning them with her feet as she stamped about. She wanted to hit Mrs. Barker, or Beatrix. Either would do. What was the good of friends if they couldn't be sympathetic?

But Beatrix had no intention of being sympathetic. "You can't do anything about it," she said. "So what's the use of talking? The Barker woman can't do anything either. Unless the tenants really have complained about your goings on."

"My goings on ... my goings on. What do you mean?" Vera had stopped by the dressing table and was fidgeting with the powder bowl.

"Well, my good girl," said Beatrix blandly. "You've brought this on yourself. Look at the way you carried on with the Dean boy till he got tired of it and went off.

Everybody knew about it—said you'd jilted him. And ever since then, you've been going round to every party you could gatecrash, jazzing about and coming home with the milk and the footling young men you pick up ... Are you surprised? *Are* you surprised ...?"

Vera suddenly picked up the powder bowl, swung round, and hurled it violently at Beatrix. It missed her by yards and splintered against the wall. A cloud of pink dust reeking of chypre blew into Beatrix's face and settled on her fair, sleek hair. She brushed a small piece of glass off the pillow and went on without raising her voice.

"Are you surprised that people do talk? You must realise if you ever stop to think of anything but yourself, that they always will talk if they get the chance. I tell you, Vera, they'll stand for a little immorality on the quiet but not for your sort of semi-virtuous racket."

"Beast, beast, beast!" said Vera, tears streaming down her face.

"You're drunk," said Beatrix, picking up her book again, and looking with contempt at Vera's swaying figure, blotchy face and wobbling lower lip. She'd had enough of Vera's nonsense—all this conceit and commotion because of her string of young men and then these airs of injured innocence when people complained.   "I hate you when you're drunk."

"If you had anybody to take *you* out," said Vera with hysterical insight, "you wouldn't lecture me because of a little fun."

"Fun," said Beatrix coldly. "My God ... Fun! D'you think I want your kind of dirty fun? Don't let me stop you. But remember Mrs. Barker, that's all." She flicked over the pages of her book.

Vera stood at the foot of her bed and pounded her fists on the rail. A wave of dark hair stood up like a frill round her head, her torn cloak dragged on the ground. She began to cry again.

"I can't bear it, I can't bear it," she said, subsiding in a sobbing huddle beside the bed.

"I wish you wouldn't cry on my quilt," said Beatrix.

"Oh, my God," spluttered Vera, burrowing her head into the eiderdown, "You're the only person I've got left in the world and now you won't stick by me."

"Stick by you, you little fool ..." Beatrix began to get really angry. "How dare you say I haven't stuck by you? In spite of Robert. You unutterable idiot. Why couldn't you see that if you didn't want him yourself ... Oh hell! It's over years ago. What's the use of arguing about that now? Get up, V., and go to bed." She pulled the quilt away.

But Vera went on sobbing into the blankets, irritating, maudlin, penitent sobs. "Oh Bee, I've been such a beast to you. I'm sorry. Forgive me, Bee darling ... please. Oh Bee, I've been such a fool, such a fool. Do forgive me. After all, we've still got each other."

"Oh, have we?" said Beatrix, beginning to read again. "Well, go to bed now anyway, for heaven's sake."

She drew the bedclothes round her shoulders and turned on her side.

Vera dragged herself to her feet. "But I don't want to go to bed," she said. "I want to talk."

"You've done enough talking for one night. Go away before I get angry enough to have a real row with you."

"I want to have a row," said Vera between her teeth. "How can you lie there reading when I ..."

"You're not going to have a row with me—tonight," said Beatrix with adamantine calm. "Go and make yourself a cup of tea and wash your face. Take the book if you like. *The Fountain of Solitude*. Do you good. All about what happens to girls who don't appreciate young men. It'll larn you, I should think ..."

"Have you finished with it?" said Vera, suddenly meek and yawning.

"No," said Beatrix drowsily. "I don't think I have, somehow. But it doesn't matter much." She turned out the reading lamp and left Vera to grope her way to the door.

V
SUSAN BEGINS TO THINK

THE quarrel between Vera and Beatrix simmered for a few weeks, then subsided and was finally forgotten in the summer holidays. But it left its mark: Beatrix and Vera ceased to take each other for granted. Instead, they were constantly aware of each other, so that sometimes they bickered with unreasonable venom, sometimes they were closer friends than they had ever been, and sometimes there was a watchful truce between them. And Alice, seeing their moods vary so much from day to day, wondered how long the uneasy friendship would last.

But though she was quite fond of Vera, Alice did not worry much about what happened to her: she was one of those that would always fall on their feet. Besides, if she was going to worry over anyone, it would be over Miss Susan, who had unaccountably regained the colour and gaiety she had when she was first married. 'I'd like to think Mr. Kennedy had something to do with it,' Alice said to herself as she scrubbed and peeled potatoes in the Kennedy kitchen. 'But I'll stake my word he hasn't.'

That evening, she knew. For John Abbot came to supper to talk to Howard and as Alice carried out the joint, she caught Susan's appraising glance flickering between the two men. 'And now there will be trouble,' said Alice as she stacked plates in the sink. 'What'll his lordship do, I wonder? He's not the kind to let go of what he's got. Regular British bulldog he is.'

The same thought flitted into John's mind as he listened absently to Howard who was being emphatic about the position of civil servants and the iniquity of trade unionism. But Susan did not think about it at all. Just as she had taken it for granted that she must love Howard because she had married him, so now when all her being was absorbed in loving John, her mind refused to consider all that this implied. She knew at last that her relationship with Howard had always been unsatisfactory. She supposed that it would go on being unsatisfactory. She knew that for the moment it was sufficient for her happiness, and presumably for John's, for her to love him, see him occasionally and kiss him on those rare occasions when they could be alone without comment. She had no idea of the hunger and desperation that would presently assail them both or of the inevitable dislocation of their lives.

John Abbot did not make very much effort to see Susan alone for some time. He wanted to be sure himself that his feeling for her went deeper than passion; and he wanted her to have time to assess her own emotions. When he did see her again, it was by accident. Howard had been going to take Susan to a dance at a Knightsbridge hotel at the end of July, but at the last moment he had the chance of dining with a particularly valuable friend to whose advice he owed the success of one or two investments. But still he did not want to waste the dance tickets; so he asked John Abbot to go, for Howard was far too unobservant to see any significance in the looks which Susan and John exchanged in spite of themselves, or in Susan's sudden rush of happiness, for which he took the credit himself.

So John and Susan went together. The party which Howard had collected contained very few people Susan knew. She and John exchanged just enough dances with these acquaintances to avoid comment. The rest of the time they danced together, swaying to the rhythm of a tango, jigging to nigger jazz tunes, swooping round in the sudden darkness of a waltz.

"You do dance well, John," Susan said as they circled and dipped in the dizzy flickering spot lights.

"Sometimes," said John, smiling down at her. He tightened his arm round her body as he bent and whispered: "Let's go home, darling." Susan nodded and let him steer her towards the door.

But when they stood on the steps of the hotel, with a warm wind touching their faces, they realised that Howard would be back at Alfred House before them.

"There's no hurry after all," Susan said, turning back towards the ballroom again. "Howard will be in by now."

"I'd just thought of that," John said glumly. "Never mind, dearest. Let's walk across the Park." He took her arm, they turned away from Knightsbridge through the iron gates, along the dimly lit avenues where a shower had laid the dust and raised the scented ghosts of flowers.

Half-way across, John turned and kissed Susan without speaking. She leant away from him and he kissed her throat and her bare shoulders. Then Susan put her arms round his neck. "I do love you so, John," she said. "I do love you so." John kissed her again, then he slipped an arm round her shoulders and they walked slowly on.

Neither of them spoke again till they turned out of the gates at Marble Arch and John called a taxi. As the cab lurched off up the Edgware Road, John took Susan's hand in his.

"My dear, my dear," he said, "I want you so much. But before I let you go on loving me, I've got to make you think."

"I love you, John," Susan said. "That's all. I haven't thought about it."

"Susan dear," John said, "this kind of loving doesn't stand still. It must go forward, or it must stop."

A cold sharp pain stabbed through Susan's warm happiness. Stop, stop ... When it was life itself, how could it stop? John's voice went on but she hardly heard it.

"You're not the kind of woman for intrigues and deceits. It would show in your face. I couldn't do it either. Howard— well, I don't much like Howard really—but he passes for a friend. I'd take you right away from him—if you'd come openly. But I can't—you can't—cheat and deceive him."

Susan nodded and drew away.

"I care enough to make a break for it, Susan," John was saying. "But do you?"

"I think I'm only alive since you've loved me," Susan said. The taxi jerked to a standstill. John got out, paid the man off and together he and Susan climbed the stone stairs. Outside John's flat, John took Susan's hand again.

"I don't believe I can stop, Susan," John said. "Nor do I, John," said Susan. But there was a new sad note in her voice, and she went upstairs, limping a little, as though she were very tired.

When she clicked the light on at her own landing, she looked down at her feet which had suddenly begun to hurt and noticed dully that her satin slippers had been cut through by the stones and gravel of the Park.

As she considered them she began to think, and as she thought she came to see as clearly as John that three people's lives must be broken up and pieced together again before she and John could belong to each other. And like John she wondered whether any of them could endure it. She loved him both too much and too little to take the risk.

All through the summer holidays she thought about John: and when she got back again to Alfred House, she took care never to see him alone any more. For Susan had made up her mind: if ever John grew desperate and could do without her no longer, she would go to him. But if he could do without her it would be better for him.

CHAPTER 10

I

1930 "NOTHING BUT THE TRUTH"

THE Probation Officer did not help Leonard very much—for one thing, Leonard bore him too much malice. Still, he did find him a job late that summer—a poor sort of job as an errand boy for a greengrocer. "No temptations there, my boy," said the Probation Officer. Leonard pedalled miserably through the streets, delivering goods fairly punctually, taking crazy risks as he skidded through traffic because it was all the amusement he had. Early in 1930 he lost that job because the greengrocer had his eye on a nephew just leaving school who would do the work cheaper. So Leonard, nearing eighteen, was out of work again. "Well," said the Probation Officer, "you've got a reference, anyhow. I dare say we'll find you something else."

But Leonard did not find something else. He did not try very hard; he just lounged over to the Employment Exchange in Silver Street, drew his juvenile unemployment benefit as long as he could and began once again to back horses. Alice watched him anxiously. Len was going to seed and nobody seemed to mind very much. She could not help him and, beyond twitting him sometimes with last year's disgrace, his father was quite indifferent.

At last Alice spoke to Miss Snow. For the best part of a year she had avoided all mention of her children so that both Susan and Miss Snow had been careful never to talk of Leonard. Both of them knew; as Care Committee workers they heard that kind of story. But Miss Snow, listening to

Alice as she told it, staring out of the window at the railway lines and twisting her apron, pretended that it was all news to her.

"Dear, dear," she said. "So unfortunate. Such a blow for you. Of course you and I know very well that it was just meant to be one of Leonard's clever deals."

"That's right," said Alice. "He meant no harm. He was always one for being too clever by half. As full of tricks as a monkey. But he deserved what he got. I only wish he could see that."

"Well, now," said Miss Snow, polishing her spectacles and getting out a notebook in her most businesslike way. "The thing is what shall we do with him next? Of course that Probation Officer ... but there, they're busy people. And they don't know the boy as we do." She wrinkled her brows. Then she said: "Have you ever thought of having a talk with Mr. Perkins? He was always interested in your children."

"I don't like to bother him," Alice said. "After all Len's done him no credit, has he?"

"I'll talk to him," said Miss Snow. "Don't you worry. We can't let Len go on like this."

So she went to Mr. Perkins with the story and a week later Mr. Perkins asked Leonard to go and see him in the Boys' Department after school hours. Leonard went reluctantly: he only remembered Mr. Perkins as a loud voice in the Boys' Hall at Hubert Street School. He didn't want to go and see him again and be treated like a blasted kid. But Alice insisted and somehow since he'd got the sack that time, his mother took a tone with him he had to notice.

So he went, slouching along the corridors where he had swaggered as a little boy, but pulling his hands automatically out of his pockets as he came towards the headmaster's desk.

Mr. Perkins looked up, a little greyer, a little yellower, a little more tired than he had been the last time Len stood there.

"Hallo, Gedge," he said. "Nice of you to come along. Glad to see you. Bring a chair over and sit down."

Len's greeting stuck in his throat. He pulled over a chair and sat on the edge of it, looking at his shoes and twiddling his cap.

"Been up against things a bit, haven't you?" Mr. Perkins was casual.

"Yessir."

"Did you like being in business? Or did you find it disappointing, eh?"

"Wasn't much fun, sir," Len said.

"Keep you busy, eh?"

"There wasn't enough to do," said Len. "Least-ways, not for me ..."

"Didn't your schooling come in handy?"

"Nothin' did," said Len drearily. "There didn't seem any way out of it all. Just bein' an office boy for years and years and then a clerk ... no chance to make money."

"So you made your own chance, eh?" Mr. Perkins began to dip a piece of chalk into the ink pot, without looking at Leonard. "I'd like to know how you worked it, you know."

"Well," said Leonard, dropping the 'sir' as he sensed the genuine interest in Mr. Perkins's voice, "it was meant to be just a bit of a deal. And it worked real well for a month or two. I made a fiver easy and no one the worse or the wiser either. You see it was this way ..."

Mr. Perkins leaned forward: Leonard stopped shuffling his feet as he talked.

"That was a good scheme," Mr. Perkins said. "Only two flaws in it."

"Two?" said Leonard.

"The money wasn't yours to begin with. And the luck wouldn't have held. You ought to know by this time that you can't always back winners. What would you have backed last week at Kempton, eh?"

"I did have a bob on Blue Boy," admitted Len.

"Exactly. So did I. But a wretched outsider romped home. There you are, you see. Mug's game."

"That's right," said Len, settling himself to wait for the moral lecture that was surely bound to come any time now. But Mr. Perkins did not talk of Leonard Gedge or morals. Instead he talked about the men who had made good in business and of the men who had failed, of the great financial schemes which had crashed and left thousands of people stranded. He spoke of Victory Bonds. He told how his own and his sister's savings had vanished in a day. Forgetting his audience, he talked more slowly of the grandeur of starting an enterprise from rock-bottom, building it up—"doesn't matter what it is, a school if you like, a shop if you like, or a farm, so long as it's your own. It's a grand thing to work yourself blind for a thing you're building. It's the work, not the success, that saves a man," said Mr. Perkins, and Leonard sat and stared at him and caught the echo of his creed with a mind that had always been taken up with shoddier dreams of quick returns and slicker deals. Suddenly Mr. Perkins turned to the boy beside him.

"Want to get back into business, Gedge?" he asked.

"Not much," Len said. "I've bin a fool. Besides, it don't pay not to run straight. An' I couldn't run straight if I was in business."

"No," said Mr. Perkins. "You're right there, Gedge. You'd always be looking for short cuts. You're too good at tricky

193

deals. Always were. Why, when you were here, you were always swapping things off here there and everywhere. And the other fellow was pretty nearly always had, wasn't he? But you've had too much education to be happy heaving coal." He drew circles absently on his blotter, with an eye on Leonard.

"Still, you know, a fellow can't pick and choose his chances these days. Times are too bad. If I find you something to do, will you get down to it, whatever it is?"

Len got up grinning: "Me benefit's up come Monday. I'll take anything you find. T'ain't fair to Mother to stop at home drawing nothing."

Mr. Perkins held out his hand. As Leonard took it, he looked up at him again. "Ever thought of the Colonies, Len?" he said.

Leonard shook his head. But he looked past the older man to the coloured posters of Empire Trade which hung on the wall. Men were growing oranges, cutting trees, lassoing cattle, building bridges.

"You might think about it, Len. There's more room out there for fellows like you—climbers who'll take a risk or two. You might end up your own master. Think it over, will you? I'll be seeing you again one of these days and we can talk about it then if you like."

Some of Len's old self-assurance came back to him as he turned and marched off down the corridor, clattered down the stairs and turned towards home.

When he let himself in and went through to the kitchen, Alice was sitting at the table, a pile of mending in front of her.

"Well, Len?" she said, in the quiet, dull voice she kept for him now.

"Old Perkins isn't half a bad chap, ma," he said. "I'm goin' to Canada, or Australia, or New Zealand, or South Africa. Any of 'em will do. Gee, that's a life, that is."

Alice's heart seemed held in an ice-cold clamp. She could not speak. She wanted to take hold of Leonard and never leave go. But as the tears rose in her throat her pride in him came back. She stood up and kissed him for the first time in a year.

Early in April Leonard joined a party organised by the Church Army, bound for New Zealand. He bought his own kit with money earned in the temporary jobs Mr. Perkins had found him, and Alice saw him off at Waterloo.

As the train drew out of the station, Alice stood and waved mechanically. Once before she had felt part of her own life leaving her for ever. But that was years ago, when she said good-bye to a grey officer she never saw again; at Victoria, in the War.

II

MRS. TOBIAS'S LAST QUESTS

INFLUENZA had broken out again in Alfred House that year. Everybody had it, but this time Mrs. Tobias did not get better: her heart gave out and she died, just as her eighty-sixth birthday was coming round.

Every day during her illness, the nurse pinned a bulletin on the front door. All the tenants stopped to read it on their way upstairs. Then one morning it was not there, and Mrs. Barker, draped in a black shawl, brought the news of her death.

Miss Snow at once asked when the funeral was, though she looked none too well herself, thought Mrs. Barker. Susan

Kennedy was away, but Miss Snow went round the other flats collecting money for a wreath and asking what people thought about going to the funeral. "I shall go, of course," she said. "But it would please her if some others did."

"How's she to know?" said Beatrix abruptly and Miss Snow looked sadly at her.

"I don't know," Vera said. "She might. I'd have gone to her birthday party. So I ought to go to her funeral."

Beatrix teased and bullied her afterwards, but Vera merely shrugged and went round her friends borrowing black. She and Miss Snow were given seats in the last carriage in the procession. There were a great many carriages and wreaths and Vera shivered as they rumbled slowly along towards the cemetery at the top of the hill in Silver Street. It made death unbelievably real. Miss Snow was sobbing gently, not out of sorrow for Mrs. Tobias but for the memory of all the other deaths she had mourned and for the knowledge that every year her contemporaries were dying off and the world was changing.

At the cemetery, there was another crowd of mourners, the lesser relations and friends and a number of quiet humble people to whom Mrs. Tobias had been kind. They all walked with bent heads behind the heavy bier, jerkily and a little out of step.

Inside the chapel, it was very cold. Some people were waiting in the pews already. Miss Snow and Vera pushed into the back row. There was only one man in it. Vera sank to her knees without looking at him, but as the congregation rose, she flicked a glance in his direction. His eyes were already on her: it was Robert Dean. He smiled.

As they sat down for the lesson, his elbow touched hers. There was comfort in it, for they were alive and young. At the graveside, Robert slipped his hand in hers.

"Don't go too near," he said.

"Dust to dust and ashes to ashes ..."

"Never mind," said Robert. "She was very old."

When it was all over, Miss Snow was swept off with the other mourners, but Robert and Vera hung behind.

"What made you come?" asked Vera.

"I saw the notice in the papers. And I thought if it had been her birthday party, I'd be coming to that. And she'd like me to go to her funeral just as much. So I came."

"Funny," said Vera, "that's just why I came."

"I had another reason," Robert said. "I always saw you at Mrs. Tobias's parties ..."

He drew her away from the gravel path into a lonely stretch of sodden winter grass and kissed her by a carved imitation marble angel. And Vera let all her pride go and clung to him, for she was cold with the fear of death and here at her side was life.

Afterwards they walked quietly down to Silver Street where they took a bus and sat very close together on the front seat and swung down to Piccadilly. Then they went to a cinema and to a crowded restaurant, loud with the noise of jazz, for a late tea. For neither of them could bear to think of that flower-lined quiet grave.

On the way back to Alfred House, Robert took Vera to his one-roomed flatlet in Marylebone; and there he kissed her desperately and taking his signet ring off his finger, he set it on hers.

"Yes, I'll marry you, Robert," said Vera. "Whenever you like, my dear. Only we won't tell anyone till it's over."

"April?" said Robert. "We'll have to find a bigger flat."

"April will be lovely," said Vera meekly.

Beatrix wondered what Vera had been up to when she came home that night, but as Vera did not tell her and as she was hardly on speaking terms with Miss Snow, she did not find out. Even Alice never guessed, and the only person who ought to have known was Dulcie Gedge, for the day after she left school at the end of the Easter term, she went to see Miss Gray in Alfred House. Nobody knew about this except Dulcie, for she had a plan.

She was still wearing her school uniform, because she had no other tidy clothes. Her fair unwaved hair gleamed with brushing, her tie was faultlessly knotted and the collar of her blouse was smooth and spruce. Even the girdle of her gym tunic was tied with an air, for Dulcie had inherited her mother's trick of wearing clothes along with her quiet bearing and soft voice. Like Alice, too, she knew exactly what she wanted.

She came at a time when Vera was glowing with suppressed happiness and the fun of getting a trousseau surreptitiously together. If Vera had been a Catholic, she would have burned candles to her saint: as it was she helped Dulcie Gedge.

For Dulcie wanted to get a job all on her own. With Len gone and Mother not so well, it was time she began to bring in a bit. And Miss Gray would surely know about jobs ... yes, of course, there was the Labour ... and the After Care, come to that. But she wanted a really good kind of job and what did Miss Gray think?

Vera sat back on her heels in front of the open trunk she had dragged into the sitting-room to pack while Beatrix was out and considered Dulcie. A pretty child and probably a clever one. She began to ask her questions. Yes, Dulcie typed ... yes, she could write shorthand, but not very fast. She knew French too and book-keeping and filing and the history of commerce, for she had learned these things in her last year at school. Something secretarial, Dulcie had in mind. In the end Vera gave her the name and address of the staff supervisor at her own library and promised to put in a word for the child the very next day. And Dulcie took down in laborious shorthand the wording of the letter she ought to send.

"That's right," Vera said. "I daresay you'll have quite a good chance. But don't count on it. "I say," she added, as Dulcie backed towards the door, "what about clothes for business?"

"I don't know," Dulcie said, blushing all over. "I've only got school things just yet."

"You wear them for the interview. There's nothing you look so nice in at present," said Vera firmly. "But I'm getting some new ones as it happens, and you're welcome to my others, you know. Most of them are a bit shabby but some aren't so bad. Here, you can have this and this and oh, here's a hat. I don't think it's very dated. And shoes you'll want. Oh bother, your feet are bigger than mine. Well, that can't be helped. There's my blue coat in the passage too. I'll give you that. Only promise you won't tell your mother yet, about my—new clothes, I mean. Can you smuggle them home?"

Afterwards Dulcie did wonder how she had failed to guess that something unusual was happening to Miss Gray, packing like fury in the sitting-room and giving away half her clothes and talking so fast and with such a queer light in her eyes. But at the time, she was too excited and too shy to think of anything but herself. She went away with a large untidy parcel in her arms and wrote her letter to Miss Gray's friend in the library. Two days later, she was summoned to an interview with the staff supervisor and Vera Gray left Alfred House for good.

She went out as usual in the morning but rather late, leaving a note for Beatrix and a cheque for a quarter's rent on her dressing table. Then she married Robert at Marylebone Registry office and drove away with him in his shabby car. And that night, while Vera and Robert slept in a pagan happiness, Beatrix came home from a party and found Vera's note. She read it through, burnt it and posted the cheque to her bank. Then she pulled on her broad-brimmed felt hat again and wandered miserably out into the streets.

III
MISS DULCIE GEDGE

THE news of Vera's marriage swept, a fortnight before Easter, through all the flats in a day. The person who was most genuinely pleased was Miss Snow; at last Robert was going to be happy and she would see him again, for he even sent her a post-card from Carlisle. The person who was most aggrieved was Mrs. Barker: she thought of all the time she had spent watching Vera and how she had nearly caught her out and how unremunerative it had all been. And now before she had had time to get another line on the girl that might bring in money, the hussy had gone and got married. Besides, now that old Mrs. Tobias was laid away, there would be no one to make complaints about the tenants and their behaviour and their noise—for there was no one else with her old-fashioned ideas. Mrs. Barker mourned Mrs. Tobias as a source of income which had expired. But still, she reminded herself, there were other people in the flats worth watching and if she couldn't count on tips for smoothing over matters with the landlord or Mrs. Tobias, she might get well paid to keep her mouth shut in other quarters. The trouble was that none of the likely tenants allowed Mrs. Barker inside their flats: for some obscure reason they preferred that Alice Gedge and she was such a close one that you couldn't squeeze a titbit out of her, not even if you as good as said you were prepared to pay for it.

But a week afterwards Mrs. Barker had a stroke of luck. The tenants of Alfred House had hardly got over the shock of Vera's runaway marriage before the routine of their daily lives was upset again by Alice's illness. It began with a chill caught seeing Len off at Waterloo, in the rain. As usual she had kept on at work—she wasn't one to stay away for a stomach ache, as she told Susan when questioned. But one morning she came over really queer in Miss Snow's flat, while she was washing the paint. Fortunately, Miss Snow was in. She took charge at once, put her on the sofa with her own quilt and hot bottle, and rang up the doctor. And half an hour later, Dr. Hawkes diagnosed appendicitis and rushed Alice in to hospital. Susan and Miss Snow spent the morning arranging for her to have a bed in a small ward and both of them waited in the corridor till she came round from the anaesthetic.

For nearly a fortnight, she was on the danger list: Thomas hung dejectedly about the hospital, clasping the faded flowers he always brought and invariably forgot to give the nurse. Then Alice took a turn for the better and Susan came round with grapes, Miss Snow with chicken jelly and extra butter and eggs, while Dulcie called for news on her way home every evening.

When Alice was really getting better at last, Dulcie went into the ward to see her. Alice was lying with the wireless head phones on; she was feeling blissful, for the pain was gone and her body, worn with twelve years of unceasing overwork, was luxuriously at rest. She could enjoy Miss Snow's eggs and Susan's grapes, and the flowers Mr. Abbot had sent—a great sheaf of jonquils. And nearest to her, in a tooth glass, were Thomas's faded anemones. The April twilight was creeping over the room when Dulcie came in, but Alice recognised the clothes at once.

"Miss Gray?" she said in surprise.

"Miss Gedge, Ma dear," said Dulcie, pulling off Vera's hat with one hand and taking Alice's fingers in the other. "It's all right," she said quickly as Alice's eyes darkened with worry. "You don't need to fret. Miss Gray gave me all her old things before she went away. Only to think I never guessed."

"Well, my word, you do look smart, Dulcie, don't you," Alice said, "but however did you come by those shoes, dear? Miss Gray's feet are tiny."

Dulcie drew herself up. "Bought them with my week's money, Ma," she said, "You always said it pays to get shoes good." She stretched out her feet and looked lovingly at the neat quiet shoes which were so unlike Len's taste. But Alice was no longer interested in them.

"Dulcie, you've never got a job, have you?" she said.

"Been in it a whole fortnight. At the library where Miss Gray was. Up in the clerical department I am. There are twelve of us and I'm the youngest typist. Only of course I do odd jobs too. Just you look here," Dulcie snapped open her bag and pulled out a small buff envelope with her name on it. She held it up and then laid it on the quilt.

"You open it, Ma," Dulcie squeaked, hopping with excitement. "I saved it for you. We're paid every Friday. Tea-time."

Alice wrenched open the flap, and pulled out the crinkly note and spilt the shillings into the palm of her hand.

"Twenty-five shillings, Dulcie, twenty-five! My word, that's grand," Alice whispered.

Dulcie took the money, nodding proudly. "Bit of a help, eh Mother?" she said.

The nurse came in then with supper trays on a trolley and Dulcie kissed her mother and went jauntily away; and Alice ate her supper and finally went to sleep with Dulcie's pay envelope in her hand.

It was a month before Alice could leave the hospital and then Miss Snow and Dr. Hawkes arranged for her to go to a convalescent home for another month. And all that time, Dulcie kept house for her father, brought home her twenty-five shillings regularly and settled down steadily and happily to work. For there were girls of her own age to talk to in the library, and besides, she liked the ordered routine of her day. There was drudgery, of course, but the clerical department was well managed and the dull work was shared out among the juniors. And Dulcie was methodical by nature: when she typed, she liked to set the words out so that the page looked nice: she enjoyed clipping and filling carbons: she was fascinated by the innumerable details of the work and learned them easily: her manners were good and she was popular among the clerks and the senior officials with whom she came in contact. By the time Alice was back, Dulcie was on the permanent staff of the library and considered to be the most promising junior that the staff supervisor had had for some time. Dulcie did not know this, but Alice did, for Vera, back in London, and in touch with the library still, wrote to tell her that Dulcie was a success. And Alice longed to praise and pet Dulcie; but she held back, thinking of Leonard to whom she had given the best of everything; the first glow of her affections, the biggest helpings, the best clothes, the most pocket money. It didn't do for mothers to make their children's lives too easy, that was about it, she thought with a sigh and turned her attention to her clients in Alfred House. It was time she got back to them, for she felt in her bones that Mrs. Barker had been up to no good.

And as usual she was right. Alice's illness gave Mrs. Barker just the chance she was itching for. She was able to go in and out of the flats—not into number eight, of course, for Miss Wood would never have her inside the door. Not into Miss Snow's either, for the same reason. But that did not matter, for there was nothing interesting about Miss Snow. It was Mr. Abbot of number seven she was interested in, because of number nine where the Kennedys lived.

John Abbot allowed her to come and do for him because he had to have somebody to clean his flat and cook and he could not see that it much mattered who did it. But Susan protested. She wanted Howard to let her manage by herself, but he said that she did not cook well enough and that Mrs. Barker was a decent sort and they might as well give her a trial. "Might be better than that Mrs. Gedge you're so keen on," he said. "And it's handy to have someone on the premises."

So Mrs. Barker took over Alice's work and for nearly two months did just enough of it to escape serious censure from Susan without overworking herself. She used to potter about in her dirty velveteen dress and bedroom slippers, disdaining an overall, and wearing a greyish apron instead. And the flat soon lost the bright, well-cared for look that Alice managed to give to every room she cleaned.

Susan used to wonder what it was. "You'd think she brushed dirt into the carpet," she said to Miss Snow once, and found afterwards that this was almost the truth, for Mrs. Barker could never be bothered to empty the carpet sweeper, since this involved stooping. When Susan found out, she complained. At first she patiently explained the principle of carpet sweepers and then, stung by Mrs. Barker's insolent contempt, she threatened to dismiss her. But Mrs. Barker went to Howard at once with a long story of her wrongs. Of course if the master wished her to go ... but Mrs. Kennedy was a little impulsive, perhaps? And easily taken in by such as Mrs. Gedge? There was no doubt Mrs. Gedge had had things all her own way. Mrs. Barker was quite concerned, for instance, about the butcher's book.

So when Susan complained to Howard about Mrs. Barker, he taxed her with unreasonableness and began a lecture on extravagance. He told Susan that Mrs. Barker was a far better worker than Alice Gedge and several shillings cheaper. Why, she had even taken the trouble to lay out his dress clothes because she'd overheard him say he was going out that evening.

"She scamps her other work to do it. Can't you see the woman's a toady, Howard, making up to you because she wants to do Alice Gedge out of a job?"

"My dear, you must allow me to exercise my own judgment. You've been a married woman nearly six years, I know. But you've given all your attention to this foolish unpaid work and as a result your poor old husband has to keep an eye on the home himself."

"Don't be an idiot, Howard," Susan said impatiently. "I could run this flat by myself and make you just as comfortable as Mrs. Barker does and go on with my other work too. I'd sooner do it than have that creature about the place."

"Really, Susan, you are a most difficult woman," said Howard. "I'd be very glad to do without a maid—I'm a poor man—if I really thought you could manage the work. But there it is—you're no good at housework, and for some reason I can't make out you think it's beneath you."

"If you weren't such a pig-headed brute," said Susan, goaded, "you'd know that I'm a perfectly good house-keeper. At any rate I know enough about it to tell you that your Mrs. Barker is incompetent and lazy and ..."

"That'll do, Susan." Howard held up his hand in an almost ecclesiastical gesture and stalked away in his bath robe looking like a pompous little flat-footed Roman, while Susan made a face at his back.

That evening she was positively glad to see him go out to dinner at his club and settled down thankfully to a lonely supper. Somehow for the last year, ever since the Robert and Vera affair had first roused his curiosity, Howard had been a daily exasperation. Sitting there in the warm June evening, Susan allowed herself to consider Howard. She thought of him in bed, a heavy, inconsiderate, blatant lover. She thought of him in the mornings, liverish and short-tempered and supposed that all men did look as ugly as that in their pants. She thought of him as he dogmatised at breakfast, contemptuously dismissing every point of view but his own, she heard his vulgar voice plaguing her with limericks, probing her with questions, mocking her work, belittling all that she admired; she saw him patronising Alice and everyone else who was poor or old; she heard him praising up Mrs. Barker, and she got up feeling sick. She walked round the room and out into the sitting room and back very hurriedly to the bathroom. When she had been sick she felt better, but horrified and frightened of herself.

'I must get away for a bit,' she thought. 'Even a week-end.' She sat down at her desk and wrote to an aunt who lived in Sussex and asked her if she might go to her for a day or two and then she found a stamp and went out to post the letter.

She did not think of John whom she had hardly seen for months, but when she met him in the empty hall, she ran up to him at once.

"Oh John, John," she said and began to cry.

"What is it, my dear, my sweet?" John said, taking her hands, as they went upstairs. "Come in for a few minutes and tell me about it."

Mrs. Barker had been watching from the basement stairs ever since Mr. Kennedy went out. She saw John meet Susan and watched them go upstairs. Then she crept out into the hall in time to see John's door close behind them both.

But Susan did not stay with John: she was too miserable to talk to him and too frightened by the sudden violence of her love for him to bear to be with him long. John, too, was worried, for now that Susan was really desperate with unhappiness, he could not endure to stand aside. 'If only Howard would be decent,' he thought. I wonder if Howard could ever see ... But of course he wouldn't listen to Susan. And if I went, he'd never believe ... I wonder if there's any way out of this ...' Aloud he said:

"Don't worry too much, my dear. We'll find a way out."

He took her up to her own flat and opened the door for her. Mrs. Barker was now on the landing below and by leaning back against the stair rail, she could just see their two shadows on the wall. She was disappointed when Mr. Abbot came down again alone, for say what you would, Mrs. Kennedy hadn't hardly been in with him long enough for anything important. Still, it all pointed the right way and no doubt Mr. Kennedy would be interested. Not like some gents what wouldn't hear a word against their wives, no matter how true it might be. She must get a chance of a word with Mr. Kennedy just to see how the wind was in that quarter. Slow and steady does it, thought Mrs. Barker in her basement. Best to take your chances where you find them.

IV
MRS. BARKER DRIVES A BARGAIN

MRS. BARKER'S chance came the very next day.

Susan went out to supper, ordering one chop to be cooked for Howard. It was an innocent, long promised excursion with a school friend and Howard had been told of it several times. But he was feeling irritable with Susan and paid no attention to what she said.

He came back that evening to find Mrs. Barker deliberately frying two chops and no signs of Susan. As she dished up for him he asked her petulantly when Mrs. Kennedy would be back.

"I couldn't say, sir, I'm sure. If Mrs. Kennedy didn't think to tell you, sir, she'd 'ardly mention it to me," said Mrs. Barker piously, wiping a smear of gravy off the dish with her apron.

"It's very tiresome," Howard said. "I don't like to see good food wasted and it's no use waiting for Mrs. Kennedy now. Are you sure she didn't mention where she was going?"

"Mrs. Kennedy is a little absent-minded sometimes, sir, if you'll excuse me saying so. I'm sure I 'ope I'm giving satisfaction," she added irrelevantly.

Howard cleared his throat. "Yes, yes," he said. "But it's a pity to waste that second chop. Is Mr. Abbot in, by the way ? He might care ..."

"Mr. Abbot is out, sir. Too," said Mrs. Barker.

"Out too, out too? What do you mean?" Howard snapped irritably.

"I was never one to make trouble, sir," said Mrs. Barker, wiping her hands with the dish cloth. "Besides, naturally I thought you bein' her 'usband would know ..."

"Know what?" said Howard, thumping down his knife. "Look here, Mrs. Barker, if there's anything you think I ought to know it's your duty to tell me ..."

"I never 'ave thought it was quite right," said Mrs. Barker reluctantly, "fer a married woman to go off with an unmarried man, 'ere there and everywhere. But I'm sure I thought you knew, sir. I've always thought you was a very patient 'usband, if you'll excuse me, sir."

"Do you mean," said Howard, breathing deeply, "that Mr. Abbot is accustomed to take my wife out without my knowledge?"

"Not out," said Mrs. Barker. "With him havin' a flat an' all they don't need to go out do they? Not unless you're in, sir."

"And when have you seen my wife in Mr. Abbot's flat?"

Mrs. Barker whimpered. "I don't want to make trouble, sir. This is going to make it very awkward for me, sir. If trouble was to come of what I might say ... well, I don't want to mix up in it, sir. T'wouldn't 'ardly be worth me while."

Howard glowered at her.

"I don't believe you," he said, with a desperate attempt at dignity. "My wife and I are on the best of terms."

"Reely!" said Mrs. Barker, edging to the door. "I'm sure I'm very glad indeed to 'ear it, sir. I'm sure for a long time I've thought ..." She paused, surveying him out of the corner of her eyes, her expression an artful blend of commiseration and malevolent knowledge.

Howard looked up at her, then down again, fiddling with the salt cellars and pepper-pot on the table. His dignity slowly wilted beneath a mounting curiosity.

"Thought what?" he said at last.

"Oh, sir, I'm sure I couldn't never bring meself to tell ..." Mrs. Barker began to scuffle sideways again, glancing over her shoulder at the door.

"You'll have to tell me," Howard said, stepping in front of her to cut off her retreat. But Mrs. Barker shook her head.

"I'm not sure it would be right. After all, I 'aven't 'ad a word with Mrs. Kennedy yet, nor Mr. Abbot neither. Besides I got to think of Number One, 'aven't I?"

Then Howard understood. He sat down again; and pulled out his note case, considered it, and threw ten shillings on to the table. Mrs. Barker shook her head, pursing her lips. He added a pound note and Mrs. Barker ignored it virtuously. Then Howard floated down another and put his case back in his pocket. Mrs. Barker knew her man. She picked the notes up, leant nearer and whispered.

It made a good story as Mrs. Barker told it. Her psychic experiences had developed her narrative powers. When she had finished, she shuffled away and Howard sat alone in the kitchen, his greasy chop uneaten before him. He licked his lips and loosened his collar. Then he got up, shivering a little and went into the sitting-room, to wait for Susan beside the unlit gas fire, his shoulders drooping, his hands idle at his sides. He had neither pride nor mannerisms left. If Susan or John had come in then, he would have listened to everything they said. He might even have tried to understand.

But John, coming home early from a meeting, paced his own flat worrying over the future and never guessed that he was missing Howard's chance and his. And by the time Susan came in-Howard had swollen himself up to his normal size with righteous indignation.

When she came into the sitting-room Howard got up and took her by the shoulders.

"Susan, where have you been?"

"With Mary Macgregor, of course," Susan said in amazement. "I've told you about it heaps of times."

"I don't believe you. You've been out with John Abbot."

"John Abbot?" said Susan, genuinely surprised. "What on earth d'you mean?"

"Mean!" said Howard violently. "I mean that my wife has been cuckolding me with my best friend long enough."

"Howard!"

"It's no use your looking at me like that, my milk and water madam. Weren't you with John Abbot?"

"I was not, And if I had been, it's no excuse for shouting at me."

"You're lying. I happen to know. Mrs. Barker saw you."

"Mrs. Barker what? You mean to say that you've discussed me with Mrs. Barker? Then that's why you want that woman round, is it? As your spy?"

"There you are. You admit it. You were out with him."

"I do not. I wasn't. I don't even know whether John's out or in. Ring up and find out. Ask him where he was ..."

"Oh, you've both got some story ... But you can't fool me. What about last night? In his flat weren't you? Mrs. Barker saw ..."

"Howard, will you stop?" Susan wrenched her shoulder free and pushed him away. "How dare you say such things?"

"In his flat ..."

"Yes, I went in on my way upstairs. I ..."

"What for?"

"To borrow a book." As she said it, Susan knew that it was only the first of the many lies she would have to tell because Howard would be incapable of understanding the truth.

He laughed. "To borrow a book ... to borrow a book. Think of something better than that." He seized her wrists and twisted them. "Listen to me, Susan. I—will—have—the—truth. Are you ... Are you ..." Susan turned her head away so that Howard should not see her eyes when for John's sake she denied loving him. But Howard finished his sentence slowly.

"Are you John Abbot's mistress?"

"No, no, no! Let me go, you bullying beast," cried Susan with all the emphasis of her relief.

She pulled her hands free and faced him, her palms pressed against the panels of the door.

"And as for you, Howard," said in a perfectly steady voice, "you may as well know. Now. I loathe and despise you. I've loathed you for years. I'd married you, so I hid it. But now when you and that woman, that foul, ugly woman, go spying on me, and making up indecent stories about me ..."

"Come now, Susan," said Howard. "If what you say is true, we'll leave it at that. I'll say no more. Probably you may only have been a little indiscreet. In that case there's no harm done. You'll have learned your lesson, I expect."

"But I loathe you," Susan repeated.

"Now Susan, you mustn't talk in that wild way. You know you have a duty to your husband. Mrs. Barker may have been mistaken, but she only acted for the best and I'm sure I'm very glad to be able to think that you've kept your marriage vows after all. I'm a tolerant man, Susan," Howard said with a twisted smile, "and a patient one, I hope. I'll overlook this foolishness if you'll do your best to ... er ... play fair in the future."

"In the future," whispered Susan, " in the future ..." She saw a panorama of the years she would have to spend with Howard, tolerant and patient, before either of them could die. "No, Howard, no," she said shrilly. "I can't go on, I can't go on."

"You get so excited, Susan, my dear," said Howard, who was now quite calm again, his injured pride soothed by his own magnanimity. "You'd better go and get ready for bed quietly. In the morning, you know, things will look ..."

But Susan did not wait for the end of the sentence. Howard heard her go into the bedroom. It was a pity she was so overwrought. She was hardly likely to be lying when she denied the implications of Mrs. Barker's story. But still, she had been foolish. She deserved a fright. After it, no doubt, she would settle down again. But still he would have to find out exactly how far ... Perhaps a talk with John would clear the matter up. Probably Abbot had just been humouring her. But better go cautiously ... one did not want to look undignified. He would go to their room in a few minutes, just as usual. He sat down to wait, satisfied with himself again. But presently he heard a door close softly. What was Susan up to? He got up feeling that really his patience had been a good deal tried that evening, and went into the bedroom. It was empty, so he went down the passage to the bathroom, hoping that Susan hadn't taken all the hot water. The light was on. But there was no sign of Susan. Then his attention was caught by an empty hook: Susan's sponge-bag and toothbrush had gone too.

CHAPTER 11

I

SUSAN WALKS OUT

WHILE Howard was searching for her in the bathroom, Susan was crossing Silver Street at a run, terrified that he would take it into his head to look out of the windows. It was so important that she should get away without being seen. For if she were caught and had to go home, she knew she would never dare to start out again. On the far side of the street she drew into the shadow and looked back. But no one was about: perhaps Howard had not even missed her yet: Perhaps she was really escaping from Silver Street for ever.

Susan decided to walk across the bridge rather than risk taking a taxi at the rank on the corner: a driver might recognise her or Howard might make inquiries. So she went quickly on, keeping to the shadows, making plans and quite unaware of the heavy case that was dragging at her arm.

At last she hailed a taxi and drove to Victoria. Her schemes were laid: at the station she paid the cab off and walked through the Booking Hall to the Grosvenor Hotel, where she registered with bold invention as Mrs. Groves from Taunton. Then she went up in the lift to a small ornate bedroom where she fell childishly asleep directly she got into bed. No dreams of a pursuing Howard, no anxious regrets, no thoughts of John, disturbed her night's rest.

When she woke up, an immense satisfaction settled on her mind at once. She rang for tea, stretching luxuriously in the big bed. There was no point in hurrying—or was there? What about money, for instance? She reached for her bag and counted the contents while she sipped her tea: three pounds—not much. But it would be better not to go to her bank, because Howard would probably go round there and ask questions. No, the best thing to do was to send a wire and go straight to Aunt Mary in Sussex, for Howard did not even know of her existence.

Two hours later she was alone in a carriage, rocking over the bridge across the Thames in the train for Midhurst. Soon, she knew, the squalor of the imprisoning streets would be behind her and the untroubled welcoming country surround her instead. How easy it was to get away from London: how easy it had been to get away from Howard. Why didn't more people leave their homes when it was such a simple thing to do? Susan settled back in her corner and watched warm meadows, where placid cows grazed among buttercups, and solemn ranks of trees edging fields of hay, or strips of yellow mustard and green corn spattered with crimson poppies.

At Midhurst she changed and took a branch line towards the sea. She was the only passenger for Clattering Fords and her aunt, a small elderly person in smoky blue tweeds with a golden retriever and a border terrier at her heels, was already on the platform, peering up and down the train.

"There you are, darling," she said, coming towards Susan triumphantly as though she had just succeeded in picking her out of an immense crowd, "how nice of you to come!"

"It's lovely to see you, Aunt Mary. Are you sure you didn't mind my coming a few days earlier?" Susan stooped to kiss her small aunt, and slid a hand along the retriever's squirming back. How easy it all was!

Aunt Mary squeezed her arm, waved a drowsy porter towards her suitcase, and bustled both of them out of the station to an absurd governess cart drawn by a fat pony.

"You mustn't think I haven't got a car," she said as they drove away, "because I have. A Morris. 1924. The best year. But somehow Bessie goes so much more quietly, so I always take her when I'm just driving in the neighbourhood. Come up, Bessie, will you?" She slapped the reins on the unperturbed brown back. "You see," she went on, looking at Susan curiously out of the corner of her eye, "when you're my age, you don't want time to go particularly quickly. It's no advantage to me to be able to drive to the village in five minutes instead of twenty. I like my days to last as long as possible." She whisked the governess cart round a sharp corner into a chalky lane, and Bessie settled down to a steady jog between hedges filled with ragged robin, hemlock and the promise of blackberries, towards a tree-crested curve of down.

Aunt Mary prattled on, breaking off now and again to chirrup to the retriever which was prying into rabbit holes. And Susan nursed the terrier and looked about her, soothed by the luxurious quiet of the summer countryside. It took them half an hour to reach Aunt Mary's home—a rambling place which offered a satisfying compromise between antiquity and modernity. Some skilful architect had propped up an old white thatched cottage and added a wing of bathrooms and kitchen. The garden blazed with snapdragon and marigolds and Sweet William, and the kind of roses which flourish without much pruning. The pony stopped at the gate of its own accord. Aunt Mary flung down the reins, jerked herself out of the governess cart and then wandered up the path calling for Joseph, till a squat black-eyed man in blue dungarees came reluctantly out of a wooden shed filled with the buzz of engines, and took the pony away.

Susan collected her bag and gloves and followed her aunt and the leaping dogs towards the house and up to a low room with bulging, cream-washed walls and a sloping floor. Bright chintz curtains flapped at the window and the smell of hay and summer flowers came floating in.

Afterwards, Aunt Mary brought Susan down to lunch, which was laid on a lawn flanked by lupins and delphiniums, adjoining a paddock where ponies grazed, and sheltered from the wind by a shoulder of down.

"Better than London, eh, Susan?" said Aunt Mary, flapping her napkin at an interested bee.

"It's glorious," Susan said enthusiastically—and wondered what to say next. To her surprise she found conversation difficult. And she felt tired. Surely the joy of escape couldn't really be wearing thin already? That couldn't be it—it must be her overpowering relief that made it so hard not to tell Aunt Mary and so impossible to talk about other things. Susan still thought that it ought all to be so simple: there was nothing for her to do except to stay with Aunt Mary for a bit, and then, when things had blown over a little, to go to her family and either stay there or find work of some kind. But Aunt Mary was speaking.

"Of course I haven't seen you since your marriage, you know. Except for that one evening at your mother's this spring, just before you left again for London. I don't think I've ever met your husband, have I? You should have come down to see me before, you know, both of you. Why didn't you?"

"I didn't think you and Howard would mix," Susan said, stung into honesty. If Aunt Mary was going to persist in talking about Howard it would be impossible to hedge and prevaricate. Better in the end to tell the truth at once.

"How sensible to be so candid! Relations so often don't mix at all. I wish more people would be wise enough to keep the ones that don't apart."

"Yes. No. Yes," said Susan absently, wondering how little she could say, and shrinking alike from argument and sympathy. "How lovely your garden is, Aunt Mary!"

"Susan," said Aunt Mary, "you're exactly like your mother. I could always tell when she had something on her mind, and sometimes she would keep it to herself for days. But she always told me in the end." She patted Susan's knee and gave her a cup of coffee and a cigarette. "But whatever it is," she said, "you'd better laze in the garden to-day, and to-morrow you can give me a hand with the ponies. I'm showing three of them at the local gymkhana and I could do with a little help. Joseph's all right, but the colt has taken such a distaste to the man that he won't go near him. Joseph won't, I mean."

"I think I'd better tell you now, Aunt Mary," Susan said quickly. "I've left my husband for good."

"Dear, dear! How trying for you both. I heard something a little time ago from your mother, which made me wonder— Has he been ill-treating you, poor child? Is he likely to come here and fetch you back, the creature? If he does, Joseph and I will be more than a match for him, I think," said Aunt Mary with spirit.

"Oh, heavens, no," said Susan, appalled. "He doesn't know where I am."

"But hadn't you better tell him?"

"No. I ... I daren't. If he knew, he'd make me go back. I feel—safe, here."

"Safe? Of course you're safe here," said Aunt Mary. "But still—"

"Why should I tell him?"

"The man might be worried."

"Howard? Worried? About me!" Susan said with a high light laugh. "Oh dear, no."

Aunt Mary looked at her, wondering for a moment which was real—the shallow modern woman who talked so brightly of abandoning her home, or the tired, anxious, young fugitive she had met at the station.

"It's quite simple," Susan went on. "I just can't bear him any longer. So I've come away. I don't want to drag people into this—my family or you or anyone."

She looked so miserable that Aunt Mary instantly became partisan again. But the sooner the girl realised that there was nothing more complicated or more calculated to involve one's relations and friends than trying to escape from marriage, the better. Besides, she thought, even if Susan's flight was unpremeditated, it was highly likely that some other love had provoked her to it. Aloud she said:

"My poor Susan! You won't be able to help dragging people in … If there's anyone you mind about specially, you ought to let them know where you are. And it's only decent to let your husband know that you're safe, even if you don't send him your address at present. Think about it, my dear! There's Joseph calling. All right, Joseph, I'm coming. It's the colt, is it? Well, leave him alone till I get to you!" And Aunt Mary stubbed out her cigarette and ground it under her heel. She patted Susan's shoulder. "Think about it!" she said again. "I'm glad you came to me. You'll find I'm a good conspirator." She strode away across the lawn, leaving Susan to watch the warm air quiver over the lupins and the butterflies rise battling above the thatch; and finally, reluctantly, to think.

II

SUSAN'S SUMMER

DIRECTLY Howard was convinced that Susan had really gone, he went downstairs to John, cautiously turning over in his mind what he should say to him. When he found John in and alone, he did not know what to do; for either Mrs. Barker was completely wrong, or else John and Susan had concocted an extremely clever scheme between them. But John's amazement was so clearly genuine that Howard dared not even suggest that he knew anything about Susan's disappearance.

In fact, John was desperately anxious to help Howard to find her; for he did not believe his shamefaced story of a slight tiff—"You know what women are at times John, old man." He could not bear to think of Susan, so miserable at last that she was driven to flight, rushing off alone in this crisis when they ought to have stood side by side and disposed of Howard once and for all. John knew that he had failed Susan.

When Howard found that Susan was not with John he stopped worrying at once. Obviously the girl had gone off in a temper, either to friends or to her own home. It would be quite simple to find her and bring her back. It was Howard who went upstairs to bed and to sleep and John who stayed awake and finally went out and began a series of futile inquiries.

The next day there was no news of her: Howard wired Susan's people, rang up all her friends, went round to her bank and finally confessed his complete inability to trace her. John was far more anxious than Howard: for if Susan was so desperate that she could leave her husband, without even letting John know where she was, then she must have been wild enough for anything. So it was John who urged Howard to ring up the hospitals and get in touch with the police, for though he hated the idea of seeing Susan dragged back to the flat, he could not endure the suspense; he lived in a nightmare in which it seemed more than probable that Susan was dead.

But before he could persuade Howard to such drastic measures, a wire came, handed in at Portsmouth, where Susan had driven in the old Morris. It said: 'Not returning no use following quite well Susan.' John's relief was so overwhelming that he wondered why Howard's suspicions did not wake again. But Howard was too insulted to care for anyone else's feelings.

Two days afterwards, Alice came back to work. For reasons of her own, she was quite pleased to find Mrs. Barker at number nine, and she contrived to listen with suitable horror to her lurid story of Mrs. Kennedy's doings. But she was glad to get away from her in case the old fraud really had got second sight and could see through Alice's apron to the letter which was burning in her pocket. For Susan had written to Alice, saying that Alice had always been so kind and would probably understand that she simply could not go on living with Mr. Kennedy any longer. So she had run away. She did not want anyone to know where she was at present, but there was one friend who, like Alice, had always been kind and who might be worried. Did Alice think she could pass on the enclosed note?

Alice did. Not that she approved of Susan's running away like that: in Alice's class people did not leave husbands, however unpleasant they were. But she knew from experience at Everton Court that even before the war marriage was more easily undone among the gentry. 'But it's a bad business,' thought Alice, 'and I doubt if Mr. Kennedy will agree to it—he's not top drawer, however much side he puts on. It'll be a rare pity if this can't be straightened out, with Mr. Abbot caught up in it too.' She sighed and went to John Abbot's flat.

He was having breakfast when Alice came in, rather red, and looking uneasily down the passage before she shut the door behind her.

"I'm glad to see you back again, Mrs. Gedge," he said. "I do hope you're really quite strong now. Don't overwork yourself, whatever you do!"

"Thank you, sir," said Alice. She looked at him disapprovingly, feeling that somehow he was to blame for part of the unhappiness Mrs. Kennedy would have to bear. Then she laid the note on the table in front of him.

"And mind," she said, "I don't know where it came from, or what it's about. And I don't want to know. If you'll read it, I'll see it's burnt at once. I don't want anything left about that might get my Mrs ... somebody I'm fond of into trouble."

John took it and turned away from her. Susan just said that she had run away, and that if he wanted to see her he could take the ten o'clock train from Victoria to Midhurst on Saturday and she would meet it.

John's sudden happiness lit up his face so that Alice thought him almost handsome for once.

He nearly slipped the note into an inner pocket, then, reconsidering it, he meekly handed it to Alice, who was waiting, match-box in hand. She took it gingerly, and tore it in half; then lit a match and burnt it, fragment by fragment.

"Don't worry, Alice!" he said. "You've been a brick. And if it's any use to you, I think you've probably done as much as anybody to help Mrs ... somebody we're both fond of."

Alice nodded. "If you'll take my advice, sir," she said, scooping up the ashes, "you'll be very careful of what you might say to Mr. Kennedy; and if you should be going to meet anyone, well, Mrs. Barker is sharper than she seems, and not above accepting money for trifles she overhears."

John thanked Alice. He kept out of Howard's way for the rest of the week: when he left on Saturday, he took his golf clubs with him, and noticing Mrs. Barker in the hall, he called a taxi and said loudly that he must catch the 9.45 from Waterloo.

It was a soft, grey day when John went down to Midhurst, and he sat in the train trying to see the country as Susan must have seen it when she ran away to Sussex. He guessed at her immeasurable relief as the train ran out of the dreary suburbs, and the quiet, green country gave him something of the same welcome.

He did not know what he would say to Susan when he saw her: he was not sure whether he would find her happy or frantic. When at last he caught sight of her, standing by an ancient Morris in the station yard in her shabby riding breeches, with a rather dusty beret pulled over her bright hair, she reminded him of a truant school child. She gave him both her hands without a word, pulled him quickly into the car and let in the clutch. The engine was running raucously, so that speech was impossible. Susan swung out into the main road and then off it again down a narrow lane. As she rammed the gears into second for the hill she leaned towards John and shouted: "I've brought sandwiches. We'll park the car at the foot of the downs and climb. You don't mind?"

John shook his head.

"Good. I want to keep Aunt Mary out of this."

John clutched the side of the car as they rocked round a corner. He was a cautious driver himself. Presently Susan turned through a gate and drew up.

"We can leave her here. She'll be all right."

She rummaged in the dickey for two parcels of sandwiches and two bottles of beer. Then she gave his share to John, stuffed hers into her pockets and set off up the hill at a pace which made him gasp.

'She's happy just to be away from Howard,' John thought, amused at the way Susan took charge of the situation. Presently he turned and took her hand. They walked over last year's leaves under vaulted beeches. Neither of them spoke. Susan was thinking: 'How lovely it is to be away from Howard, able to walk in woods with someone who loves them! Howard would have said a dozen times that these are fine old trees.' John was thinking that Susan seemed still quite untouched by anything that had happened to her, and wondering if she could understand the urgency of his own need. But when they reached the open downs again, and she dropped on to the crisp turf sprinkled with the small blue flowers of milkwort, and eyebright, and yellow tormentil, and pulled him down beside her, he knew that she did.

He kissed her then, but without passion, knowing that she must have had enough of it. Presently Susan drew away, and he saw that her eyes were filled with tears.

"Oh, John," she said, "I've wanted you so much. I didn't at first. It was enough just to have run away—to have one's bed to one's self and one's days to fill without being afraid that he would come in and wreck it all. It was such peace—"

"But you did want me?" John said, reassuring himself.

"Oh, yes, I did. I can talk to you. I want you because you're a person I like and trust, not just because at times I've been mad and loved you."

"Yes," said John consideringly. "I know what you mean. I like you like that, too. Only I'm in love with you. More than ever, I think."

"Look, John!" said Susan. "That's the sea over there."

"Is it?" said John.

"And that's Wittering, where I bathe."

"Yes."

"And that's Heron's Edge, where I ride. D'you see?"

"Yes, I see," said John, who had never taken his eyes from her face.

"Oh, John," said Susan, "I wish you could stay down here and see it with me every day."

"Then you would marry me if you were free?"

"John, dear, of course I would, if you wanted me to. Do you? Do you really? Want me as much as all that, I mean? Enough to risk having me as a wife, after I've made such a mess of it once?"

"Why, of course."

Susan rolled over and hid her face on her crossed arms.

"I'm so proud," she said. "I'm so proud you want to marry me. I'd have done anything: I would have been glad to be just your mistress."

John put an arm round her. "That's just it, Susan, my sweet. Where the trouble comes, I mean. I don't want you as a mistress, to have a week-end cottage with, or odd sneaking nights. I want you in my everyday life, all the time. Day and night. I want your children, too."

Susan sat up and pushed her hair out of her eyes. John agonised over the two grey hairs in it. It was appalling to think that time could touch Susan and he couldn't take her away at once and defy it. In a couple of years, perhaps: in a year, if things went well. But not yet.

And Susan, chewing grass stalks, seemed to read his thoughts.

"Oh, John, it is hell," she said. "Will I ever be able to escape from Howard altogether, and marry you?"

"You shall," John said, looking up defiantly at the fleecy grey sky. There was an uncertain gleam about it. Was it sun or rain?"

"Let's eat!" Susan said. She tugged her sandwiches from her pocket and began to munch. "And let's talk ... make plans. If I had a plan, I think it would make things easier when your train goes to-night. You see, until to-day, I didn't want one. I thought things would settle themselves. But now that I'm going to marry you ..." She paused. "I *am* going to marry you?"

"Yes, my dear," said John. "Yes, yes."

"Well, it's different now. You see?"

John nodded. "Howard doesn't know where you are at present," he said. "But for some reason, I think he's fearfully suspicious of me. If he had the faintest notion that I knew where you are, he'd be on my trail at once. And I don't somehow think that he is likely to be particularly generous when his vanity is hurt."

"I ought to hate Howard," said Susan. "But I don't, now. I just dislike him so much that I don't think I could ever bear to be in a room with him again. Tell me, John, he's not going to be really hurt by this, is he? Miserable, or broken up, or ill?"

"No," John said, "I don't think so. Frankly, I think he's convinced that you'll go back to him in a day or two, when he knows where you are and can fetch you himself. He's in communication with your family, so I don't suppose it will be long before he finds out. Your family can't keep your whereabouts secret for ever, you know. But of course when he knows that you aren't coming back, he'll be pretty sore. But I shouldn't worry about his side of things, you know, Susan, for I'm sure that he won't worry much about yours."

"Well, of course, Howard won't offer to let me divorce him," Susan said. "It would be against his principles to put himself in the wrong. And even if it weren't, any sort of divorce would spoil his career. I mean, being a Civil Servant makes it so ..." She stopped and looked at John in dismay. "I never thought of that. You're one, too. So, if Howard brings you in—oh, we must stop that, we must stop that."

"I saw that," said John, "long ago. It would be a pity, of course. But it doesn't weigh in the balance with you. I daresay if we tried we could manage without a job. We'd be dreadfully poor, though. Would you mind?"

"Not however poor we were. But I haven't any money at all, except the dress allowance my family still give me. It'd help—if it went on."

"Well, I have a little money," said John. "We shouldn't starve. But it would be better if we could do it some other way."

"Can women find odd men to go off with?" Susan asked. "Because if so, I will."

"Good God, *no,*" said John.

"I don't mind. I don't care what happens if I get you in the end. Perhaps that would be best. I could send Howard hotel bills from Bournemouth or Torquay or somewhere."

"You can't," said John.

"But why not? It's my fault. I'm the one who made the muddle, so I ought to get us out of it."

"A woman can't. ..."

"I don't see why women should hide behind men ..."

"But it's so sordid. You don't know what you're in for, Susan. I couldn't let …"

"I don't care. It won't hurt me, and I'd feel better if I had to pay for it. As if Fate wouldn't bear me a grudge. D'you see?"

"My dear!" said John. "Shall I find out? Would it be a help?"

"Yes, it would," said Susan, jumping up. "Oh John, oh John, oh John! When it's all over, how lovely life will be!"

She took his hand and stood beside him, looking across the valley to the sea, where the sun was shining. John put his arms round her and kissed her, and then they walked slowly back down the hill and through the wood to the car. On the way, they passed a derelict cottage.

"There you are, Susan!" said John gaily. "That's the sort of place for us if Howard does me out of my job. We'll live there and I'll grow potatoes and you can keep a pony in the field."

Susan drove back slowly to the station, and John held her left hand nearly all the way. The winding lane, the tangled hedges and the distant downs were photographed indelibly on both their minds. Slower and slower Susan drove, but the minutes raced on. In the station yard John squeezed her fingers and ran through the barrier to the platform without looking back. Then she drove quickly away to the top of the hill and watched the curl of blue smoke from his train till it disappeared among the woods on the far side of the plain.

III
SUMMER'S DONE

AFTERWARDS Susan drove the car up hill and down till the petrol gauge showed only half a gallon and she turned hastily home. Aunt Mary was pottering in the garden and met her at the gate.

"So it was all right, my dear? I thought it must be when you weren't in for tea."

Susan tucked her hand under Aunt Mary's rough tweed sleeve. "We had a lovely day. And we've fixed everything."

"Oh dear, I suppose that means a divorce," said Aunt Mary. "Do you think Howard will ever do it for you? He doesn't sound a very—generous person."

Susan shook her head. "I wouldn't ask him to do it. But I don't suppose he'll mind divorcing me."

Aunt Mary looked across the garden. Between the long shadows of the apple trees the wagtails were still strutting across the sunlit lawn. "You must love this man very much," she said rather forlornly.

"John? Of course," said Susan.

They took the path by the delphiniums again in silence. Then Aunt Mary became her dry, practical self once more.

"And meantime, my girl, the first thing I want you to do is to take that colt in hand for me. If Joseph goes near him much oftener he'll have the back of the loose-box kicked in. You'll be here another fortnight or so, won't you? That'll just give you time to take a first with him at Midhurst."

"It would be fun if I could," said Susan. "And John will let me know what I have to do in heaps of time, I expect. We shall have to arrange things, you know."

"Hotel bills..." said Aunt Mary, and shivered suddenly. "Let's go in, my dear! I've got a twinge of my rheumatism. We'll have a glass of sherry before supper."

So Susan stayed on at Clattering Fords and schooled the pony while she waited for John's directions, which came at last, discreetly typed and unsigned. If she had really made up her mind, he suggested that she should go to Bournemouth the next week with a man he could trust.

The gymkhana went off well and the colt was awarded a first. But as she jogged home along the road she had driven with John, tired and contented, a sudden suspicion crossed her mind, devastating as a lightning flash. She pressed the affronted pony to a trot, flung the reins to Joseph in the stable yard, dashed into the house and wrenched Aunt Mary's floral calendar from the wall.

"My dear child!" said Aunt Mary, at the sight of her desperate face. "What in the world ...?" Then, as she understood: "What nonsense! You've caught a chill."

But Susan shook her head and reeled upstairs, dizzy and sick and trapped.

Next morning Aunt Mary pooh-poohed her fears, but said she had better stay on for a few days. The other plans could wait. And Susan agreed, sending a non-committal letter to John at the address of his trusted friend. But every day she grew more miserable. She took the temperamental colt out for long gallops, she tired herself cutting chaff and carrying water for the stables. Nothing that Aunt Mary could say would stop her, and at last she could stand it no longer.

"My dear, you must stop carrying on like a mad thing. Go up to London and see your doctor and have your mind put at rest. You'll have trouble enough to face anyway, and it's not a bit of use making yourself ill."

Susan went that afternoon. She took a fast train and watched the suburbs and the slums of London close mercilessly round her again. When the train reached Victoria, she took a taxi to Dr. Hawkes' surgery at once, and then had to wait her turn with all the other women.

Dr. Hawkes looked her over thoughtfully. "When I asked after you the other day," she said, "Miss Snow told me that you'd been called home suddenly—illness in the family. But I've only to look at you to know that isn't true."

"No," said Susan, "I left my husband."

"For someone else?"

"No. I left him because I couldn't stand being with him any longer. But—yes, there is someone else."

"I see. And whose baby do you think you're going to have?"

"Oh—*Howard's*," said Susan.

Dr. Hawkes watched horror darken her eyes, and turned her back on her as she filled a glass of water.

"I'm afraid you are," she said. And then: "Sit still for a little and rest!"

But Susan picked up her gloves and bag. "I'd rather not. Thank you. But I'd rather not."

She went carefully down the steps into the street. 'I shall have to go back, I shall have to go back, I shall have to go back ...' she said to herself. And the drone of the traffic echoed her: 'Go back! Go back!' She noticed a telephone box. It was half-past five. John might be home. She called his number, heard his voice without amazement and said:

"It's Susan. Something has happened. I'll be in the A.B.C. at the corner of Silver Street," and put the receiver back.

Then she went into the shop and sat down at a corner table to wait. The waitress brought her tea and she sipped it, looking down at her own body. Soon it would be hideous. Perhaps it would die. It would serve it right for betraying her and bearing Howard's child.

Presently John came in. His anxious eyes found her at once in the half-empty room and he came to her quickly, taking her hand. She pulled it away. "Listen, John—"

"Tea or coffee, sir?" said the waitress.

"What? Oh—coffee."

231

"Black or white?"

"White."

"Large or small, sir?"

John glared at her desperately.

"Large," said Susan quite calmly. Then she looked at John for the first time.

"It's no good," she said. "I'm trapped."

"What d'you mean? Has Howard—?"

Susan gripped the cold edge of the marble table with colder fingers. "I'm going to have his child," she said.

"Oh, my God! But—but it doesn't matter. Nothing matters. Nothing's got to matter …" began John wildly.

"Oh, yes, it does," said Susan. "I thought it didn't either, at first. But it does. I've been dreading this for days. And now I know. I can't take Howard's child away from him. And neither you nor I could face Howard or each other if we did. That's true, John—you know it is. There's nothing we can do."

She stood up, resting her hand on his shoulder for a moment. But he did not move or speak, and the crash and jangle of tea-cups and spoons deadened the slight sound of her feet. When John at last dared to look up, she was gone.

Susan took a taxi and told the driver to go to Alfred House. As they went back slowly along Silver Street, she thought of nothing but the familiar landmarks they were passing. If she missed any one of them, she thought laboriously, something very terrible might happen to John. There was the shoe shop, then the hairdressers, the picture dealer farther along on the right, then the Dairies and the sign that said 'To the Foresters' Hall.' Then the cinema, the paper seller by Worcester Terrace, the railway bridge. And Alfred House.

She took out her latch-key and gave the driver five shillings without looking at the meter. Then she went upstairs almost at a run. Somebody had been painting the banisters. Mrs. Tobias's old flat had been turned into two and one of the new ones was let. She looked the other way as she passed John's door; she climbed the last flight and pushed her latch key into the lock of number nine.

As the door shut behind her, Mrs. Barker put her head out of the kitchen. "Well, I never!" she said insolently.

Susan went across the passage to the sitting-room. Howard was sitting on the sofa just as usual. He looked up as she came in.

"Well, my dear Susan," he said loudly. "Welcome back to your own home. I knew my little wife ..."

"Howard," Susan said, "stay where you are! I'm going to have a child, your child. So I've come back. I'll bear your child. But that's all."

She went into the bedroom and locked the door.

CHAPTER 12

I
DULCIE GETS ON

ALICE was recalled to number nine the day after Susan came back. Howard himself dismissed Mrs. Barker, with a show of reluctance, though actually he was glad to be rid of her before she could make trouble or demand money for unsuccessful espionage. Besides, Howard was relieved: after all, Susan had just gone off by herself for a week or two. There was nothing in it. Didn't everybody know that all women turned a bit queer when they were in a certain condition?

But Susan's life did become a little easier, for Dr. Hawkes was sufficiently worried about her to pay an official visit to Alfred House. She produced what she called a tonic for Susan, knowing from experience that bromide can blur the blackest tragedies out of recognition. With Howard she took a very different tone. If, said Dr. Hawkes, he set any store by the child, he had better be careful how he treated Susan.

"I know nothing about your relations with your wife," she said, "but it's no use pretending that there hasn't been a fuss of some kind. Your wife has obviously had a serious shock."

"I assure you—ah—er—Doctor," said Howard, who still grudged that title to a woman, "that nothing I have done ..."

"Quite. But you see, Mr. Kennedy, it is your responsibility to see that nothing of any kind can occur to upset your wife again. You should, I think, make it your duty to consider her wishes in every way during the next few months. London does not really suit her, you know. If she has any relations in the country and could go and stay with them for part of the time, it would be wise to send her."

Howard said sulkily that he would consider it, and for some time after that he treated Susan with unusual deference. She, for her part, was thankful to sink into the mental stupor of pregnancy. She stayed as long and as often as she could with her own family, and when she had to be at Alfred House she spent most of her evenings in her own room, doggedly reading and knitting. It was some time before she even noticed that John had left Alfred House.

It was Alice who told her. Susan did not take much notice. She just went on fiddling with the ruffles on her bed jacket and stared unwinkingly at the window.

"The best thing he could do," Alice said. "You know, Miss Susan, I'm sorrier for him than you. You'll have the child to take up your thoughts."

"It'll be Howard's."

"Bless you!" said Alice. "Babies belong to their mothers at first. The fathers don't seem to show, not in the baby years. He'll take after you, never you fear."

Susan shrugged.

"These things wear off," Alice said. "Believe me, ma'am, I know. Us poor women make the same mistakes in all walks of life. And husbands are mistakes you can't get rid of. If you make your bed with a man you've got to lie in it. That's life, that is," said Alice, tilting back the mirror to dust it, "and as you grow older it don't seem to matter so much. There's the children, whoever fathered them."

"How are yours, Alice?" said Susan. For Alice was right. Life went on all round you and it was better that it should take you with it. "It's ages since I heard about them."

"I had a letter from Len yesterday," said Alice. "Seems they've just arrived, or had when he wrote. He'd enjoyed the voyage—

grand, he says it was. And the others are a decent set, he says. Been drafted to a farm. Somewhere in a desert or something. I don't know how he'll like that, without even a gramo, but maybe it'll make a man of him."

"And Dulcie?"

"Oh, Dulcie—she's that grand you wouldn't know her, Dulcie is. You knew she'd got a job in Miss Gray's library. … Well, she began as a typist a couple of months ago. It seems she may get promotion soon. Oh, yes," Alice said, collecting the waste-paper basket and her polishing cloths, "business suits our Dulcie all right."

Business went on suiting Dulcie until the middle of December. By that time she had got to know the library and had assessed the prospects it offered her. If she went on steadily, she would earn £2 10/- as a stenographer at twenty-one; if she transferred to the library service proper she might earn £3 a week in time, and there were several minor posts she might get after that. At first, the height of Dulcie's ambition was to get a transfer to the library, a thing within the bounds of possibility but sufficiently rare to be coveted. But by December, Dulcie had come to the conclusion that the library was not such a good opening as she had once thought. If she went into it, she would have to compete with all the University trained young women and the cultured young ladies fresh from finishing schools who were drafted on to the staff from time to time. Dulcie was quite sure that she could be as good at the work as any of them; but she doubted whether she would ever keep pace with their knowledge of books and people, let alone take the lead among them. And Dulcie meant to lead. So she decided after careful thought that the time would soon come when she must leave the library and look for something else.

It came sooner than she expected. Just before Christmas, the staff supervisor sent for Dulcie and told her that she was to be transferred to the library, where she would start as a message girl. "It's a splendid chance for you," the supervisor said. "Why, in time you might get to be a real library clerk."

Dulcie thought this over for a few minutes. Then she said that it was very kind indeed of the lady to offer her the chance; but she would sooner stay where she was.

"It's no kindness, my good girl," said the supervisor. "I'm not in the habit of being kind. If you don't like the change, you'll have to put up with it. I've engaged someone else to do your job. Take your chance or leave it!"

Dulcie looked down at her neat feet, then looked up again and politely said she would leave it. She accepted a week's notice from a staff supervisor who was pale with indignant unbelief.

When she got home that night, Dulcie told Alice, adding:

"You've not got to worry, Ma dear. I know what I'm about."

"You need to," said Alice, "throwing away twenty-five bob a week like that! But there—it's your life. You've got to live it."

"Oh, Ma!" begged Dulcie. "Don't be down on me! I'm only bettering myself."

"That's all right, Dulcie," said Alice. "Only don't tell your father, till you've got whatever it is you want. I suppose there is something big you're after."

Dulcie smiled her small secret smile. "You're right, Ma. Been thinking about it a long time, I have. But it doesn't do to talk."

Alice held aloof from Dulcie's scheming; but inwardly she was just as excited. What would the child be up to next?

Early in 1931, she knew. Dulcie had been round to see her old friend Miss James of Hubert Street soon after she got her job in the library, and Miss James, when congratulating her, said that if she ever wanted a change she might do worse than apply to the Warrington Bureau. They were good people, always on the look-out for decently efficient secretaries, and they had had several of Miss James's old girls. Directly Dulcie got her notice from the library, she went round and saw Miss Frobisher of the Warrington. She was a small, red-faced woman of about forty-five, with wisps of grey hair that got entangled with her glasses. Dulcie's amazing luck held: there was a vacancy, temporary only, but you never knew. If Dulcie were up to the work, she would be kept on. Anyway, she could come for a week or two while a junior member of the staff got over scarlet fever.

Dulcie went home and walked into the kitchen, very quiet and composed, but rather pale. She took off her hat and ran her fingers through her new permanent wave. Then she got out her manicure set and began polishing her nails.

"For goodness' sake, Dulcie," said Alice, who recognised the symptoms, "tell me what you've been up to!"

"Nothing much, Ma," said Dulcie, "I'm starting work at the Warrington Bureau on Monday."

She paused to see the effect of her words. Then, as Alice got up and came towards her, she threw away her grown-up indifference and skipped across the room, flinging her arms jubilantly round her mother's neck. "And now we'll tell father, because I'm getting thirty bob there," she said.

At first the Warrington Bureau was all that Dulcie hoped. The work was hard but immensely varied. Dulcie typed memoranda and agendas and reports and MSS and balance sheets and inventories and minutes, till her fingers nearly dropped off. There were only seven other girls. Three of these, the grandest, were sent out to people who needed secretaries, and four stayed in the office. It was a long, half-furnished room, with a tall window at one end, bare boards, two long deal tables, four typists' desks and two stationery cupboards. Miss Frobisher sat at an elderly office desk with a green reading lamp and a telephone and half a dozen wire baskets full of finished work which she checked before it was sent out. The three senior girls only paid brief haughty visits to the office between jobs; for they were in great demand among the philanthropists, business men, authors and society ladies who were in trouble with their correspondence. They were well paid, for they earned four pounds a week and a bonus for every new customer they introduced. Dulcie could quite easily see a future for herself there; but for the time being she was content to do routine work, draw her thirty shillings regularly and go out to the flicks with the faithful Reggie Baxter.

Alice did not consider Reggie Baxter much of a catch: he was only something to do with wireless. But he got Thomas a set dirt cheap. It never worked very well; but that suited Reggie Baxter too, because he was always in and out of the house in his vain efforts to put it right. And whenever he seemed to succeed, Thomas asked him to supper and let him take Dulcie out afterwards.

Now that he had got the wireless, Thomas spent less of his time at "The Feathers," and his intense pride in Dulcie's achievements proved a new bond with his wife. And Alice, less tired now that she could afford more leisure, was quite content to sit by the fire with him of an evening. He was no hero, but when you came to think of it, he was better than most. There mightn't be much romance about him, either, but there—after all, he was Alice's oldest friend.

Alice often thought that Thomas and Mr. Kennedy were much the same under their skins, and she hoped that Mr. Kennedy would mellow as well. If he did, Mrs. Kennedy might have quite a happy middle-age.

But Susan, back again from another visit to her family, was not thinking of the years ahead, but only of the cold rainy days of February when her baby would be born. For seven months now she had nerved herself to go through with this particular duty to Howard, for she felt that its performance might acquit her for all the other ways in which she had failed him. The minor ailments, the unfamiliar unwieldiness of her body, the continual fatigue, had produced in her a fortitude sufficient to oppose them. But she noted the date, the 25th, as though after that she would not need to go on living.

II
MOTHERS' MEETING

ONE afternoon in February, Susan was sitting by the window wondering whether she really ought to go out for a walk or not. It was all very well to prescribe exercise, and quite another thing to climb the stars again afterwards. She decided to stay in: she was feeling uneasy, and Alice was about, doing some extra cleaning. It seemed a pity to go out when for once there was company indoors. She would stay where she was a little longer, and go through to the kitchen and talk to Alice later on. She flipped over the pages of her book and wondered vaguely why the door bell rang. She hoped it was nothing she would have to attend to; but Alice would almost certainly be able to deal with it.

"Can't you see to it, Alice?" she said, as the sitting-room door opened.

"It's someone you'll be glad to see, ma'am," Alice said coaxingly, "Miss Gray that was. It'll do you good, you know. And besides, you've a lot in common. I'll bring her in."

Alice slipped into the passage before Susan could protest.

"Mrs. Kennedy will be so glad to see you, ma'am," she said. "Will you come in?"

Susan could hear Vera's voice, then the door opened again and she saw Vera herself, a Vera who had changed completely. She wore an opulent fur coat, and a loose scarf that hid the generous lines of her figure, her once pointed face was almost round, and she reminded Susan at once of a sleek contented black cat that might begin to purr at any moment.

As Alice went into the kitchen to make a cup of tea for everybody, she decided that her Mrs. Kennedy's baby should arrive about a month sooner than Mrs. Dean's. Well, the two ladies would cheer each other up, and how marriage had improved the looks of Miss Gray!

"Oh, Susan dear," said Vera, "it's years since I saw you. But somehow I couldn't pass Alfred House without coming in. D'you mind?"

"Of course not. I'm awfully glad to see you again. How's Robert?"

"Robert's splendid. His work is growing so. Oh, life's marvellous."

There was a pause. Vera and Susan looked at one another, Susan shyly, Vera with quite brazen interest. Then Vera said: "I see our news is the same, darling. When's yours?"

Susan, who could never take the changes in her own figure for granted, blushed and said: "Any time. Next week, I think."

"You are lucky," Vera said. "I've got another whole month to wait. Aren't you excited? I am. Robert is, too. We're having a baby this year and a car next. Can't afford both at once." She pulled off her gloves and hat, and flung back her coat.

"Robert wants a girl and I want a boy. Robert says it had better be twins and then we shall have done our duty to the state. But I think that'd be a pity. I want to do it again."

"Perhaps you won't feel like that when it's over. After all, we haven't got to the worst part yet," said Susan.

"Why, Susan, are you frightened? I never would have thought you would be. But perhaps you don't want it. Oh, forgive me! I shouldn't have said that. Only you look peaked. Robert says it suits me ..."

She rattled on, and Susan, leaning back in her chair, agreed that life was suiting Vera. Marriage seemed to have made her simpler and kinder. It must be because she loved Robert so much. Susan found Vera's love for Robert unbearable: it was an echo of her own love for John which she was still trying to forget.

By the time Alice had brought in tea, Vera and Susan were comparing baby clothes, and Alice was glad to see that Miss Susan seemed to have come to life a bit. Mrs. Dean was teasing her about her sewing, holding up a lop-sided nightgown and laughing herself silly over it.

"Well, Susan, it's a disgrace. I can do it better. I never would have thought I'd beat you at sewing, would you, Alice?"

"I would never have thought to call you domesticated in the old days, ma'am," said Alice, smiling.

"I am now. I mend and cook. But tell me, Alice, how are you all? My husband's sure to ask. He said if I saw you I must be sure to give you his love."

Alice stayed to tell Vera proudly of Leonard and Dulcie and to ask after her Mr. Dean. Then she left the two ladies together again and Vera began to tell Susan about her own ailments, which were few, and about confinements, which Susan found alarming.

"I think it's exciting," Vera said. "People don't die much nowadays, you know."

"It's a funny thing," Susan said to Alice when she had finally seen Vera off in a taxi, "but Mrs. Dean never once asked after Miss Wood, and they used to be such friends."

"Fancy!" said Alice absently, running an expert eye over Susan, who was walking restlessly up and down.

"Yet I wonder she came to Alfred House if she wants to avoid Miss Wood. They might so easily have met."

"They wouldn't have much in common now, would they?" said Alice. "Miss Wood's that literary. Quite taken up with it, hasn't she?"

"I suppose she has," said Susan, thinking of the last time she had seen Beatrix walking rather slowly down Silver Street, her broad felt hat set at a rakish angle on her fair eton-cropped hair, looking angular but handsome in her square-cut coat and skirt. She began to wonder about Beatrix, about Robert, about Vera—anything to take her mind away from her own sudden discomfort.

"Are you all right, Miss?" she heard Alice say.

"Indigestion ... it's only indigestion," Susan whispered.

"Not if I know it," said Alice, making for the telephone. "Always take you by surprise, babies do. Go and sit down a minute, dear, while I ring up the doctor!"

Susan did as she was told, till Alice came back. "It's all right, Miss Susan dear," she said. "Dr. Hawkes is making arrangements with the nursing home. And she'll be round in an hour or so. She says you can go straight into the home if it's not a false alarm, which I can tell by the look of you it isn't."

"An hour?" said Susan, her face already drawn with anxiety. "Mayn't it be too late? How can I ... ?"

"Goodness me, no," said Alice. "A first baby? They're more trouble than that. You just stay where you are and put your feet up. I'll go and get the baby things and pack a case for you. There's nothing to fuss about," she added severely, as Susan begged her to stay with an imploring gesture.

Half an hour later, Susan dragged herself up and went to find her. "Alice, are you sure it's safe to wait? The pain's quite bad, you know," she added apologetically. But Alice laughed at her. "Don't you worry," she said, "when you're in mortal agony it'll be time to get anxious. You're nothing like that yet."

"No," said Susan meekly, "I don't suppose you could call this mortal agony. But I wish Dr. Hawkes would hurry."

"Don't take on, now, dear," said Alice, "and I'll get you a cup of tea. Would you like me to get Mr. Kennedy home? He'd come, I expect, and if he took a taxi ... all right, Miss Susan, I needn't do it if you don't want me to. I can always say I was too taken up with looking after you to give a thought to him. Men are out of place at these times, when all's said and done."

She went on placidly with her preparations, and Susan wandered restlessly about till Dr. Hawkes arrived, reassuring, sympathetic and unperturbed. "Well," she said to Alice, "it's a mercy you were here when this began. They always get upset the first time. You'd better get her round to the home in a taxi. I'll leave a message for the husband if you like. Now, Mrs. Kennedy, you're doing splendidly. Go on being sensible! I'll see you again later on."

Susan went to get her hat and coat and picked up a couple of books, feeling that no one was making quite enough fuss about her. Leaving a husband, having a baby—perfectly commonplace events if you took them that way.

"I'm ready, Alice," she called, and let Alice take her arm and help her downstairs to the taxi. "I wish you could stop with me," she said when they got to the nursing home, so cold and unfamiliar and smelling of ether and disinfectant.

"Never mind, dearie," said Alice. "I'll be in to see the two of you to-morrow." She handed Susan and the suitcase over to a nurse, paid off the driver, and took a bus back to Silver Street. She might have called at Alfred House and broken the news to Mr. Kennedy, but she thought better of it. A bit of a shock never did him any harm.

Howard, however, rose to the occasion and was as tiresomely anxious as tradition demanded. He rang up the nursing home at regular intervals all through the night, stayed away from work the next morning to pace the nursing home waiting-room, and spent the afternoon fuming in Alfred House after large quantities of beer and bread and cheese. Anxiety told on a man so. A night and a day of it. Surely most people had babies more quickly than that? In the evening he returned to the nursing home, and stayed there till a harassed matron drove him away. He meant to ring up regularly during the night again, but sleep defeated him, and Susan's baby was ten hours old before he heard about it. At ten o'clock the telephone roused him, and a cold official voice informed him that Mrs. Kennedy had given birth to a fine child at midnight and was doing fairly well.

And then, much to his annoyance, he was not allowed to see his wife. Dr. Hawkes was taking no risks with Susan, who had borne the pain well and made no fuss, but seemed not to mind whether she lived or died once she heard the child was safe. Dr. Hawkes felt that the sight of Howard might prejudice her against life. So Susan was left to herself till the baby was a week old, and she had had time to test Alice's statement that babies belonged to their mothers and gave them a claim on life.

III

DULCIE GETS OFF

THAT summer, Susan's baby throve in the country and Vera's grew large and fat in London. Alice went to see it sometimes, but although it was admittedly a very fine child she was convinced that it could not be as nice as her Miss Susan's. She said this unguardedly to Miss Snow, who did not agree with her; for she adored anything that belonged to Robert and had been comforted and flattered at being his daughter's godmother.

"I never really thought quite as highly of Mrs. Kennedy as you did, Mrs. Gedge. Making all allowances—and between ourselves, Mr. Kennedy is not perhaps quite—you know what I mean —but still, making all allowances, she did run away from him once, and I often wonder if she will come back from the country at all. I mean to say," Miss Snow added, looking over her spectacles at Alice, "Mr. Kennedy is a man ..."

"And that's something, after all, ma'am," agreed Alice. "Us women can't be too particular nowadays. All the same, I should be sorry to see my Dulcie saddled for life with a mistake like that."

"Oh, surely she's too young to worry about yet, Mrs. Gedge," said Miss Snow, who clung to the illusion that the Gedge family were still school children. But Alice said she was not so sure. Reggie Baxter was too much in and out of the house for her to forget that Dulcie was grown-up, but somehow she did not think that Dulcie was serious about Reggie. Dulcie had her own ambitions and an indifferent mechanic was hardly likely to be one of them.

She was right. Towards the end of the summer, Dulcie asked if she might bring a Mr. Vincent home with her—quite a gentleman, he was, said Dulcie proudly. Something to do with the Bank. Alice said that she might, and in view of the young man's refinement she sent Thomas out for the evening and gave Mr. Vincent supper in style.

He was a tall, sallow creature, with a large nose and dark hair and eyes. His clothes were subdued, but double-breasted, and his tie and handkerchief were perhaps a shade ornate. He looked at Dulcie adoringly all through the meal, and treated Alice with tolerant politeness. Dulcie appeared to know him very well. She teased him a good deal in a coy, cold way. When they had gone out to the Palais de Dance, Alice washed up and decided that she knew what Dulcie's intentions were, though probably the young man did not. But she was vaguely disappointed in Dulcie: she would sooner that she had set her hopes on something more genuine. Imitations were never the same: they did not wear well. To her own amazement, she found herself comparing Dulcie's debonair young man with Thomas, and not to Mr. Vincent's advantage.

But though Dulcie looked forward to a future which included marriage with Mr. Vincent or somebody exactly like him, she did not let such hopes interfere with her work. It would be years, most likely, before Mr. Vincent could afford to get married, and meanwhile it was most important to do as well as she could in her own profession.

During the spring and summer she went rapidly ahead from junior to senior typist, and during the holidays she actually did the work of one of the visiting secretaries. This had been entirely successful and Dulcie hoped that one of the senior's shoes would soon be empty so that she could step into them.

At this point, however, Dulcie's luck changed. In the summer months, she had been several times to a Lady Barbara Romilly, who combined very profitable journalism with the ordinary social round. She took a fancy to Dulcie, who was so quiet and so nice-looking and made up letters so well that Lady Barbara was saved a great deal of time and trouble in putting her scattered thoughts together. However far behind Lady Barbara was with her article for the Sunday papers, Dulcie always seemed to get the thing finished in time without fuss or confusion.

When she got back from Scotland, Lady Barbara rang up the Warrington Bureau and asked to have the usual secretary sent round at once, because she was all behind with her articles and her correspondence. Miss Frobisher glanced round the room: who had been going in the summer? She always liked to humour clients as far as possible. Miss Stubbs, Miss Gordon, Miss Brown ... ? No, of course, it had been Miss Gedge. Well, that was quite out of the question. Miss Stubbs had better go.

So Miss Stubbs, who was incidentally Miss Frobisher's niece, went and was sent back in a taxi with a note demanding the nice girl with fair hair and her wits about her, that Lady Barbara had had in July. This put Miss Frobisher in a quandary. She wanted to please her client, but she hated to push Dulcie Gedge forward. Juniors were all very well in their way, but however bright they were, they needed to be kept back and put in their place. Still, there was nothing for it. Dulcie, pink and jubilant, got into the taxi, and the tearful, plain Miss Stubbs finished Dulcie's typing.

Dulcie came home to Alice that night in such excitement that she could not hide it. She was convinced that her own success was assured: hadn't she been chosen over the head of the most senior secretary by a celebrity? All she had to do was to demand promotion to the status of visiting secretary, and collect the clients that Lady Barbara would undoubtedly bring her.

But Alice was not so sure. "Sounds nice, Dulcie," she said. "Don't think I'm trying to crab it. You've done very well indeed,—it's splendid. I only mean that perhaps you'll find that things don't work out so easy every time."

"Well, but Ma, I don't see how it can fail to come off. Look here, Lady Barbara is one of Frobisher's most important people—she simply can't afford to cross her. Well then, she'll have to employ me to satisfy Lady Barbara. And if I do well, she'll be jolly glad to have me for what I can bring her. Things aren't any too good at the Bureau, you know. Frobisher's not much use: she can't make up her mind when to stick out for her price and when to cut it down."

"If I were you, Dulcie, I should go slow," Alice said. "If I were you, I wouldn't ask for a rise or even insist on being sent to Lady Barbara every time. I'd go very slow till I saw how the land lay," said Alice.

But Dulcie was too young to go slow, or to give up an immediate chance for the long view every time. So she did go to Miss Frobisher, and demand promotion to the status of a visiting secretary with a visiting secretary's salary and first claim on Lady Barbara's work. And Miss Frobisher grudgingly gave it to her. Dulcie noticed with a certain triumph that her easy popularity with the other girls was rather dimmed; but she took it as a sign of success. "There you are, Mother!" she said. "It's come off. I told you it would."

Dulcie's success lasted for exactly three months. Like everyone else, she was aware of the financial crisis which overwhelmed the country in the autumn of 1931. But she did not bother much about it: her money came in and she could buy what she wanted with it. Besides, she hadn't got a vote, so the elections everyone was talking about were no concern of hers. She never thought that the repercussions of the crisis would affect her own life. Work seemed to go on much the same. It was not until the end of November that she realised that it was not going on quite as usual. Then she found that she spent three days out of five in the office, that the pile of typing by her desk was insignificant, that the telephone hardly seemed to ring at all. And Miss Frobisher spent most of her time chewing a wooden penholder and twisting her wispy ends of grey hair as she worked out sums on the blotter instead of checking work. 'I shall have to sack somebody: that's about it,' she said to herself. 'It's the same on all sides. People that hardly know how to hold a pen for themselves are too hard hit to hire a girl for a day. There isn't the work.'

She said this every day for three weeks. Then she got the bank book out and saw that her sums were more than correct. Unless she discharged three of her clerks, she would not be able to keep the Bureau over the New Year. She looked down the row of girls. The two juniors could go, and one of the others. Either Miss Brown or Miss Gedge. Of course, Miss Gedge was a help with Lady Barbara —not that she wanted a girl as often as she once did. But still, she was a good customer—better keep Miss Gedge perhaps.

The telephone rang and she lifted the receiver. "Yes, Warrington Bureau speaking ... Yes ... Lady Barbara Romilly? ... What can I do for you, Lady Barbara? ... Oh ...

yes ... I see ... Yes, it's the same for all of us ... Perfectly ... quite ... good-bye."

Miss Frobisher set the receiver down and scrabbled with her pen on her blotter. Better do it now, if it had to be done. "Miss Gedge!" she called sharply.

Dulcie got up, slipping a sharp pencil through the loop of her notebook. 'That'll be Lady Barbara for me,' she thought. 'And a good thing too. I'm fed up with slacking about here.'

"You called me, Miss Frobisher?" she said as she came to the desk.

"I did, Miss Gedge. I'm afraid I shall have to ask you to take a week's notice from to-night."

"But—but what for? What have I done?" Dulcie stiffened in amazed defiance.

"I'm afraid, Miss Gedge, that if this comes to you as a surprise, you must be a thoughtless sort of person. Haven't you seen for yourself how slack we are? Don't you know there's been a crisis in the country—that no one's got any money for luxuries like fancy secretaries any more?"

"I'm sorry, Miss Frobisher," said Dulcie. "I've noticed, of course. And I know it must have been a very trying time for you. But surely I've a right to know why you've chosen me. After all, Lady Barbara—"

"You needn't worry about her. Lady Barbara Romilly has just telephoned to say that she regrets she'll not be needing a secretary, as the Sunday papers are not taking any more articles from her at present. And I'm beginning with you, Miss Gedge, because you're one of the newest members of my staff ... No, I've no complaints. You've only one fault— you never knew your place. You can go, Miss Gedge—right now if you choose," said Miss Frobisher, feeling suddenly tired.

"I do choose," said Dulcie in a fine heat of indignation, and went straight to the peg where her new hat hung.

Alice heard Dulcie's story without comment. It was just the sort of thing she had foreseen; but she was careful not to say so.

"Well, now, Dulcie," she said. "You'll just have to see about something else. We shall be all right without your money for a bit, so you don't need to worry. I suppose you got your testimonial all right? Let's have a look at it."

"Testimonial?" said Dulcie in a temper. "No, I didn't get a testimonial. And what's more, I'm not going to ask for one either. I'll never set foot in the place again."

Alice said nothing to this either: she just asked Dulcie if Mr. Vincent were coming to take her out that evening. It would be a good thing to have Dulcie out of Thomas's way when they were both likely to be upset. Dulcie nodded crossly, and was still sore about her wrongs when young Mr. Vincent came round and was extremely sympathetic over them. But he shook his head over the slump. In his view the country was not near the bottom of it yet. And as for the banks—he grew mysterious: no one guessed what the banks had been through. People just didn't know where to turn for money, he added. Winning the sweep was about the only chance some people had. Alice listened thoughtfully and after supper, when Dulcie had hurried off to get ready, she took Mr. Vincent on one side herself, rummaging in her bag. Ten shillings changed hands.

Next day, Alice set herself to improve matters for Dulcie. She did not see why the child shouldn't have a testimonial: in fact, she was not sure that Miss Frobisher could refuse. It was probably only a matter of asking, and evidently she had better be the one to ask. So the next afternoon she took a bus down Marylebone High Street and found her way to the Warrington Bureau. She walked straight into the long room and up to Miss Frobisher's desk.

"Good afternoon!" she said smoothly. I believe you're Miss Frobisher. I'm Mrs. Gedge, Dulcie Gedge's mother."

"If you've come to ask me to take your daughter back," said Miss Frobisher, "I'm afraid it's a waste of time."

"I shouldn't dream of such a thing," said Alice. "These things have to be. Dulcie quite understands the position. But there's just one little matter ..."

"It's a waste of time," said Miss Frobisher again, clipping some papers together with a desperate air of urgent affairs.

"I won't keep you long," said Alice. "I can see you're busy. But Dulcie tells me she never asked you for a testimonial."

"I don't know that I feel inclined ..." said Miss Frobisher. "Your daughter was very highhanded, Mrs. Gedge."

"Girls are foolish," Alice said reflectively. "But I'm sure you wouldn't be the one to stand between a girl and her living, Miss Frobisher. And you know what it is in business—no girl would stand a chance of a job these days if she hadn't a testimonial."

"Oh, well," said Miss Frobisher. "I'm sure I don't bear the girl any malice. She can have it." She took up her pen and filled half a sheet of notepaper with a cold record of Dulcie's employment and ability. While she wrote, Alice looked round the room: it was so long since she had been in an office. She savoured the familiar atmosphere, the faint smell of carbons and ink and gum and gas fires. It was a nice little place: it seemed a pity that Miss Frobisher should be so disheartened about it.

Miss Frobisher folded the paper, pushed it into an envelope and handed it to Alice.

"It's most good of you, Miss Frobisher, when you're so busy."

"I'm not busy," said Miss Frobisher with sudden bitterness. "It's no good pretending I am. I'm just sitting here, making work for my clerks, till I have to close down. It's the slump."

Alice nodded. "There's not a business but feels the pinch," she said. "The worry of it must be terrible for you. I've been in business myself, and I know."

"It was a nice business once," said Miss Frobisher. "I daresay we could pull through now if we had a bit of capital. But I might as well wish for the moon, of course. Good-bye, Mrs. Gedge. I'm glad you came in, and I hope your daughter finds something soon."

IV

SILVER LINING

BUT for the next few weeks Dulcie, crestfallen now, found nothing. Early in February, young Mr. Vincent came to supper again, and as he sat down he winked at Alice, slipping an envelope into her hand. "Got it for you all right," he said. "Gave your name as Silver Lining. Seemed appropriate, somehow."

"Get along with you!" said Alice. She locked the envelope away: it was an awful extravagance to gamble on the National. She couldn't think what had got into her. At such a time, too, with every penny counted twice over. The Derby—well, that was another matter. She'd quite often won a pound or two on that. But there were other things to think of—a letter from Len saying how fit he was and doing quite decently, he thought. Even better was the letter from the organisation which was keeping a paternal eye on him. The Superintendent wrote to say that Leonard looked like making good: he was a steady worker and getting quite an eye for cattle. His employer was really pleased with him.

And Alice was busy again at Alfred House, giving regular help to the Kennedys and spending several afternoons with Miss Snow, who needed looking after a good deal these days. So she was taken by surprise when she saw the evening paper placards blazoned with red letters: GRAND NATIONAL: Luck of the Draw, A to Z. She was dishing up in the Kennedys' kitchen, and Howard came gloomily in with his paper. He stood by the supper table reading down the columns of names.

"No luck, as usual," he said. "Nor anyone we know." He fluttered the page away in disgust.

Alice stooped to pick it up and noticed a headline: Silver Street's Luck. 'Well, that's near home,' she thought, and read the paragraph. It said: "Silver Street has been lucky again, and the Favourite, STAR DUST, last out of the Drum to-day, has been drawn by Silver Lining of 10 Tuffnel Road, just round the corner. We have not yet ascertained the winner's name."

Alice stood stupidly in the little kitchen, with the Kennedys staring at her and the potatoes burning black on the stove. Almost before she had taken it in, there was a terrific clatter on the door, and Dulcie appeared with a handful of telegrams.

"Ma, what have you been up to?" she said breathlessly. "Look here—it says 'Congratulations Silver Lining L89765 draws Stardust.' Is it you or is it a mistake?"

"It's me all right," said Alice, sitting down rather hurriedly in Howard's chair. "It's me all right. A bit of luck after all these years!"

Susan went down for Miss Snow, and in a mysterious way the small flat was soon crowded with people. With surprising affability Howard produced a bottle of sherry, and they all drank to Alice's luck.

"My word!" Howard said. "Thirty thousand! You're a rich woman, Mrs. Gedge. You'll be too grand to know us now."

"It's not thirty thousand yet, by a long way," Alice said. "It's a thousand for drawing a horse. You never can tell with National: it's a cruel race. And look at my potatoes ..."

At last she and Dulcie went home. At the corner of Silver Street and Tuffnel Road there was quite a crowd of press photographers, journalists and neighbours who had come to share the celebrations, and were being entertained by Thomas all over the place. In fact, one look at Thomas told her that he had lost no time in celebrating the occasion himself. But at last they were able to have supper, and afterwards they left Dulcie and the godfatherly Mr. Vincent to bar the door to visitors and wash up, while Thomas tucked Alice's hand under his arm and took her out to celebrate all over again. He began at "The Feathers" with beer for himself and port and splash for Alice. And Alice was never quite sure afterwards how she managed to get him home.

The National was the one topic of conversation in Tuffnel Road during the days beforehand, while on the morning of the race itself none of Alice's friends in Alfred House could settle to anything. Alice herself was far less excited. After the first surprise she had refused to discuss any aspect of the situation with a single soul. "I'm not worrying," was all she said.

"I am, though," groaned Thomas, "with a fortune dangled in front of me nose and whisked away again as like as not. Enough to turn a man's hair grey, that's wot it is. And no sympathy, neither!"

He wanted Alice to stay at home and listen to the result on his wireless. But Alice would do no such thing. "I've got my work to do," she said, "if you haven't." And off she went to Alfred House. But Thomas came too. He hung round all the time, sitting first in the Kennedys' kitchen and then in Miss Snow's, and begging to be allowed to turn on Howard's wireless to listen to the race. In the end he got his way, and Howard came home specially to stage-manage things.

They were all grouped round the wireless under his direction a quarter of an hour before the race was due to start. Howard sat nearest, so that he could turn the knobs. Thomas sat beside him, fidgeting to be allowed to tune in himself. Susan, holding Alice's hand, sat beside her on the sofa, the nursemaid and baby were by the door, Miss Snow was in the best arm-chair, and Dulcie sat on the floor, white and open-mouthed, her eyes fixed on the loud-speaker.

The delay seemed interminable. They were ready to shriek with impatience as the announcer described the crowds, the weather, the state of the course. Thomas nodded knowingly as he dealt with the horses and said that STARDUST was looking fine. They all held their breath and clutched their chairs as the start was described.

"They're off ... STARDUST well to the front, lying close to the rails: she's being splendidly ridden ... Now the first fence ... all over ... they're going well ... STARDUST holding her own ..."

He paused, and they could hear the animal roaring of the excited crowd.

"STARDUST's losing a little ..."

"No, she's holding her own ..."

"FIREFLY's down ..."

"BLACK BEAUTY's gaining ..."

"They're coming up to the fence ..."

"STARDUST's over ... No! ...What's that? She's down! She's fallen at the last fence. Bad luck, bad luck! ... BLUE BOY's ahead ... He's in. PRETTY LASS second. Can't quite

257

see who was third till the colours go up. Yes, I thought so—GREEN GARTERS. Someone's made a fortune. Well, good luck to them! ..."

Susan turned to Alice, weeping with disappointment. Howard's mouth sagged open: "Too bad, too bad," he said. "Unplaced, too." Thomas just sat and groaned with his head in his hands, and Dulcie positively screamed with exasperation. "Dear, dear!" said Miss Snow shakily, "dear, dear! We must try to believe that it's all for the best." They were all startled into silence when the bell rang. The small nursemaid went to open it and came back in a moment: "Mrs. Barker's compliments," she said, "and she thought Mrs. Gedge might like to know that STARDUST didn't get home at all. An outsider won, she said."

"We know all that," Howard said. "Tell her to go away!"

"Oh, Alice," Susan said. "I'm so *sorry*."

But Alice was smiling. "I don't know what you're all taking on so for," she said. "Some people may have lost fortunes; but I haven't."

"You haven't won thirty-thousand, anyway," said Thomas in an aggrieved voice.

"I never thought I would," said Alice. "Ten thousand's enough for me."

"But you don't get ten thousand just for drawing a horse, Alice," said Howard. "You don't understand. You only get one thousand. Not that that isn't a nice little bit, but ..."

"Yes, that's right," Alice said. "I'd forgotten that. That makes eleven thousand in all."

" 'Ere, wot's all this?" roared Thomas, roused from despair.

"Out with it, Ma!" squeaked Dulcie.

"I don't know what you're shouting for, Thomas," said Alice indignantly. "I've had ten thousand pounds in the bank since the day I sold half my ticket on STARDUST. I've got some sense, I have, even if I'm not an expert at the street corners. What d'you take me for?"

"And now what about it, Dulcie?" she said, when the first flurry of amazed congratulations was over. "Shall we set up on our own, you and me? I've always had a fancy for running an office. And there's that Bureau you were so keen on. I daresay we'd get it cheap ..."

KALEIDESCOPE
ARMISTICE DAY, 1932

Vera and Robert

Vera and Robert walked slowly through the park, wheeling their baby in its heavy pram. Robert's hand closed over Vera's on the handle-bars, so that he did all the work. They dawdled to let the baby watch the whirling autumn leaves; but they hoped to get to Marble Arch by eleven.

Beatrix

Beatrix was in her flat in Alfred House, typing laboriously. Her third book had just been recommended by the Book Club, and now she must begin her fourth. She considered the words she had written, stroking her sleek cropped hair and adjusting her sombre tie. Then she pulled out the page and slipped in another. She had forgotten the date.

Isabel Snow

Miss Snow picked her way through the crowds in Oxford Street. How much gayer people were than they used to be! They took The Day so irreverently now. But what did it matter? She was going to lunch with Vera and Robert and there was a Committee meeting in the afternoon. Another day gone.

John

John sat in his office signing letters fretfully. Another quarter of an hour before the signal went. Fourteen years since the War ended, fourteen years since he and Howard had vowed friendship by the lions in Trafalgar Square. And two years since he had seen Susan. Was it possible that love lasted as long as life?

Howard

Howard picked up his hat and coat and went out into Whitehall. He always liked to be in the centre of things. What a crowd! And what a lot of elderly people about! It seemed only yesterday that he and John Abbot had got so drunk together. And yet here he was with a wife and family, all serene.

Susan

Susan picked up her plump baby and went over to the window. Soon it would be eleven, and all the traffic over the bridge would stop. Fourteen years ago she'd been at home in Wiltshire. She held up the baby on her shoulder so that it could see the buses and trams, loitering now because they would have to stop in a few minutes. Fourteen years more and she'd be almost old.

Alice

In the long room of the Warrington Bureau work was still going on. Four junior clerks were typing manuscripts, filing papers, sorting letters, stamping envelopes. At the far end of the room the duplicating machine was champing out agendas under Dulcie's supervision. Every now and then Dulcie looked up at the clock and across at her mother, who was placidly checking work at the big desk. Then she looked down again at Mr. Vincent's showy stone on her fourth finger. In a year or two now she would marry him and they would have one of the pretty houses on a building estate, all nicely furnished up to date on the hire purchase. Out at Kenton, perhaps, or Ealing or the new suburbs at the end of Silver Street. My word, Len wouldn't half envy her, with a home of her own and a business as well, with cinemas and dance halls just round the corner.

And Thomas, sitting patiently on a deal chair by the door, waiting for Alice to give the word, thought of Len too; and with a sudden return of the roving spirit that had once sent him into the navy, he envied his son and the way he had got to grips with life at last. He didn't quite know why: he only knew that all this machinery and jimcrackery and refinement made him sick. Why didn't Alice hurry up?

But Alice was still checking letters at her desk opposite the window. A bunch of Flanders poppies stood by the pile of letters on her heavy leather-edged blotter. She looked up at the clock—only another minute or two now. Deliberately she wiped her pen on a felt blotter, adjusted the green shade of the reading lamp and moved her desk telephone out of the way. Then she looked down the long room, nodding to Thomas and Dulcie: the girls were working well this morning, and there was plenty for them to do too. Nice little business it was. Funny to think it had taken her fourteen years to get back to where she'd been.

Well, mustn't grumble. There they were, Thomas and Dulcie. And Len—Len who'd been outwitted and disgraced. If he was going to make a better thing out of it than Dulcie in the end, nobody but Alice would ever guess. Fourteen years ... She stretched out her hand to the buzzer and spoke quietly to these girls for whom the war was not a memory but a legend:

"In ten minutes you may go."

THE END